Go West!

Will Riley Hinton

John 5:24

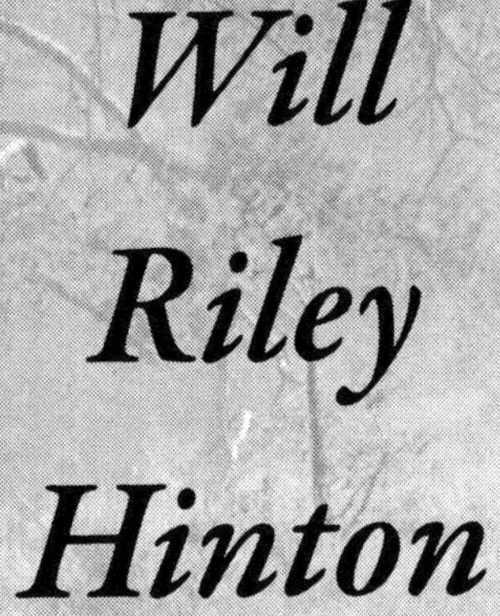
Will
Riley
Hinton

Shadow of Vengeance

Book three in the Rocky Mountain Odyssey adventure series.

Published by White Feather Press. (www.whitefeatherpress.com)

ISBN 978-1-4537038-2-3

Printed in the United States of America

Exterior cover photo ©iStockphoto.com/ Holly Kuchera
Exterior cover photo ©iStockphoto.com/ Steve Cukrov
Interior chapter head photo ©iStockphoto.com/ Clint Walker

White Feather Press

Reaffirming Faith in God, Family, and Country!

Dedicated to the memory of
Ralph Wenzel.
He was truly a friend
in spite of our never having
met in person!

Thank you, Sharon,
for sharing him with me.

"He that dwells in the secret place
of the Most High shall abide
under the shadow (protective cover)
of the Almighty."
Psalm 91:1

Preface

As I complete this final chapter of the Rocky Mountain Odyssey series I simply can not think it is truly finished. These characters have written their names and personalities on my writer's heart and I refuse to say we are parting ways.

I may, in the future, have to bring them back for a reunion or else lose sleep as they prowl around in my dreams. They have enriched my imagination and blessed me in doing so!

Much of this story, Shadow of Vengeance, reprises occurrences from Lonely Are The Hunted and Rocky Mountain Odyssey. If the reader has not read those two works, this may be a bit disconcerting, but I do believe this book is capable of a "stand-alone" read.

My editors have asked so many questions concerning certain terminologies through the process of developing these three stories that I have decided to include a short glossary in the back.

The editors pointed out that a non-western reader will be confused about certain things that I take for granted. My initial response was, "Then let them figure it out like I did." However, that's a rather closed minded approach. It also tells me, (or should tell me) that I may be developing NEW western readers through my stories. What an exciting privilege that is!

With that in mind, please refer to the glossary ahead of time if you're new to the western genre.

I jokingly claim to have graduated from the University of Zane Grey with a master's from Louis L'amour tech. While those are fictional schools, those two writers, more than any others, shaped my life as a pre-teenager. Coupled with my privilege of growing up on a horse, (or horses,) I'm afraid I rather became completely immersed in the waters of western slang.

This, mind you, is not an apology, simply an explanation of the need for a glossary for those new to the western genre. It is my wish and prayer that you not only learn to love the west as I do, but grow to love the history of the second greatest time period in all of creation. The Biblical period is the greatest, at least in my opinion.

May you lose yourself in the Rockies as you read.

Acknowledgements

I want to acknowledge these great folks for the way they stand by me in spite of me!

First, my wonderful wife, Donna. Without her belief in me, I would never have the courage or the energy to continue. She also does a great job of editing.

My two children, Doug and Beth, who never once have said their dad wasn't capable.

My dear friend, Mary Mueller, who tirelessly edits my work in spite of having to deal with a rebellious student!

Thanks to Sharon Wenzel for her selfless proofreading efforts. She is truly a professional. You make me look good, Sharon.

My publishers, Skip and Sara Coryell, of White Feather Press. You are the greatest – your unique approach to your authors is the absolute tops! God bless you.

To Greg Burkholder, the designer of my two web sites. You make so many good things happen in my life, thank you!

To all those readers who have urged me to keep writing because you want more; what an inspiration you are! I am truly humbled.

And finally, and most importantly, I must speak of my Lord and Savior, Jesus Christ. He is the One Who has given me any positive talents that I may posses. I owe ALL to Him.

Shadow of Vengeance

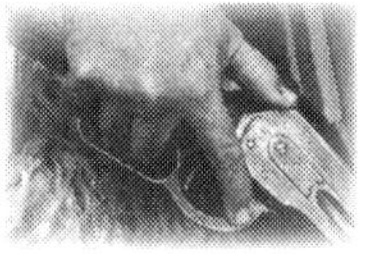

ONE

A shrill, high-pitched cry pierced the tranquil setting of the canyon as the monarch flew high overhead surveying his kingdom. The eagle was exceptionally large and soared back and forth, eyes passing over and marking every detail of the floor below, the walls and rocks beside him, and any small creature that might fall prey to the mighty talons with which he was armed.

In the plush grass carpeting of the canyon floor below grazed a small herd of horses, mostly mares, while their champion stood off to the side, nervously pawing the ground as he stood with neck arched and silky, soft nostrils flaring as he caught the scent of a small grizzly just to their north and to his left. The huge claws of the bear tore at a cedar deadfall as he tried desperately to roll the log from its place in order to get to the little creature he had seen dart to safety underneath. This was not to be the final day on earth for the little fellow, however, and after much grunting, growling, and rocking the cedar back and forth the bear finally gave up and went in search of easier prey.

As the eagle banked left his keen eyes caught the scurry of a marmot as it ducked into the protection of a small crevasse, only to turn and peek out to see if the hunter had seen him. While that was the case, he was safe in his shelter and would soon be back out, sunning himself on the nearest rock.

Another shrill cry pierced the air and seemed to declare to

the mere earthlings below the supremacy of one who had "broken the bonds of earth" on eagle's wings. After one final pass over this section of the canyon, the hunter turned south in an attempt to find richer hunting.

The eagle, bear, and stallion were three separate rulers of three different kingdoms living in a strange harmony of survival whose lives were forever intertwined by the forces of the creation in which they existed. Each had but three instincts to drive him: to eat, survive, and to procreate. All else in life hinged and depended on these three drives. Each was a ruler of his separate kingdom in his own right. Each had not only survived, but had prospered.

Ten miles in a southerly direction, positioned on the west bank of the Twin Forks River, Dan Kade sat on the front steps of his ranch house. It was a long, framed structure situated some two hundred yards from the river and just in front of the mountain behind it. The ranch buildings were situated on a shelf of land that was some thirty or so feet higher than the river's edge. Though the shelf dropped away gradually it was quite pronounced, while the other side of the river bottom stayed level for nearly three hundred yards and ended rather abruptly against an earthen bluff some fifty feet high and shrouded in scrub brush. The ranch buildings consisted of the original house that was the southernmost structure, plus the new house in which Dan and Allison Kade lived, and then the barns and corrals north of that.

The original house was used as a bunk house for the other three partners in the ranch and one hired hand, Skinny Robins. Skinny was only sixteen years old and was constantly kidded by the others. Two of Dan's other partners were Comanche Indians who embraced the white man's lifestyle while still maintaining their heritage. They were Red Elk, commonly known as Reddy, and Five Ponies, whom they called Joe. Reddy spoke like a Texas cowboy, while Joe had mission school English and seldom spoke improperly. The last of the partners was a mountain of a mountain man named James Anderson "Bear" Rollins. He topped the six foot mark by a full four inches and weighed in at least sixty pounds over two hundred. He was all muscle and bone.

The four had been partners on several wild horse gatherings over the last five years and were as close as brothers. You challenged one, you challenged four, and it was a very bad idea.

Dan himself was a slender yet muscular six footer who loved horses nearly as much as he loved people. His parents were horse ranchers, as were the parents of his wife, Allison. Dan's folks lived in Arizona while Allison's were just two hours' ride east of them.

Southern Idaho has an area where the mountains release their hold on the land and allow an area roughly seventy-five miles wide to be rolling, mostly grassy terrain. The area is interrupted near the western side by a cluster of smaller mountains that arrogantly plopped down there to stay, but they are of minor consequence in the scheme of things. The McCord ranch of Allison's folks was just to the east of those mountains' southernmost point. The little town of Twin Forks was situated twenty miles north of the ranch with the same name. It was rapidly becoming farming territory around the town.

In the grass in front of Dan was a little toddler with the bow legs of one so tiny and unaccustomed to walking. Especially with the bunching of his diaper in the way of those tiny legs, he waddled left and right as he toddled around the yard clad only in the diaper and a little shirt. He made his way to the large leg of a horse grazing in the same area and latched onto it with a squeal of delight. The animal appeared to ignore the toddler as he continued to munch grass. The little guy was nearly lost to sight when holding onto the leg, as this stallion stood well over seventeen hands at the withers and weighed in at over twelve hundred pounds. He was a blue roan, having the typical mottled coat of such an animal, with an unusually large head and ears that resembled those of a mule. Most people considered him just plain homely, but to the Kades he was beautiful. Known to all simply as Blue, the beast was dedicated totally to Dan Kade. He was allowed to roam free because where Dan was, Blue would be.

The horse had been wild when caught on Dan's first horse hunt and seemed to have just been waiting for Kade to find him. His intelligence was legendary and his speed and endurance even more so. Little Ira Kade soon tired of trying to climb the leg and waddled off toward the river, pausing every few feet to squat down to pick up a stick or to try to catch a moving bug he happened to see. Dan watched closely as Allison came out on the porch, set herself down by Dan and snuggled close.

"How far do you think he'll get this time, Dan?" she asked.

"Not far; Blue just looked up."

It wasn't long before the big steed left his grass, walked past the youngster and then turned so he was in the child's way. Little Ira went right, but the horse went with him. Then he went left, and Blue backed up to stay in front of him. Before long, Ira became a bit discontent with the game and charged under the horse's belly toward freedom and the thrill of investigating that new thing below formed by running water and rippling sounds.

"Watch now," said Dan.

Finally, apparently realizing the child's quest was not going to be easily thwarted, the big fellow reached down with those huge jaws and fastened his strong teeth on the shirt. He picked the now irate boy child up by the back of his shirt and started carrying him back to the porch. Ira was slowly slipping down out of the shirt and would soon be stripped from it if allowed to go on like that, but Blue arrived in front of Dan and Allison with his tiny cargo and deposited a most unhappy little fellow to the ground.

Allison retrieved her son while laughing loudly with Dan, then went in the house with him to change the shirt that was covered with the horse's slobbers. While Blue was a good guard dog, he was a messy one.

Anyone who had watched this sort of byplay take place would be amazed at the actions of the horse, for even Dan and the Indians claimed that Blue wasn't a horse at all, but a big dog in disguise. It appeared that the animal was so dedicated to Dan that he sensed the relationship of father and child.

"Dan Kade, why are you here watching your son while the others are cutting hay? Aren't you shirking your duties?" called Allison from inside the house.

"Not at all. If I can get the woman of this house to fix them a lunch, I'll take it to them. I was up the draw behind us trying to see if I could pot that grizzly that took down one of our colts last week. He's been prowling around during the day some, and I thought maybe I could get a shot at him."

"I don't suppose it had a thing to do with how much you hate haying, now did it?"

"Aw, Allie, you know I do my share. Bear suggested it."

"Well, I think you should leave that sort of thing to Bear. He's the one who is part animal when it comes to hunting."

"Hey girl, you just do up a lunch for those four and let me do the job assignments here, okay? They're bound to be hungry by now."

Allie stuck her tongue out at him and told him to get busy and fix it himself, she was busy. Dan chuckled and went about that very task. As soon as he was done he found his two loved ones, kissed them warmly, and headed out the door. He discovered the horse was gone from sight and called out his name. Heavy hoof-falls sounded from the side of the house and the big fellow appeared with a mouth full of grass he was energetically chomping. Dan waited until it was gone before putting the hanging bit back in the mouth of his friend, then tightened the cinch, grabbed the sack with the others' lunches and mounted. The other three, plus their hired hand, Skinny Robins, would be more than ready for the meal by the time he reached them.

He crossed the river and turned north, following the meandering flow for nearly a mile before coming to the expansive bottom land they kept fenced to allow them to grow their hay for winter feed. This was the first place with a wide enough area this side of the river for any endeavor of that sort.

He saw Skinny in the distance to the east driving a team hitched to the new-fangled sickle-bar mowing machine they had shipped in from "out east" the previous summer. Dan chuckled as he remembered the look of consternation on Skinny's face when they told him he had to drive the machine all the way home from Boomstick, a two day ride by horseback. By the time Joe took pity on the lad and explained that they were bringing one of the hay wagons to haul it home, the lad's relief was such that Joe was assailed by a hug very unlike the boy. Poor Skinny had envisioned a week on the road on the slow and rough-riding machine.

Six foot swaths of standing hay fell to the cutter bar as the team drew it along while another team, driven by Joe, drew a dump rake of ancient descent along, making windrows of the fresh, green nourishment to facilitate the drying and gathering. It would get turned over in a couple of days if it didn't get rained on so it would dry further.

A half mile further to the east he could see the hay wagon where Reddy and Bear Rollins were loading already-dried hay in preparation to hauling it the mile back to where they would stack it in the narrow bottom land directly across the river from the ranch buildings.

This was May, and by late fall they would have many stacks ready to sustain the main herd of breeding stock through the hard winter. With each of the two previous winters they had discovered their planning to be lacking in good hay so they continued to increase the amount grown and stacked. That was the only way they could continue to increase the size of their herd, and there were valuable contracts to be had with good horses to sell. Truth be told, they all enjoyed the haying but Dan, even though they were riders at heart.

Dan made his way to the wagon after dropping off a lunch for Skinny and one to Joe and grabbed a pitchfork as the other two stopped to eat. The wagon was already half-loaded and he had nearly finished the forward half by the time Reddy and Bear finished their lunches and decided to help once again. The "Johnny-come-lately" hassle Dan had expected never came, so he figured the other two must be either tired or deep in thought over something. Once the wagon was loaded and they were on their way back to the ranch area, with Dan riding the wagon and Blue following behind, they finally spoke.

"I assume yu didn't see thet griz' or yu woulda told us by now."

"Right, Bear, no sign of him anywhere."

"I sure hate the thought of losing any more colts to thet critter," spoke Reddy. "He seems tu pick on the best when he goes after them."

The rest of the way was spent in silence until they came

within sight of the bottom land where they stacked the hay. As they trundled to a stop, Reddy spoke in low voice. "Riders comin', fellas. Two of them down over the high bank on the east."

It was automatic that three hands slipped the thongs off of the hammers of their six-guns as a matter of precaution. Then two of them slid off the wagon and each went a different way, Reddy around the front of the team to be the one to meet the riders, Bear strolled around the back of the wagon while Dan stayed on the hay load. They waited in expectation until Dan recognized the man on the right.

"Relax boys, that's Paul McCord's bay on the right. I don't know the other fellow."

Paul was Allison's father and therefore Dan's father-in-law. When he got closer, Blue trotted out to meet him. The two had become friends during the first weeks of Dan's time at the McCord ranch when the four partners first arrived in this territory. Paul had bribed the big horse with sugar cubes, carrots, and apples he kept in his pockets to cement their relationship.

When they rode up to the wagon, they dismounted and came forward to meet the three partners. Paul McCord was a big-boned, husky six footer with the muscle development of the typical working rancher. He showed his relationship to Allison in his handsome face. He shook hands warmly with the three before introducing his companion.

"Boys, meet George Searcy of the Union Pacific."

They greeted the older, graying individual with strong handshakes and received the same in return. Searcy was a tall, slender man with a neatly trimmed mustache, dressed in the typical riding garb of the times. He wore a leather shell belt showing decades of wear, with the wooden handles of an equally worn Colt protruding from it. It swung low on his left side and was tied down, indicating the weapon was not for show.

"I'm happy to meet you fellows. Mister McCord has been regaling me with tales of your exploits all the way here, so I've really been looking forward to this."

"Mister Searcy, I'm afraid my father-in-law may be a bit inclined to rather enhance the facts of some things he tells about the Twin Forks crew."

"Well Dan, if half of it is accurate, you are the men I want to talk to. You'll remember that three years ago we had planned to build, or rather, extend the existing spur, from Boomstick to Twin Forks but there was a lot of crooked dealing going on to try and acquire the entire valley for monetary gain. The home office decided to forego that extension until things had time to settle down, but now it is still needed, and in fact, even more so. The farmers north of here want to expand their tilled land, but the transportation problems are just too much to allow it. We have the potential to make a lot of money for all concerned, including you horse ranchers who sell to eastern interests. That's why I'm here; we need your help."

Bear's gravelly voice spoke up, "Jist how can we ranchers help yu, sir? Seems tu me yu must have folks who know what they're doin' tu build such a road."

"Yes, as far as the actual building goes, you're absolutely right. However, we need horses, lots of them, that are large, good stock for the road excavating equipment and such. Not even ordinary work horses are up to some of our tasks with the heavy stuff. We need draft horses for that. I'm looking for thirty teams of drafts, along with another twenty teams of regular work horses. Paul, here, says he knows you can help very little as far as the drafts. He can help me some, but we're falling way short. He thought you fellows might know where we can find our needed help."

Dan spoke up, "Wow, I wish we had a hundred horses to sell you, but Paul is right on that issue. We have a few drafts here that we got from him, but we need one team ourselves and have yet to multiply the herd as far as that end goes. We have most of our other work horses spoken for by those same farmers up north, but maybe you could work a deal with them to buy and then sell back, or whatever they might come up with. After all, this is to help them so they should be willing to help out somehow."

"Well, I plan to try just that, but I'll still be short on the big fellows. Any suggestions?"

Bear spoke up once more. "I know a rancher fifty miles

south of here who may be able to help. Yu could telegraph him tu find out. His name is Jim Branson, and he's a real honest feller. He lives by a town called Sunny Springs in Utah."

"Thanks, Bear, I'll contact him as soon as I get back to Boomstick. But first, I have to go to Twin Forks to see some people there for land acquisition. That brings me to another thing we need to talk about, the railroad's right of way through your ranch. How far north does your ranch run?"

"We go right up to the town. East, we run into Paul's ranch."

"Then we need to purchase a right of way from you. Any objections? The U.P. will pay going prices."

"And cut our own throat by putting up a fight, not on your life. You tell us what you need and draw it up and we'll go along with you, right fellows?"

He received nods from both Bear and Reddy so the deal was agreed to.

"One more thing to cover, then I think I can mark this day down as a total success; are there cattle ranches in the area? We are going to need cattle to feed our men, and lots of them."

"There are some north of here, all good men. Not a one of them has caused trouble for the farmers moving in like you hear about in other places. They buy the farmers' produce and the farmers buy their beef. In other words, they act like people should." Dan had long been critical of some of the land wars in other areas and looked upon his area as one of distinction.

"You apparently haven't noticed the telegraph line along your route as they surveyed it? You can send one to Jim Branson from Twin Forks." Reddy smiled mischievously as he said this.

Searcy smiled back and replied, "As a matter of fact, I had nothing to do with the surveying. I received maps and specs and was handed the job on rather a minute's notice. So thanks for telling me. I probably would have noticed the line as I rode into town." His grin was just as mischievous as Reddy's.

The three talked a bit further, establishing how many horses could be furnished by the two ranches, and then the railroad man rode off to the north on his quest for the town while McCord went east and the three partners resumed their haying. The long-awaited railroad was on its way at last.

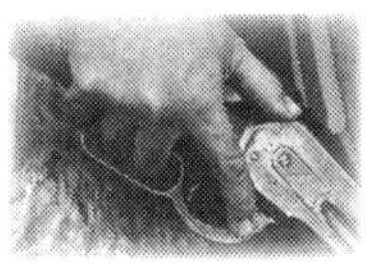

TWO

The Union Pacific westbound slowed as it rolled into the station just north of Salt Lake City and as it did, three scurvy-looking characters jumped from the open cattle car near the end of the train. They gathered their meager gear, including one saddle; then, avoiding the main part of the town, they went directly to the "lower" end to a rough, dirty, noisy saloon.

The individual with the saddle stood out a bit from the other two. He showed a bit more personal care than his companions, wearing a black leather vest over a once-white shirt above black trousers of a rather expensive make. There rode on his hips the worn leather belt supporting two holstered forty-four caliber pistols with fancy pearl hand grips. Each sported notches on the handles, three on the right and two on the left. The low-riding, tied-down rig announced the presence of either a true gun slinger or a profound fake. Fact was, he was the former, with the name of John Smoots; at least that was the one he was currently using. The notches on his guns only represented those he had bested in face to face shootouts; there were others who had seen less or no chance to defend themselves, men he had been hired to kill whom he had needed to dispatch quickly.

Number two train-jumper was a little man with two weeks' growth of beard, in flannel shirt and too-large bib overalls, with a single shell belt holding a black powder revolver of southern construction and shells for the Henry rifle in his hand. He would have been eagerly accosted by the proper authorities for desertion had the South still had an army. His name was James "Jimmy" Flanders.

The third man proved to be the leader of the trio. His was a bulky and powerful build encased in a six foot frame of bone and muscle. He carried a Sharps fifty caliber buffalo gun and a nondescript and seldom used six-shooter. He depended mostly on the Sharps or the huge Bowie knife at his side. He was known simply as Cannon and he was a totally ruthless and cold-blooded killer. He was on a personal quest.

"We ain't too fer from thu gurl, but I want to get that mountain man first. To do that, we gotta go north a bit more. We'll stay here tonight, get a little sleep, a lotta drink, and try to ketch the train north to a ratty little town called Boomstick tomorrow. Somebody there can tell me where to find this Rollins guy." Such were Cannon's instructions to the others. They simply nodded and bellied up to the makeshift bar, a plank laid upon two empty whisky barrels.

The targets of Cannon's quest were a girl named Melodi Branson and the Twin Forks partner, Bear Rollins. Melodi had been kidnapped by Cannon and others a year before and Rollins had rescued her. During the several months involved, all of Cannon's cohorts had been either killed or jailed, including himself for a few nights while in Salt Lake, Utah. It was there he and Bear had come close to a fight to the finish, but the law had interfered. He nursed a deep-rooted grudge that he intended to satisfy before kidnapping the girl a second time. He was bound and determined to get the big money he felt her father "owed" him.

The very nature of the establishment fostered trouble each and every day; this was to be no exception. The fact that the local constabulary kept a close eye on it made absolutely no difference. As Smoots bellied up to the bar his twin holsters caught the attention of a local would-be gunman, one looking for a reputation as such. The notches on Smoots' guns may have been gaudy show-off material, but they were the real deal, earned at others' expense.

"Looks like we got us a real live bad man here, fellows. Either that, or he's awful careless with his knife around those show-off gun handles," growled the youngster.

He was a grubby-looking kid of around twenty-two years with a growth of peach fuzz all over his homely face. There was an occasional "real" whisker dotting the area and that made him look even worse. With a really bad over-bite and tobacco-stained, protruding buck teeth, he was a fine example of the town's best. Or so he thought. He followed the cutting remark with a hand reaching for the left holster of Smoots only to pass into unconsciousness with huge bloody lump on the side of his head. John simply drew and clubbed all in one motion; a motion that to others was nearly indistinguishable because of the quick, fluid movement of his right hand. The form on the floor never moved as the gunman stood over him.

"This scumball was lookin' for a killin' and isn't up to the task. Someone dig him outta the sawdust and tote him home to his momma."

The bartender looked Smoots over before answering. "No need to drag him out. He'll likely come to in a while and walk out on his own. Ain't worth the trouble to drag on him. Been lookin' for this for a couple o' weeks now. I don't care if he croaks; I'm tired o' him hasslin' folks and glad I don't gotta shovel-blood soaked sawdust outta here when I close.

"You gents have one on the house, an' then I'd advise moving on before the depity makes his hourly check. That'll be in about fifteen minutes. The locals is awful picky 'bout what goes on in here and don't mind pushin' the law hard at people."

"Then give us a bottle to carry out with us an' we'll move along," growled Cannon. They took the bottle, tossed the money to the 'tender and stalked out.

"Why didn't you just shoot that stupid kid, John?" asked Jimmy.

"With what Cannon here has planned we don't need to be noticed in this territory, you fool, that's why. Besides, I don't like killin' unless there's good pay for it or it just can't be avoided. That kid has no idea what to do in a fight. He won't last another month."

"That's good thinkin', Smoots," came from Cannon. "No need to cause folks to remember us."

"What's next, Cannon? We stayin' in this town, movin' out to dry camp, or what? I'd not mind some good food tonight instead of grubbin' around for hand-outs."

The three had been on the grubstake trail for a week, traveling without horses and keeping to the rails to get to their destination. Both Cannon and Smoots seemed to have plenty of cash when needed, so clandestine movement had to be their purpose.

They made their way to an eatery that promised home-cooked food, sat on the stools at the counter and found the home in which the food had been cooked must have been that of a grease merchant. However, the oily fare went down easily enough for three who were used to bad trail food. They hogged it down as quickly as a wolf on the prowl and were soon trekking their way back to the railroad yard.

After a bit of searching, they found a switch rail that hooked up with a branch pointing north. After a brief consultation with a track inspector, they found it went to Boomstick and so began walking along the rails, John Smoots carrying his saddle over his shoulder and trailing behind the other two by several feet. The tack was going to get heavy quickly.

Neither Cannon nor Jimmy knew the measure of the man accompanying them, or they might have been less accepting of his company. John Smoots had been born and raised in the east, son of a lawyer father and socialite mother. His parents' expectations had been only theirs and not his own. John was lazy and was not about to apply himself to studies or other hard work if he could escape by doing things other ways. He was of higher than average intelligence and therefore became quite adept at maneuvering those not so blessed to accomplish gain for him. He became a real con-man.

Banished early on by his ladder-climbing parents, he soon found those willing to pay for his cleverness and eventually ran afoul of the law. That led to grabbing a train to Ohio, a place he quickly learned to hate. It was there he had killed his first man.

When he was just seventeen years old, a philandering wife of a rich merchant had wooed him and convinced him to kill her husband for her with promises of big money rewards and herself. He fell "victim" to her wiles, killed the merchant, and found his safety in the town quite wanting. The lady had quickly identified him as the assailant and he found himself to be much in need of a way out of town. The westbound train served his purpose and he stayed on until he was far on the western side of the Mississippi.

It seems those inclined to live outside the law have a magnetism between them, and he soon fell in with like-minded people. Discovering he had an innate skill with a revolver did nothing to dissuade his further development as an outlaw and, soon after that, a gunslinger. What Cannon and Jimmy failed to know was the complete lack of integrity in the man, and therefore they had no way of knowing he intended to take anything they could swindle, steal, or otherwise for himself. John Smoots wanted a life of ease and luxury and was scheming at all times with a cold approach to finding the means for achieving his desires.

"Why don't you dump that heavy saddle, gunslinger? They make new ones every day. Seems you spend a lot of wasted muscle on a hunk o' leather," commented Jimmy.

"It's my muscle," Smoots replied with no emotion. "New tack costs money, which I don't have. Besides, I happen to like this saddle. That okay with you, Flanders?"

Jimmy Flanders wasn't a brave soul, or a foolish one, and he recognized the coldness in Smoots' question, so he merely grunted an assent.

They made their way north along the tracks of the spur that pointed the way to Boomstick, their current goal. About a quarter mile out they found a likely spot for boarding unnoticed and settled down with a meal of cold biscuits saved from the days before, washed down with the cheap whiskey. Cannon and Flanders proceeded to drink continuously while the gunman eased back against a large rock and closed his eyes. John never drank more than a swallow of liquor at a time, he was too aware of the restriction of reflexes inherent to the brew.

Twilight started its slow approach before the puffing of a steam engine roused them from their ease. That was good timing, for it was more likely to be a successful boarding without notice in the poor lighting. Now, if they could only find a car with the door open. They hunkered down behind the boulder previously serving as their back-rest and waited.

It wasn't long before a freight car showed up with a gaping side door advertising its emptiness within. The train wasn't gaining speed yet and Smoots had less trouble tossing his saddle in and climbing aboard than his two whiskey-laden comrades. However, they were relaxed and sleeping before he had stretched out in a corner with his saddle arranged as a pillow. Boomstick was about to receive three new inhabitants.

§ § § §

It was fully dark and around midnight when the train finally pulled into Boomstick. The town had been established as a point of contact for the settlement of the Idaho territory, and the railroad had built the branch strictly for that purpose. It was located at the outlet of a pass through the mountains from the east, allowing for wagon trains from that direction as well as the trains from the south. The name had derived from the local Indians' comments about the use of dynamite to clear the way through many boulder strewn fields and passes. In the earliest days of the tracks' approach there had also been more than a couple of Indian attacks thwarted by the use of the very effective explosives.

It had become a really peaceful little settlement since the completion of the tracks, with well-established law enforcement, telegraph, huge general store that supplied all the people for a radius of over thirty miles. When the small town of Twin Forks was started some fifty miles to the west, the store owner had built a branch there as well, so owner John Miles was a well-to-do man and highly respected in the whole territory around southern Idaho. He had helped build the railroad and just stayed when the work was done.

Bill Hanson was the local and territorial law, having served as marshal of the territory and then as local sheriff. He had married John's sister and the two constantly feuded over who had married the better cook. They were as close as brothers.

The livery stable in town was also huge and boasted of a very large herd of stock, both riding and harness, that all around knew could be had at fair prices and honest dealing. All in all, Boomstick was a thriving little place that called the surrounding settlers to its bosom with more frequency than was probably necessary. However, the normal, quiet routines and tranquil atmosphere of the great little town were turned upside down at the present time; the railroad building crew had moved back into the vicinity.

When the three outlaws jumped from the now slowly moving train, it was on the opposite side from the camp, and they slipped behind a large bush until it had passed them by. John Smoots swore softly at the scratches his saddle received as the result of being tossed out, retrieved it and started toward town.

"Where the blazes ya think yore goin'?" grumbled Cannon.

"Hotel room and a bath."

"Ya don't need no bath, and we ain't stayin' in no hotel, neither. We'll settle in at the tent camp 'til we get the lay of things and find out where this Rollins character is."

"Cannon, you want to sleep in a tent another night, go ahead. You want to keep smelling like a goat, go ahead. But don't get the idea I work for you or take orders from you like that. I signed on to this caper for the money and only the money; you get my gun and nothing else. I'll look you up tomorrow." With that, the gunman turned his back and walked away, heavy saddle over one shoulder.

Cannon stood looking after the slowly receding figure for several minutes, seething with anger at the smaller man's audacity. His hand unconsciously fingered the large knife at his side as he did so. John Smoots should have been scared of a man his size. He should have cowered down and obeyed. Smoots would have to die for that as soon as he was no longer a benefit.

The big man finally shook himself and proceeded toward the tent city. Jimmy Flanders knew this was no time to be slow to follow, so he scurried to Cannon's side and remained silent. Silence was safer than talking right now. They found a tent that was much larger than the others, with men coming and going as though it was the center of activity for the camp, which was actually the case. This was the "office" complex for the project. They found a table manned by two men in suits with papers and maps strewn before them where others were congregating as they awaited instructions.

The younger of the two noticed the arrival of Cannon and

Flanders and motioned them over. “What can I do for you gentlemen?”

“What kinda jobs ya got?” asked Cannon.

“Well, we have about anything you can think of, sir. I would guess you to be a hunter from the cut of you. We need meat supplies on a grand scale to feed these hungry track-layers. If you take the job, when you’re not bringing in large game, you would be butchering cattle once we get them here. That may be a couple of weeks, so the hunting is very critical right now. We have only one other hunter at this time, so the hours will be long. Interested?”

“We’ll take it. My friend here can butcher for me.”

“Fine and dandy. Now, your names, please?”

“I’m Cannon and he’s Flanders and that’s all we use. Don’t abide much in first monikers.”

“Okay, you are now on the payroll of the U.P. Step outside and ask for Con Richards and he’ll give you a tent. You can take your horses to the picket line after that.”

“Ain’t got no horses, came in on yore train.”

“In that case, tell Con to set you up with two horses and a pack animal. We’ll reclaim those from you when the tracks are done.”

They exited the large tent and were immediately approached by a short, stocky Irishman actively stuffing an apple into his mouth one huge bite at a time. He noted their exit from the main tent and stopped them.

“I betcha just got jobs in there, right?”

“Yeh, what’s it to you?” Cannon growled.

“What it is to me, big man with the lousy disposition, is that I’m Con Richards and what you do for this railroad is totally my business and what I tell you to do better be what you do, or you’ll soon be orphans again. What’d they hire ya to do?” All this came out in a distinctive Irish brogue and with forceful meaning. Con Richards had been with the U.P. from the beginning, working his way up to construction supervisor for the entire western branch. He was used to rough, cantankerous men and could handle the worst of them.

“I’m a hunter and he’s my butcherer,” growled Cannon.

"They said to give us horses. And a pack horse."

"Good, good. You'll need ammo for that cannon you're carrying. I'll show you where to get supplies in case you end up staying out a night or two. I hope that won't be the case, as we need meat each and every day! The picket line is out there to the west edge. Just tell whoever's keeping watch what you need and that I sent you and he'll take care of you."

He led them down a "street" between two rows of tents to an actual building where he introduced them to the storekeeper. As soon as they finished there, Con took them along the same "street" to a small tent clear on the edge of the complex, pointed to it, and left them with nary another word. They stood looking after the squat man as though he had just taken their last bite of pie.

"If that don't beat all. Just leaves us here and traipses off. No telling us when to start or nothin'," Flanders said.

"We start when we want," growled Cannon. "That's tomorrow at first light."

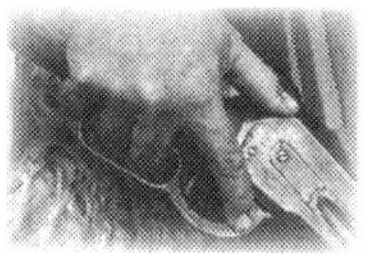

THREE

George Searcy rode back into the Twin Forks Ranch at dusk two days later. Allison greeted him and welcomed him into the house, setting a cup of coffee before him as he eased his tired frame into a chair.

"Thank you, Missus Kade. This old body doesn't handle days on horseback the way it used to."

She smiled down at him with a knowing look and replied, "I'm afraid I understand all too well, Mister Searcy. My dad is in the same situation, much to his consternation. Dad just can't admit that he can't go all day for several days without stopping once in a while."

"When we men get a little long in the tooth we tend to ignore it and keep trying to do as always. By the way, it's just George, no Mister allowed for my friends, and you folks have certainly befriended me."

"Okay, George. And that means that I am just Allison, or Allie, if you prefer. We are so thrilled to have the spur coming into the area. It's going to help all this wonderful ranching and farming land become a prosperous territory."

"I have been very well received up north of here. The farmers and ranchers alike have endorsed the 'road with enthusiasm like yours. I sense a real spirit of unity between the two factions. That is NOT what I've found in other areas. This is quite refreshing."

They stopped talking as the sound of horses arriving rang

forth from the front. Within moments the door was filled with five dusty, sweaty bodies as the Twin Forks men filed through. Dan was leading and smiled broadly with pleasure as he recognized Searcy.

"Hello, Mister Searcy, good to see you back!" The greeting was echoed by the three partners while Skinny just nodded.

"First, it's George, not Mister. Second, thanks. And third, I really need help! That's why I came all the way down from the road to Boomstick."

"What's the problem, George?" Reddy was in the process of pulling off his boots as he asked this.

"I have had absolutely no luck in finding horses around Twin Forks, but I just received a reply telegram from Bear's friend down in Utah and he'll supply horses, but needs for a rep to come down and pick them out and to verify the deal as being real. Not that I blame him; I'm sure there are a lot of horse thieves around."

Bear spoke up, "Wal, George, Jim had his share of horse stealing happen jist a year or so ago, so I'm sure he's extra careful. Iffn ya want, I'll take a ride down thar tu act as yore rep. It'll be good tu see Miss Mel again, and rumor has it thet Ted showed up and is staying on thar. Don't surprise me none," he chuckled with delight. "He and Miss Mel were really taken with each other. A man'll ride a long ways fer a good-lookin' gal iffn she's friendly-like." He looked at Allie as he spoke and received a poke in the arm for his trouble. Her look told him he was lucky it wasn't harder. Except for Skinny, who was still easily embarrassed around any female company, all the men at the ranch continually gave Allie a hard time, but they received just as much in return from the "little sister" of Twin Forks. Dan tried his best to stay neutral, but with little to no success. Either side would often attack him for not taking sides.

"Bear, I'm grateful for that. How soon do you think you can go? I have men already at Boomstick waiting to start construction right now. They can do some work with what we now have, including the teams you and Mister McCord have let us have, but I need thirty more teams as soon as I can get them."

"I'll be gone at first light tomorrow. I'll see iffn I kin find enough help tu drive what Branson kin furnish. I gather yu want them driven tu Boomstick?"

"No, drive them due east to the spur that runs from near Salt Lake City to Boomstick. I'll have a train waiting to load up on a siding there, and the engineers will keep watch for you. Telegraph me in Boomstick as soon as you start the drive, and they'll be warned well in advance. That will get the herd there in just a few hours instead of a three days' drive from the ranch, if you could even make it that quickly."

"Got my doubts about thet; more like four with a herd thet size."

"I'll be back in Boomstick day after next, so I should have things set up in plenty of time."

Bear left the room to prepare for his ride and the others continued talking business and railroad while Allie fixed the supper meal. Skinny went out to put the horses away and do some chores until meal time. Joe and Reddy talked a while, then left to help Skinny finish up. Dawn the next day found Bear already ten miles south on his way to Sunny Springs, Utah, on his quest for the U.P.'s sixty horses.

§ § § §

The red stallion was stretched out in a full run, belly to the ground and raising dust like there was no tomorrow. The girl on his back risked a look over her shoulder and saw that her pursuer actually had gained ground. Her hat flew back behind her on the chin strap as she turned back to the front and frantically cried into the ear of her steed to go faster or they would be caught.

A long-limbed steeldust gelding with nose stretched out long and legs pumping like pistons slowly gained on the girl and her mount. The rider in pursuit leaned far over the horse's neck and also cried out to his racing animal for more speed. The rider was a wild-looking individual with low-slung, tied-down sidearm and long flowing sandy hair trying to escape from his hat. The worn jeans and run-over boots only served to accent the range rider look of one used to life on a horse.

The girl finally saw the ranch buildings come into sight and felt a sense of relief as she counted on her mount's endurance to make the safety of the ranch yard ahead of the steeldust with its determined rider. The path to the buildings curved around two outlying corrals and she panicked when she realized the rider behind had turned his horse to go around the first of these to try to cut her off! It was a possibility and she let out a scream of frustration at the sight of the bigger horse coming at the opening that would cut her off. Then the red stallion found one last burst of speed and thundered into the yard between the stables and the house.

She pulled the horse to a sudden stop that set him to his heels and threw dust into a rising cloud. The sound of her scream while still outside the corrals and the hammering of the two large horses' hooves brought Jim Branson on the run from the larger of the barns. He had taken to wearing a gun at all times since the kidnapping of his daughter Melodi a year and a half previous. and the holster flapped wildly as he ran. He hauled up short of the blowing, prancing horses and took the reins of the red steed, holding him down from too much nervous movement.

Melodi dismounted and stuck her tongue out at the cowboy still on the steeldust. "Thought you said that nag could catch Flash! Well, didn't you?'

The smiling pursuer chuckled through a handsome face turned dark brown by years in the sun. A Texas heritage showed plainly and no one who knew anything at all about Texans could mistake the brand on him. When he dismounted he stood on the bow legs of a life-long horseman, worn Levis showing themselves to be shinier in the seat than the rest of the garment from the hours of rubbing the leather of a roping saddle.

A Colt resided in a low-slung gun belt that was tied down and spoke of many days of constant practice at the art of the quick draw and marksmanship. The sombrero trying to manage the unruly sandy colored and nearly-shoulder length hair was likewise obviously a very experienced member of the outfit. Those run-over-at-the-heel boots with the huge Mexican spurs completed the appearance of this likeable-looking individual by the name of Sweeny. Ted Sweeny, late of Texas.

"Well, are you ready to eat crow, Ted? It looks to me like that steeldust has really been EATING dust!" And with that comment, Jim Branson broke into laughter at his own joke.

The slow Texas drawl came quietly through that laughter, effectively silencing Branson. "Wal, Jimmy, my lad, if ya take note of whar Dusty was when we came into this yard and stop tu think of the fact he was carrying aboot twenty more pounds o' saddle than Flash and maybe five or six more pounds o' rider, he coulda won hands down in a fair race."

"A RIDER WHO'S FIVE OR SIX POUNDS MORE!? Ted Sweeny, I'm going to make you regret the day your mother decided to marry your dad! I'm going to…I'll…You're going to die a slow Indian torture death, you horrible Texas bum!" shouted Melodi.

The laughter erupted once again from her dad and was supplemented by that from the cowboy, and the two ended up leaning against each other to keep from collapsing. The unhappy girl promptly pushed both of them hard enough to topple them had they not seen it coming, yelling at them all the while. Both horses shied away and trotted off to the stable on their own. If one looked the two of them over closely, they saw a sorrel stallion with remarkable lines of breeding with speed and endurance practically glowing about him, while the steeldust, standing a full hand taller at seventeen hands, was of even more impressive build.

He had a chest that promised lungs the size of a kitchen stove and rangy limbs shouting of never-slowing strides exceeding those of most thoroughbreds. He had the head of an Arabian on the neck of a thoroughbred and the body to do justice to both. Sweeny had won him in the only poker game he had ever taken part in. When he had showed up with the horse after a week away from the ranch and was asked how he could buy a horse like Dusty, his reply had been that "Ain't no Texas cowpoke ever could BUY a hoss like Dusty! I stole him." He had never confessed to a different story, no matter what persuasive efforts Melodi had applied. When she finally approached her dad about it, he only smiled and assured her the mischievousness of Texas cowboys was as natural as breathing to them and she would probably never know the truth, except that she could be sure Ted had not stolen the steed.

“Ted Sweeny, if you think you can get out of saying I weigh almost as much as YOU without pain and misery, you’ve got another think coming! I don’t know just what I’m going to do yet; but when I do, you, mister smart mouth, are going to pray for help!”

A low, gravely voice from behind interrupted Melodi at that point with, “Well, now, Miss Mel, seems tu me the last time I saw the two of you together, yu hed a totally different thought about mister cowboy thar. Iffn I ‘member right, yu was kissin’ all over him an’ tryin’ tu squeeze his innerds out.” The big man behind the voice referred to the goodbye shared by the two young people when they left Silverton, Colorado, heading in different directions. Mel had stated her love for Ted at that time.

Melodi squealed as she turned to the voice and then yelped out, “Bear!” She ran pell-mell to the big man as he rounded the corner of the house and leaped to wrap her arms around his huge neck while throwing her legs around his waist and began kissing him all up and down his bearded countenance. He laughed as she kept a running talk going between smooches until he finally spoke through all her efforts.

“Miss Mel, I think yu better let go an’ get down afore yore daddy thar goes fer his shotgun tu start a weddin’. I’m most glad yore happy tu see me, but yore gonna wear out my welcome hyar iffn yu keep on.” With that, he gently loosened her grip and slowly lowered her to the ground, where she continued to snuggle up against him, arms now trying to reach around his waist.

Ted stalked up to their friend and the two shook hands, each placing their free hand over the other’s and just staring into each others’ eyes with the silent respect that comes to men who have been through very hard times together and strengthened one another during the journey.

Bear Rollins and Melodi had nursed Sweeny through a bout of alcoholism while in Silverton, Colorado, and had supported him when he lost his twin sister, Tessa, to suicide. It was during that time Melodi had expressed her love for the cowboy and sworn him to follow her once he had returned to Texas to break the terrible news to his parents. He had shown up at the Branson ranch nearly a year later and was quickly hired on by her dad.

"Daughter, I have to ask, just what is this display of scandalous affection all about?" Jim asked with a twinkle in his eyes.

"Oh Dad, you know very well what it's about. You don't have someone save your life and then spend two months on the trail with them without learning to love them like a brother. Oh, Bear, I've missed you sooo much! What are you doing here? Did you come just to visit me?"

He chuckled a deep sound and then, hand on top of her head replied, "I'm afeered not, little one, though iffn I was smart I'd say yes tu avoid getting' in trouble like Teddy, hyar. I come tu talk horses with yore dad fer the railroad. But afore we do thet, when's the weddin'?"

Both Melodi and Ted blushed, as Ted waved his hands furiously at Bear to hush. Melodi saw that out of the corner of her eye and stuck her tongue out at him again.

"Wedding? Why, I know nothing of any wedding, Bear. What ever can you mean, wedding?"

He then laughed outright and squeezed her before gently extracting her arms from his waist and holding her by the shoulders at arms' length.

"Don't ferget, little one, thet I kin easily toss yu over my knee and whup on yore backside fer misbehavin'. Don't be playin' innocent with yore old big brother, Bear. Do I need tu take thet worthless Texas cowpoke out back o' thu barn an' beat a little sense inter him tu make him ask yu?"

Melodi squeaked and freed herself, then ran for the house, hat and hair flying as she did so. Bear chuckled deep in his chest as they watched the girl's frantic retreat. Her dad spoke up, "Don't know as I ever seen her cowed that easily, Rollins. Maybe we should keep you around. Now, I assume you're here about the horses. Searcy and I worked out most of the details by telegraph, but I insisted on a rep from him to select the teams and verify payment."

"Thet would be my job, I came 'cause it was a chance tu see Miss Mel and Ted again. Truth be told, I miss both o' them from time tu time. Do we have tu do some round-up work first?"

"No, Ted has taken care of that. Him and Melodi make pretty good hands when they behave themselves, so I sent them out for that chore while the other two hands took care of the rest of my herds. I have two different ranges here that keep the riding stock separated by age as much as possible. The Army doesn't want young mounts and they're picky about color, so I try to make it easier to separate when their purchase time comes. The harness herd is right out that way about a mile. This is going to take about all the harness stock, except for my brood mares and stallion, that I have. Searcy knows most of the horses he's getting have never seen harness. I assume you four will care for that?"

"Dunno. Nuthin's been said about thet. Teddy, let's you an' I take a quick ride out thet way and have a look at thu herd."

"Fine by me, Bear. Let me switch horses first. Want a new mount?"

"Good idea, this fella's had a hard two days.

Ted disappeared into the stable, was gone a few minutes and then reappeared leading two fresh horses. They switched their saddles to those two, turned their others into box stalls and grained them then rode out to the northeast. Ted talked as they rode.

"This herd is all the harness stock we have. Jim doesn't rely much on anything but riding stock for right now, but I think I've got him leanin' thu other way a bit. I been tryin' tu talk him into goin' back into some cattle, too. Hed a brick wall there tu start with, may hev him comin' round a bit, though.

"Horses air alright fer awhile, but thar's only so many markets fer them. Folks always got tu eat, and beef is mostly whut they want."

"Yore right thar, lad, we been talkin' thu same way at Twin Forks, 'ceptin' we ain't got nobody but Reddy whut knows even a little bit about cattle and he hates thu critters. Mebbe we kin get you tu come up and teach us fer a year or so."

"Not likely, Bear. The Bransons air countin' on me too much. 'Sides, I cain't leave Mel alone thet long. Leastways, I won't."

"Whut's thu deal thar, Ted? I figgered yu'd be hitched by now."

"When I came here, I left two broken-hearted folks back in

Texas, my mom 'n dad. Then a few months later I got this letter sayin' they cain't stay thar, too many memories. Pop says they plan tu sell ever' thing off an' move oot o' the area so I told them all aboot this wonderful valley and aboot thu ranch jist north 'o hyar thet's fer sale. Ain't as big as they'd like, but this ain't Texas, neither.

"Mel, she gits it in her pretty little haid thet my folks might blame her fer Tessa's death an' I cain't talk sense into her. She's been actin' real distant ever' since. Any time I try tu talk tu her, or even try tu hug her, she moves away an' gets real teary-eyed. I quit pushin' an' guess I jist gotta wait her oot. I promised the folks I'd go back down tu Texas tu help them trail up hyar, but I'm afeared thet'll be even worse whar Mel's concerned. I jist don't know whut tu do, Bear. I gotta help thu folks."

"Welcome tu thu world o' love, Teddy me lad. Wish I could help yu, but ain't nuthin' tu be did about it by anyone but you and Mel. I wish yu luck, an' I gotta feelin' it'll work out. Thet girl has a real big love fer you, an' thar's no way she kin let go of it."

"Bear, my good and dear friend, I shore hope yore right. At least I know yu'll stick by me no matter whut. Yore true-blue and I love yu for it."

The two continued on to look over the harness herd, not returning to the ranch until nearly dark. During supper, Melodi sat as close to Bear as she could and pumped him continually as to his life since he had left her there at Silverton. Her kidnapping had been a harrowing experience, and Bear's rescue and subsequent weeks of travel to return her to her folks had cemented a relationship that could very well have been as close as or even closer than brother and sister.

They had met Ted in Silverton at a low point in his life. His twin sister, Tessa was working in a saloon for her husband, a lecherous and crooked individual, and ended up committing suicide in spite of Melodi's friendship. Mel had always harbored a guilt feeling over the fact that she hadn't been able to rescue Tessa in much the same way that Bear had rescued her. It was during that time that she had fallen in love with Ted Sweeny.

Now it seemed Ted was faced with yet another dilemma as

Melodi carried her load of false guilt over her failure to save Tessa from her despondency. As Ted faced up to the decision he was headed for, it became a balancing act between his love for Melodi and his love for his parents.

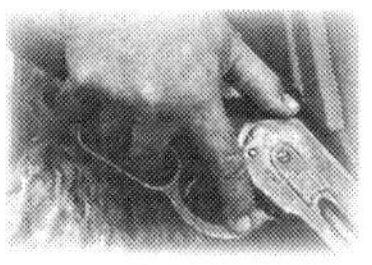

FOUR

All but Bear were in a "family meeting" at Twin Forks Ranch. It was at the end of the evening meal, and the table had been all but empty when the four tired, hungry men pulled their chairs from the table and proceeded to help Allie. She had apologized for the lack of a proper meal, but the four had assured her they would get by. They all pitched in to clear the table and wash the dishes. That made Allie feel even worse about her lack of success with the day's duties. Little Ira had been ill all day, causing no end of nursing to be necessary, and Allison simply didn't have enough time and energy to care for the feeding of the men.

"It looks tu me like we need tu get Allie some help around here now thet little Ira's here. This is jist too much fer one woman." Reddy had suggested before that they should get a cook for the ranch, but Allison had always talked them out of it. Now she was beginning to drop her opposition.

"One of us needs to go to Twin Forks tomorrow to see if we can find someone. Preferably a really beautiful and single young lady," said Dan, ducking the swing of Allie's backhand as he did so.

Reddy chuckled and replied, "Then, Danny boy, yu should be thu one tu do it since yu know jist whut yu want. Right, fellas?"

Dan received a quick vote from all but Allison as to the affirmative and found himself an unwilling delegate to the ladies of the town of Twin Forks to find a full time employee. Allison stuck her tired tongue out at her husband and then issued dire promises of punishment should he bring home "too young and too pretty" a girl.

The next morning's dawn found the rider some ten miles north of the ranch as he and Blue moved in a ground-eating pace. The big horse had not been worked all that much during the first cutting of hay and was eager to go, and then go some more. Dan allowed him his head, and his response was a mild canter that set Dan's body to a rocking-chair motion of easy comfort.

Another two hours found him a full fourteen miles further north, still at the same tireless pace, when he topped a small rise and pulled the roan to a sudden halt. He was overlooking a large plowed section of land covering fully fifty acres of rich ground. He knew he was still on Twin Forks Ranch!

Pulling his binoculars, he scanned the field of vision from horizon to horizon and found a set of buildings another mile to the northwest. They shined in the morning light with the freshly peeled look of newly cut logs. Halfway between his position and the buildings he located a team pulling a plow. In the same field, following the plowing team was another team pulling a harrow instead of a disc that was knocking down the furrows.

He dropped off the rise in a gallop that soon took him to the plowing farmer. When the fellow saw him coming so fast, he stopped his team and unlimbered his rifle, held to his back by a section of leather rein, and waited Dan's arrival.

When Dan pulled Blue to a stop he found himself looking down on a medium height man of grizzled look. His five foot, eight inch frame was nearly as wide as it was high, at least that was the impression one got when looking him over. The hands were almost as large as Bear's and showed the results and ravages of hard labor. Dan knew he was looking at a bonafide working man.

"Hello. I'm Dan Kade, one of the partners down at the Twin Forks ranch. Looks like you've been a very busy man this spring!"

"Yeah, I have. Man's got to keep at it if he wants to make a decent livin' for his family. What can I do for you?" The words came out with a distinct accent Dan was unfamiliar with.

"Well, sir, I don't know just how to break this to you, but this is Twin Forks Ranch land for another five miles north. You've settled on deeded land, my friend."

"I don't see any deed, was told all the land around here was open for the settling of it. If it's so blamed important to you, why haven't you been around before this? We been here two months already. Got my house, barn, and corrals up and frankly, mister, I don't plan on moving. So I guess that means you and me have a problem."

"No, that means YOU have a problem. The law is plain, and we can just turn this over to them and let them deal with you. How in heaven's name did you get all this done in two months? You must have hired help besides that youngster over there with the other team."

"I got me two good boys old enough to work a team and another that can plant already. They run from ten to fourteen years. Now, what you plan to do about YOUR problem?"

"You planted that other section I came by yet?"

"If you have to know, yes we have. We got taters and corn in there. Seed was expensive, too. We have a lot of cash tied up right now, as well as two months' hard work. You haven't answered my question."

"You're right, I haven't. Don't plan to until I talk to my partners. I hate to see all this work and investment go for nothing, but it's still our land. Who can I say is squatting on the ranch? I'll need to know that for the law."

"Name's Cogswell. Hiram Cogswell, if you have to know. Won't do you any good to know it unless you want it on your tombstone as the perpetrator of your demise. I told you, I'm not moving, so you just better get off MY land, and NOW!"

Cogswell's eyes then fairly bugged out of his head as he was suddenly staring down the barrel of a Colt revolver that seemed to magically appear in the rider's hand. It not only pointed unwaveringly at his head, but it was fully cocked. How had that happened?

"Please don't make me cause those hard-working boys to be

without a hard-working dad, Mister Cogswell. I'll do it if you even twitch with that rifle, but I'll hate myself afterwards. Now, very gently and slowly, and I do mean slowly, lay the rifle down at your feet. Now."

All that was said quietly and almost gently, but Cogswell was no fool. He recognized the no-nonsense tone behind it. He complied, never taking his eyes off the rider. The son with the other team was approaching and would soon be there.

"Mister Cogswell, I would rather not have you embarrassed by your son seeing you under my gun. Do I have your promise not to try anything if I put this away?"

"What do you care what my son thinks if you plan to try and run us off this land?"

"I care, that's all. A man needs to have his son's full respect. Besides, it hasn't been determined yet that you'll be leaving Twin Forks property. There's always a chance of working things out, as long as both parties are willing to talk."

"You got my promise. How you know you can trust me?"

"Hiram Cogswell, I've yet to meet a hard-working man who wasn't good for his word, and it's quite obvious to me you're a VERY hard-working man. That shouts to me that you're honest as well."

Cogswell blinked as the hard blue frame of the Colt suddenly disappeared into the leather at the rider's side. How did he DO that?

The son arrived just a few minutes after and stood looking at the pair.

"Danny, come over here. I want you to meet this man."

"Danny, huh? I'm glad to know you, Danny, that's a good name. I'm Dan Kade, one of the four partners at Twin Forks Ranch just south of here."

Kade swung from the saddle as he spoke and walked over to the burly youngster to offer his hand. It was met by the hand of a youngster that gripped his like an adult.

"I'm glad to meet you, sir. What do you do at that ranch?"

"We're mainly a horse ranch. We raise horses for the army and for the farmers and other ranchers in this territory. We grow a lot of hay and oats to supply our winter needs for the stock, too, but it really taxes us to grow enough crops and do the horses as well. I'm afraid we're going to need to hire more people next year if we grow any more."

"Mister Kade says we're on their land, Danny. Claims they have a legal deed. We was just talking it over when you came up. Man says the law can run us off."

"That's right, I said the law COULD run you off, but I didn't say it was going to happen. Tell you what, can you afford to spend and hour with me, setting down to discuss this amicably, and just possibly work things out to every one's satisfaction?"

"We could do that, but let's go to the house and get some cold water to think on, and maybe some shade there. I put the house right close to the river on purpose, plan to run a pipe trough to the spring house later on, and maybe even to a pump in the kitchen."

"That's a great idea, Hiram. How high is the bank there? Twin Forks River can get really high during spring run-off. The rest of the year it's pretty tame except for heavy rains in the mountains; then it gets rather feisty."

"It's about twenty feet to the water right now. This here's kinda high ground right in here."

"Good You should be okay most of the time. Hopefully it won't reach your buildings during run-off."

The three arrived at the buildings and Dan saw that Cogswell was a very skilled builder. His house was a long, low affair with shake roof and the typical porch running the length of the house. The outbuildings were built just as carefully and strongly as the house and were amazingly large for farm buildings. They spoke of the farmer's future plans for the need for storage.

They dismounted and Dan was introduced to the rest of the family in much the same manner as he had been to Danny. They parked themselves on the porch and gratefully received the cold water brought out by the ten-year-old son.

"Well, here we are, killing time. So speak your peace, Mister Kade."

"Peace is exactly what I plan to speak, Hiram Cogswell. I see the possibility of your taking up a full section of our land here, with the hard work you've already done, and that's a lot of land. The government says a section is a mile square, right?

"You remember I told you and Danny back there in the field that we are probably going to need more hands to grow what we need for our herds? Here's what I see as possible, and please keep in mind that my three partners will need to be in on the decision process; we could contract with you to grow hay, oats, and corn for us every year. We have most of the equipment needed for harvesting if you need it, and we can work out a payment system based on a fair market price for your work and crops until you could be deeded the land. Then we would still be open to contracting with you for the provision of those products, except we would then pay cash for them.

"Later, when your boys are grown, if they want to continue farming as you do, we could talk about additional land being available for them on the same terms. By then, we hope to own more land south of our headquarters; and if that becomes the case, we could afford to release some more up here. Only if we get the extra land, you understand, but I think it's going to happen."

Cogswell removed his hat and mopped his bald head with a kerchief as he contemplated the proposal. He then looked at his son with deep affection showing. Then he showed the kind of father he was by including his oldest son in on the decision-making.

"What you think, Danny boy? Does this man sound okay to you with his ideas?"

"Yeah, Pa. That sounds good to me, 'specially the part about land for me 'n the others. I could really go for that."

"Mister Dan Kade, gunslick and horse ranch owner, if your partners agree to those terms, we have a deal. I hope to heaven they do, for I'd hate to have war over this farm with a man of your make-up of honesty and fairness, I surely would. And that isn't mentioning the slick draw that goes with it! Man that can handle a gun like that isn't too likely to be a bad shot, either."

Dan just smiled and held out a hand for each of them. The Missus came to the door and spoke, "If you're already here, you may as well eat before you go back to work, Hiram; and Mister Kade, you need to eat before you have to do it in town. I promise you better cooking than any restaurant you find there!"

Dan chuckled and accepted, enjoying the next hour with the family before continuing on to Twin Forks. His arrival in the town happened to coincide with that of several area farmers bringing wagons to town for supplies, and the main street was quite crowded. Dan pulled Blue into the hitch rail at the town's only restaurant and went inside. What better place to learn of a cook in the area, right?

He straddled a stool at the counter and motioned for coffee as the waitress approached. "Hi Dan. You finally give up on your wife's cooking and decide to come in for some real food?"

"Hey Dolly, don't you be knocking Allie's culinary skills; she feeds us too good."

"Well, if I can't win you away from her with my cooking, I guess I'll have to marry one of those other rich ranchers from down at Twin Forks ranch. Which one do you recommend?"

He chuckled and accepted the coffee as she slid it across the counter. "Not one of them is good enough for you, Dolly. I guess maybe Bear would make you the happiest."

"Bear? That behemoth of a man? Are you trying to get me squeezed to death, Dan Kade? Besides, MY man will take a bath at least once a week!"

"Actually, sweetie, Bear is in the river with soap at least twice a week! Should I tell him to come calling?"

She swatted him in the ear with her dish towel and barked out a "No!"

Dan failed to duck in time so he wiped the moisture from his head and winked at the two other patrons in the place as they laughed at the byplay.

"I hope you use a dry towel the next time; that one's getting too wet to dry anything. Listen, Dolly, all teasing aside, I am here for a definite reason, and I came to see you because I figure you can help me.

"Allison is so busy at times that she's not able to care for little Ira and do all the other things she needs to do, so we've decided to hire a cook. I don't care if she's a she or a he as long as they can cook and get along with everyone."

"Oh, you don't care if SHE'S a she? Or a HE?"

“Okay, okay, don’t get feisty on me here, just tell me if you know someone who might be interested and capable.”

Dolly grinned a mischievous grin and leaned way over the counter at him. “Allison mind if SHE’S young and pretty and out to steal her man?”

“Doggone it, Dolly, you’re no help at all. Surely you know someone. C’mon, be a good girl for a change and give me some names. Please?”

“Oh, be a good girl FOR ONCE? You’re not doing so well here, Mister Kade. Look, I’ll let you off the hook. There’s Lucinda down at the hotel. She can cook, and I’m sure old Martin isn’t paying her anything decent to make beds and sweep the place. She’s full-blooded Indian, though I don’t know what tribe, but there’s a really easy going lady and should work out really well. Go see what she thinks.”

“Thanks, Dolly. If you weren’t bound and determined to take it wrong I’d give you a hug for that.” Dan turned and left before the little lady could give a retort and chuckled as the wet towel smacked the door just in front of him as he went out. Dolly was so mischievous that most people just shook their heads at her shenanigans, and all the riders in the area tried to marry her; but she really had such dreams of what her prince charming would be like that no one had yet measured up.

Dan trekked to the hotel and entered the front door into the lobby. Old Martin Libbey was at the desk, and Dan approached him.

“Mister Libbey, I understand you have a girl named Lucinda working here. Do you mind if I talk to her?”

“Just don’t keep her from her work. She’s upstairs sweeping. And be sure she doesn’t stop while you talk to her, I’m paying her good money.”

Dan smiled and nodded as he headed for the stairs. The old skinflint was really going to be upset if he hired her away from him! He found a short, pleasantly plump Indian girl in her early twenties industriously sweeping out a room near the back of the hallway. She wore a cotton dress showing much wear and shoes to match. She had a quick smile for Dan as he leaned against the door jamb of the room.

"Are you Lucinda?"

"Yes sir, that would be me. You have a problem with your room?"

"No, I have a problem with my wife."

She drew back and eased the broom to the front while changing her grip on it to one that suggested defensive maneuvering. Dan then chuckled and elaborated.

"What I mean is that my poor dear wife is overworked and we decided we need to hire a cook for the ranch. Actually, a cook and general housekeeper. You see, we have a little toddler and he keeps her too busy to do much else but care for him.

"There are four of us as partners and one hired hand, Skinny Robins, plus my wife Allison and little Ira. I'm Dan Kade. Dolly, down at the diner, said you could cook and might be interested."

"You mean Allison from Twin Forks Ranch? I love her! She treats me like I am white, she doesn't even see the Indian in me! But, wait a minute; is Red Elk one of the ranchers? Him and Five Ponies?"

"Uuhhh, yeeess, why do you ask?" Dan thought he might have lost her there for some reason.

"My father hates Red Elk. He wanted him to marry me last year and was told, in no uncertain terms, to get lost." She chuckled aloud and the humor slowly took hold of her until she was shaking all over at the memory.

"I told Father I didn't want a husband, especially a lowly Comanche, and then they both were mad at me! It was the most fun I'd had for a long time!"

About then old Martin Libbey showed up on the run, furious as could be. "I told you to make sure she didn't stop working while you talked to her! Now you get out! And you, squaw, you'll lose an hour's pay for stopping to visit, you understand?"

"Mister Libbey, sir, you can just have your old hour's wage, and for that matter, the rest of the week, too. This Mission School Indian knows a good deal when she sees one, and I quit. You can do the rest of the sweeping yourself. And while you're at it, see if you can pry yourself loose from half a dollar for a new broom, this one is no more than a fuzzy stick any more!"

She then dropped the broom and pushed her way past Dan and the shocked Martin Libbey and disappeared down the stairs. Libbey looked at Dan and spoke, "Do you have anything to do with her quitting? You better not have, or I'll have your hide if that's so!"

Dan only smiled mildly and pushed by the irate hotel owner and left, following Lucinda down the stairs and out into the street. He stopped and looked both ways for the girl, not seeing her at all. He shrugged and went back to the diner, and there found his prospective hire talking to Dolly in excited but hushed tones. Dan stopped just inside the door and waited until they noticed him.

Dolly ran around the counter and engulfed Dan in a very unladylike hug while smooching his cheek all the while. He quickly pushed her away, scolding her.

"Dolly, I told you, that's not right for you to do. I am a married man, get it? I don't care how good a friend Allie is with you, you can't be kissing on me like that, even to make the local boys jealous!"

"I'm sorry, Dan, but I am so happy for Lucy that I got carried away."

"So, Lucinda, does this mean we've hired a cook and housecleaner? We didn't even talk salary."

"Mister Dan, I don't care what you pay, I'll be so glad to get out of this town and away from that old skinflint and the rude men around here that I'll work for a place to sleep and food to eat!"

He laughed and replied, "Well, Twin Forks pays a bit better than that. How soon can you…never mind, I imagine you can leave right away? How long to pack?"

"Mister Dan, I have so little to pack that I can be ready in five minutes."

"No, I don't think so. Dolly, can you leave here for a few minutes?"

"Sure, Dan. Dad can handle it alone for a bit. What's up?"

"I want you to take Lucinda down to the mercantile and help her get some new clothes and necessities and put them on Twin Forks' bill. It might be a long time before she gets back in town again, and we don't want her lacking anything she needs out there."

He barely staved off another onslaught of affection from Dolly as he shoved the two out the door. "Don't take too long, I'd like to get back before dark! Lucinda, you do ride horseback okay, don't you?"

He received a feisty glower at the question and proceeded to the livery to rent another mount. He found that a Twin Forks horse was still there from a previous trip and only required renting a saddle to get Lucinda properly mounted.

The girls returned less than half an hour later. Dan soon had the horses mounted and Lucinda's goodbyes said, and they were headed out of town, going south at a steady clip. He soon found Lucinda was totally at ease on a horse and realized they would likely meet his goal of arrival at the ranch before darkness invaded the land.

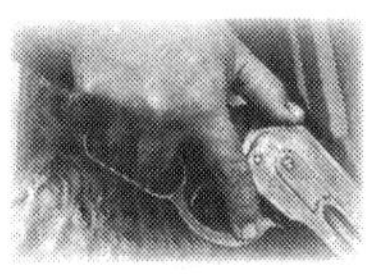

FIVE

"Look, Smoots, if I say jump, you say 'How high,' got it?" Cannon emphasized his statement by punching his finger on John Smoots' chest several times as he spoke.

"Cannon, I'll just say this once; if you ever touch me again, I'll kill you. No man touches me that way. I am NOT your man, I don't ever intend to BE your man, and you only hired my gun, nothing else."

With that he backed off two steps and poised his hand over the gun butt at his side. The move stymied Cannon; he was used to most men fearing him and this much smaller man had no fear. There had only been three men before in the recent years who hadn't been frightened by him. One had been old Joe Batt, but he had been crazy. Another had been a gunman named Banty Harris who had recruited Cannon to help with the kidnapping of Melodi Branson, but Cannon had killed Harris when he was gut-shot and suffering. He had blown the little gunman's brain to pieces just as if he were a horse with a broken leg. The third was Bear Rollins. Bear had done for old Joe Batt during the rescue of Melodi, so he was the only one until now who was still alive. Cannon planned to correct that situation as soon as he located Rollins. He now decided once that chore was cared for he would also care for the demise of one John Smoots. Once he had Melodi in hand again, that is.

The argument had been that Cannon expected Smoots to

work for the railroad the same as he and Jimmy, but Smoots informed him that manual labor was not in his plans. John had become a gunman for hire so he wouldn't have to work, and he had no intention of starting now.

"Listen, you. I'm still runnin' this show, an' the plans I make are what we follow. You signed on understandin' that, and we're gonna do as I figger on.

"Word is that there's nigh on to a hundred horses comin' this way on the rails and we're gonna cabbage onto them after they gets here. I kin get hold of a feller east of here that will pay good money, no questions asked, and we kin have operatin' cash from that. I'll tell you when we are gonna move. If yore too lazy to work, leastways yore gonna keep watch fer those horses to get here and see where they take 'em."

"That I will be more than happy to do, but it's a mistake. You want to find this Rollins guy, do it and then we take the horses. We take the horses first and we're done around here. And likely the whole territory will be warned that rustlers are about so any movement will be harder. How far is the girl from here?"

"Two days that way," Cannon answered with a thumb over his shoulder.

"Well, two days isn't too bad, but it's still closer than I like for us to be on the dodge and then trying to get the girl."

"You never mind that, you jist do as I say."

"I just do as I please, Mister Cannon. When I see the color of your money, I might be a little more flexible for a while."

They parted company and Smoots stepped down from the boardwalk into the dusty street, only to be nearly run down by a rider walking by on a mustang. He was already angry and he smacked the horse on the nose with his hand, causing it to rear and then crow-hop a bit until the rider collected the animal. Smoots suddenly found himself facing an angry Joe, who had leaped from the saddle and turned loose of the reins to let the horse trot off on its own.

"Mister, if you ever do that again I will tear your head off. Next time you step off that walk, you look first and leave the horses alone."

Smoots crouched, hands on his guns, and faced the Indian, ready and willing to kill. John was used to either being called out for a fight or doing the calling out himself. Then both parties usually faced each other while preparing to draw and shoot. The key was in anticipating when the opponent was going to draw and John was a master at that.

He therefore had no concept of an Indian stepping forward and busting him in the chops with a fist instead of drawing a weapon! He suddenly found the sky directly in front of him and realized he was flat on his back. Something hurt, a lot, and he searched it out only to discover it was the whole left side of his face.

He struggled to his feet, somewhat light-headed, and swayed a bit as he tried to stabilize his stance in the dust of the road. The angry Indian before him seemed to ease in and out of focus as he attempted to see clearly. He realized there was now no way he could safely draw a gun quickly and live. He whirled around, nearly falling as he did so, and stalked off toward the saloon, weaving a bit on the way. Joe remained ready for treachery until the gunman was out of the street and into the saloon.

He looked at the rough-looking big man on the walk who stared at him, thinking there might be trouble from the way he was being studied. He stared back until the fellow walked toward the railroad camp just west of town. Joe then caught his horse and led it to the house of Molly Clements, his favorite person in Boomstick. Molly was about as cute a little lady as he had ever liked.

§ § § §

John Smoots bellied up to the bar and ordered sarsaparilla as he endeavored to quiet his anger. Anger was a tool he seldom used, because it clouded the judgment and also the mental reaction to danger. He was a true professional gunman and worked at it as such. His thoughts were slowing down and he actually felt as though a peace was settling over him when a gentleman sidled up to the bar beside him and leaned his bulk over it to grab a bottle of the same sweet soft drink Smoots was nursing. Standing somewhere just under the six-foot mark and at least two hundred pounds, the fellow showed the results of several years of life in his slowly fading hair color as well as the sun-darkened skin of many years and hours in the saddle. The most prominent feature for Smoots, however, was the silver star on his left breast. Hanging there on the leather vest that covered his blue chambray shirt, it was worn quite smooth from years of wear. Smoots had a strange thought that it resembled the handles of a well-used Colt.

"Morning, Mister Smoots. How ya doing today?"

John responded as his nerves gave a sudden jolt at the realization the lawman knew who he was. As far as he knew, there should be no wanted posters out on him. "I'm fine, sheriff, how 'bout yourself?"

"Oh, I'm doing about as usual for a day like this. Name's Bill Hanson. I'm the law around here as well as pretty much of the whole territory as far west as you want to ride in two days, south a day, north a day, and east to the mountains. Maybe a little further than the mountains, but my horse is getting' older and don't like climbing much.

"I saw that little byplay between you and the Indian out there and thought I should give you a gentlemanly warning about starting such things in our little peaceful town, here. You're lucky that Comanche didn't part your ribs with that big knife on his belt, ya know. He's right touchy about anyone smackin' a horse. Any horse, not just his own. He's a good Indian, owns a ranch west of here with three other fellows, good men, each and every one of them. All good friends of mine, by the way, and honest as the day is long.

"I saw you in town the other day with your low-slung holsters and the notches on the handles of those six shooters. Did some telegraphing and found out several names you might wear, but after a while I pretty much settled on the right one. You got every right to be here, unless that is, you're here to do a job of the type you normally hire out for. I don't like you, Mister Smoots, because I don't like men who think it's okay for them to shoot other people for money.

"I'm gonna explain a few things to you concerning my methods of enforcing the law around here. I'm forty years old,

Mister, and I'm still alive because I have no pride in being fast with a gun. My pride is in doing my job and doing it very well. You'll notice I laid this double barrel Greener down on the bar here when I came up. When I leave my office, Matilda, here, goes with me. In fact, unless I'm riding, she goes everywhere I go. Matilda's a good ole girl, never misses. And I'll tell you this, she'll cut a man nearly in two from anywhere in the range of twenty feet.

"Ever see a ten gauge shotgun shell pulled open, Mister Smoots? I use double-aught buck and there's thirteen of them in there. Now, a double-aught buck is the same as a thirty-two caliber bullet, three hundred twenty thousands of an inch in diameter. That's over a quarter of an inch of lead ball hitting a target at a speed of twelve hundred feet a minute, just in case you're interested. There's only room for nine of those in a twelve gauge shell, that's why I prefer to carry the ten gauge, more fire power.

"Now, while I disapprove of shooting people for hire, I don't have any qualms whatsoever about shooting them to enforce the law. Sorta doesn't fit the same mold for me, ya know? I don't relish taking another's life, but I do relish keeping my own. In fact, I relish it enough to not hesitate to shoot before there's any chance whatsoever for the old noble 'even break.' I even shot a man in the back once. He was drawing down on another fellow that I knew was an honest man, so I figured the guy had no cause to be doing that. Like I say, I'm not a proud man; but I am a live lawman, and my dear wife appreciates that, as do I.

"So, Mister John Smoots, as long as you remain peaceful, you're more than welcome in our town, but you step over the line and I'll spill your guts all over this peaceful little town's street, and I'll not shed a tear over it. You have a good day, now, sir. And the sarsaparilla's on me, sort of a welcoming gift."

With that, he pushed a coin across the bar, turned his back to the gunman as he picked up the shotgun and strolled slowly out the swinging doors of the saloon. John stood there watching the receding back of the lawman and felt he had just somehow avoided physical disaster by remaining silent. Bill Hanson was a gentle man of honor but also said nothing he didn't mean, and Smoots knew instinctively that was an accurate assessment of the man. He might want to re-evaluate his purpose here.

His thoughts were interrupted by the shrill whistle of a locomotive. A train was pulling into the yards south of town and John decided to check it out. He strolled at a leisurely pace as he heard the puffing of the engine and the squeaking of the steel wheels as it eased into the siding. A ramp was pushed into place and staked down on the opposite side of the tracks, and the first cattle car was opened up. The first figure down the ramp was a huge man, bigger even than Cannon and leading a saddled horse. Dressed in buckskins and wearing moccasins, he pulled his horse to the side and passed through the gate of the corral to tie the animal inside and return to the car.

He and others began to off-load large horses from the car, and then the train pulled forward until another car was lined up with the ramp and that car was off-loaded. The process was repeated until there were upwards of sixty horses milling around, raising a dust cloud of confusion. He saw George Searcy approaching the area at a fast walk and observed the meeting of the buckskin-clad behemoth and Searcy where a warm and prolonged handshake was shared by the two.

Smoots had slowly eased their way and had gotten close enough to overhear their conversation. He was sure Searcy had called the big man Bear. If he was right, this was Cannon's main target for this area! He slipped off to try to find Cannon and share the information. After several inquiries, he gave up and decided the man had actually gone hunting as he was supposed to. How unique was that? Jimmy was nowhere to be found, either, so he returned to town and sought out the livery man to spend time in gossip, hoping to learn useful information from him. Every town had a livery stable and every livery stable possessed the town "information center." That center always walked upright, had opposing thumbs, and usually spit tobacco juice between delivering bits of "official information" and just plain gossip.

§ § § §

Just west of town was the main camp of the railroad workers, and on the north side of that was the temporary corral for the work horses. It bordered a forest that gradually sloped upwards and culminated in a ridge some quarter of a mile to the north and extended to about a thousand feet in height. That same ridge then extended west about a mile before coming to an abrupt halt in the form of a very steep decline. It was at the top of this ridge that Cannon lurked, spying on the camp with binoculars. His intention was to scope out the different routines in the camp and determine the best time and manner in which to steal horses. He had sent Jimmy out to kill game for the camp so as to fulfill the duties for which he had been hired.

Late afternoon found him watching men drive in a large herd of horses from the direction of town. They raised a dust cloud as they romped and cavorted their way into the corral. Cannon jerked all over when he spotted the huge figure in buckskins astride a rangy grey. Rollins! To be sure, he held the glasses on him until the dust settled a bit, then he surveyed the surrounding area to plan out the kidnapping strategy for taking his sworn enemy captive. He literally trembled with eager anticipation as he thought through how he would torture this captive to death. Cannon was among the most vicious of miscreants in the human race.

Jimmy showed up an hour later with three deer roped across the pack horse and the two men proceeded to make the descent to the camp. On arrival they trussed the game into a tree and proceeded to skin them. George Searcy happened to be strolling by and veered their way.

"Skinning the last three for the day, gents? Is the game holding up?"

"Skinnin' the ONLY three for the day. And yes, game is holdin' up."

"You mean this is all the meat you brought in for today? But there's still plenty of game? Would you mind explaining why there are only three deer for this day?"

"'Cause that's all we chose to bring in, that's why. These men don't need more than that. If they do, let'em get their own meat."

"I'm feeding almost fifty men here, and the cattle I arranged for aren't here yet. Three deer are only a drop in the bucket.

These men work hard, which is a concept you apparently don't understand. Get your gear, see the paymaster for your pay, and get out of this camp. You're through."

Cannon's hand dropped to his knife and he started to take a step forward but stopped as the worn forty-five of Searcy appeared smoothly at full cock and centered on his chest.

"Actually, you've not earned your pay one single day here, so just take your gear and go, I'll see you out. March!"

"Jimmy, move to yore left and separate us. This tinhorn can't cover both of us, and we're gonna get our due plus some skin from this bum."

Jimmy's left foot moved a little to his left and then he jumped straight up as a bullet tore up grass and dirt and scattered them all over his feet at the crash of Searcy's gun. The leaden missile hit precisely where Jimmy's left foot had been.

"You take one step and I'll knock your knees out from under you, little man, and then I'll kill you, Cannon. I said get out, and I'll back that up with the remaining five rounds in this pistol."

Jimmy's eyes darted from Cannon to Searcy, trying to decide which man he feared the most. Searcy won, hands down. The two grudgingly started toward town with Searcy walking a few paces behind, gun still in hand. A crowd gathered to watch the procession as they did so, but a cold look from their superintendent soon sent them back to their duties. When the two left the camp border, Cannon looked back at Searcy and threatened him with a withering look that boded no good for his future. Another was added to his revenge list.

§ § § §

Joe had just descended the three steps from the Clements' porch when he heard the shot from the camp. He started to step out to run that way when two little brown arms wrapped themselves around his neck from behind and stopped him. Little Molly Clements was on the second step and pulled him back, her face just a bit higher than his shoulder since she had a two-step advantage on him.

"You stop right there, Indian. You don't need to check out every single gunshot in the world. Let Sheriff Hanson take care of that; you haven't even kissed me goodbye yet!"

She put her head down over his shoulder, knocking the brim of his hat up with her head as she did so and causing it to slide over his left ear while she rubbed her smooth cheek against his. He had to chuckle at the girl's possessive manner as he tried to catch the hapless hat on its journey to the ground. He missed it.

"Molly, dear, you are the most shameless hussy I ever did court. Here you are in broad daylight, wrapping yourself around a man and demanding kisses. Whatever are you going to come to?"

"Maybe YOU can answer that better than me, Joe Five Ponies! What AM I going to come to? Now before you answer that and get in deeper trouble, kiss me goodbye and go on your way if you must."

Joe complied, and then turned, facing her. "Molly, I don't want to go, but I heard that train and I'm sure it had to be Bear with the horses for the U.P. I need to get over there and help. After all, that's why I came to town, to help him. I promise I'll be back as soon as I can. Okay?"

She laughed a gay laugh and nodded as she shook him by the shoulders, nearly knocking the retrieved hat off again. Another peck on the cheek and she released him. He started in the direction of the camp, occasionally looking back to see her still standing there watching. His chest swelled with joy at the sight.

As Joe exited the town he passed Cannon and Jimmy coming in. He saw George Searcy watching their departure, gun still in hand.

"Mister Searcy, what's up; you have a problem with those two?"

"Come on, Joe, it's George, and yes, they didn't take kindly to being fired. The big fellow seemed to want to skin me alive. If he had done his job and been skinning enough game, like he was hired to do, he'd still have a job."

"He doesn't look like the most pleasant of people. So, are you telling me you need more meat for your cooks?"

"A lot more, Joe. I have a small beef herd coming from over Twin Forks way, but the telegram I received said it will be two more days before they get here. You don't by any chance want a job, do you?"

"No, George, I don't, but I'll help out for a day or two. Did Bear come in with the horses? He will probably help, too. Give us a couple of good butchers to do the dirty work and we can get you plenty of meat."

"Bear is here. He helped drive the horses out to the corral. He found us a fine bunch of harness animals."

"Good. Let's go find him."

They found Bear with a foot up on the bottom rail of the makeshift corral, watching as two drovers caught horses for harnessing. The range-bred animals put up a bit of a fuss, but the drovers were experienced hostlers and soon tamed the recalcitrant steeds so that they accepted the harness. Even though it was afternoon, Searcy had ordered the work teams to start immediately. The earth-moving equipment had sat still way too long to suit him, and he wanted to get the roadbed under way. Hitches of four teams were harnessed and hitched to the huge equipment used to root up the top soil and haul in stone, gravel, and what clay soil they could find to establish a solid foundation for the bed. After that was in place they pulled large, heavy rollers in to pack the bed in preparation for the ties.

While all that was taking place, other crews were already cutting and hauling trees from the forest up on the slope, and yet another crew was splitting ties from those trees. Those would have to dry before being seated in the roadbed, but he had many piles of cured ties that had been hauled in by rail waiting to start the track-laying. Searcy figured he could lay twenty miles of track before needing the freshly cut ties. It was his plan to intersperse uncured ties for every tenth one in order to stretch the supply until more cured ties could be shipped in.

Steel rails were deposited every so often in piles, waiting their turn for spiking into place. The rail crews were helping others until their job came to the front. No one had time on their hands if they worked under Searcy, but they were paid fairly and treated right.

Bear turned and greeted Joe with a big smile and handshake and then nodded to George. "Looks like yu got yore men getting' on with the job, George. Them horses air actin' a might spunky for them but they're good men. Know what they're doin'."

"You are right, Bear, I do have a good crew for this job. They are the leftovers, so to speak, from the main crew that brought the road west a long time back. I've been able to keep them on, and just for the reason that they can all be trusted to give their best."

"Bear, George had to fire his hunters and needs meat desperately. I told him we could likely help him for a couple of days until his beef herd gets here. What do you think?"

"Shore 'nough. Let's git a couple of pack hosses and hit the hills. We got enough time tu nail down some game before dark. I happen tu know whar thar's a small buffler herd thet the hide hunters drove this way a few years back. Iffn we kin find them, jist a couple should do thu trick fer tonight. You got any skinners, George?"

"I will have by the time you get back. If you think you can find the buffalo I'll have a wagon follow you instead of pack animals."

"Thet'll work fine. Get'em ready an' me 'n Joe will be out thet way. Tell'em tu jist head out 'n we'll hunt 'em down when we need 'em."

"That's fine, fellows, and I want you to know how much I appreciate this."

The two partners nodded and headed for their horses, Bear leading his as Joe walked back toward Molly's to retrieve the mount he had left there.

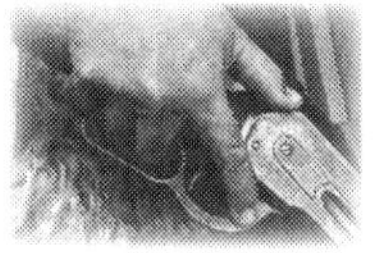

SIX

The lighter discharge of the thirty-six caliber Navy Colt sounded almost with the heavier boom of the forty-five Peacemaker, but the black powder smoke obscured the shooter for a few seconds. The holder of the forty-five peered through the smoke and then commented, "Wal, Skinny, yore gittin' tu be 'most as good as me with thet thing. Yu just keep burnin' powder and aimin' careful like and what yu hev now is a good workin' skill with thet hogleg."

"Thanks, Reddy, for teaching me how to draw and shoot, but I can't wait to get a real gun like yours."

"Now son, yu just hold on thar a minute. Now, take a look at yore arm, wrist, and hand. Hyar, hold it up along side mine fer a minute. I ain't tryin' tu shame yu or anything, but yu just ain't built the same as me or Dan or Joe. Yu got those slender arms thet keep folks callin' yu Skinny 'stead o' whatever yore real name is; an' even though yu kin hold yore own with the best of us as far as workin', this hyar heavy Colt would slow yu down and take away yore accuracy because of the heavier kick. Thet thirty-six is about perfect fer yu.

"Now, as tu a better hogleg, yu could have it changed over for cartridges 'stead o' thet smokin' black powder an, yore reloadin' would be lots easier. Thet's where I'd spend my pesos iffn I was you. Thar's a right smart gunsmith over in Boomstick thet kin do thet very thing fer yu. Meanwhile, 'til yu get the money fer thet, keep on practicin' what I've shown yu and yu'll be fine. Right now, yore good enough tu care fer any rattler thet yu might find unfriendly and settled in yore path.

"Just remember, youngster, yu only need tu carry thet thing fer rattlers, coyotes, wolves, and broken-legged hosses. The west is a getting' pretty well settled now and I don't see the need fer us fellers tu be carryin' tu protect against bad hombres the way we used to. I think maybe Danny boy has got rid o' all them types." The last was said with a chuckle.

"Is Dan really as fast as you say? Has he really shot men?"

"I'm right sorry tu say 'yes' tu thet, son. True as Dan is tu bein' a gentle sort of guy, he holds tu fairness and the law, an' he's hed some really bad stuff happen thet made the killin' of other men necessary. None of us really relishes thet, but each and every one of us Twin Forks partners hev been hed tu do it. I'm shore the others feel like I do, and hope it never needs tu happen again.

"My background is full of the killin' and stuff thet my people went through, with some really bad stuff happenin' on both sides of the spear, an' many of my people were ruthless and cruel, but the surroundin's made them thet way, right or wrong. Joe and I see the better way of the white man who wants tu just pull a livin' outta the land and be left alone tu do thet very thing. No one should hate anyone jist 'cause they hev different skin or ways or God. Jist don't make no sense, Skinny, not at all! They's been both bad and good Indians and bad and good white men. Sadly, they's been some pretty good men and women on both sides got found on the wrong end of a gun or arrow 'cause of the bad ones.

"Yu take care of yore weapon, lad, but take even better care of yore heart, an' thet's the last you'll hyar from old Red Elk on thet subject."

Skinny gazed intently on the Indian beside him, eyes wide with wonder for he had never heard Reddy be so serious and talk that way for such a long statement. He vowed to himself to always remember what Reddy had told him. As they walked back toward the buildings he was silent and thoughtful. When he had purchased his gun and belt his mother had thrown a fit, while his father had preached somewhat the same message

Reddy had just finished. His father had no first-hand knowledge of violence such as the Comanche beside him, and the presence of the dangers from many of nature's creatures was quite real and demanded each rider carry protection.

As they approached the house, twilight began to wend its subtle way through the trees and the sound of horses crossing the river invaded their thoughts. The splashing was loud and steady, and Reddy chuckled as he declared big old Blue to be the source of the sound.

"Thet hoss loves the water and he loves tu make it fly! Dan gets pretty upset when he uses his hoss tu cross a stream and gets just as wet, or maybe wetter, than iffn he waded across himself! I love tu watch him!"

When the two arrived at the house they found there were two horses in front and Dan was just about to help the second rider down when she piled off on her own. Reddy groaned audibly when he saw who it was.

"Aww, no, it cain't be. Tell me I'm imaginin' things, Skinny. Tell me thet ain't Lucinda. Skinny, talk tu me, boy!"

Skinny looked on the man with amazement at his consternation and affirmed that the second rider was, indeed, Lucinda from the hotel. That brought another groan.

"Reddy, what's the matter? Lucinda is a wonderful cook! She used to cook in the diner until their business fell off and she had to leave."

"Aww, Skinny, it's a long and horrible story, but her old man wanted me tu marry her last year. I told him just where the bear hid in the woods in no uncertain terms and she heard me. I thought she was gonna scalp me right thar. Told her old man and me both we was nuthin' but scum and thet she'd slaughter both of us iffn she could. The gurl hates me."

Dan's voice rang out with a call for all to come to the house to meet their new cook, and Reddy slunk along like a coyote leaving a henhouse with a full belly. Skinny began to get in the mood of the hour and pulled at his friend to hurry him along. The two were soon scuffling and for once, Reddy was losing.

When they walked through the door they found Allie wrapping Lucinda in a big hug while beaming from ear to ear. She had gotten to know the girl in town and the two, along with Dolly, had become great friends. They had known each other since their early teen years.

As Lucinda looked Reddy over like a butcher after a market hog, Dan pulled him aside to tell him about the Cogswell situation. When he was done, Reddy remarked that he felt Dan had shown great wisdom and patience in handling the deal. He, too, was sure the other two partners would go along with the plan.

"Dan, the other fellers shoulda been back by now. I think one of us should head over tu Boomstick way tu see what's goin' on over there. It ain't like it takes all thet long fer them tu deliver them hosses tu Searcy."

"You're right, Reddy, unless Joe is seeing little Molly Clements. I think he's getting in pretty deep with that girl. Still, Joe wouldn't be gone this long without more reason than that."

"Wal, I'll head on over thet way tomorrow and see what I kin find."

"Sounds good; Skinny and I can hold down the home fort."

§ § § §

For two days Joe and Bear had hunted game for the railroad crew, supplying buffalo, deer, elk, and whatever else fell to their guns. There were even a few wild turkeys that had ventured out at the wrong time. When Red Elk rode into the railhead camp, he was met by George Searcy.

"Man, am I glad to see you. Bear and Joe went out yesterday for their hunt and haven't returned. They've been supplying our meat until my cattle herd gets here, and when they failed to show up last night I sent a search party out for them, but they returned without having found any trace of them. The skinners that went along to haul the game came back and the men told me they just never saw the boys again after they hit the forest.. I'm really concerned because there was some trouble here a few days back and I'm quite suspicious of the two individuals involved."

"Any idea which way they went when they left, or where they were hunting most of the time?"

"No. I left it all in their hands. Not only that, but that small cattle herd should have been here two days ago. I shouldn't need hunters any more. That herd should feed the crew until the next one arrives. That's coming from just north of Twin Forks, both herds, that is."

"All right, I'll start huntin' the boys, and keep an eye oot fer the herd at the same time. I need a fresh hoss and some grub; I might be oot a few days. How 'bout sendin' a telegram tu Dan over Twin Forks way tu let him know, and tell him I'll be west of Boomstick and north into the trees. No sense huntin' them in the flat lands. They wouldn't hunt anything but buffalo there, and I suspect they would have moved into the trees iffn they was bein' hunted regular-like."

"Consider it done, Reddy, and good luck."

By the time Reddy had switched his saddle to another mount a fellow came along with a sack of supplies which were tied behind the cantle and as he swung to the saddle he spurred the horse to a run, headed northwest from the camp. The workers laying track paused a few seconds to watch the disappearing rider, then resumed work. The camp had moved five miles west from Boomstick and would achieve another five miles today. But the work was being done by very hungry workers, and the ten miles a day that Searcy was used to getting was not going to happen.

First, he had but a skeleton crew compared to the building of the U.P. years before. Second, they were making most of the ties right on the job, and that was time-consuming. He had determined that if he reached Twin Forks in a month it would be a good job. That rankled him to no end, though, for he knew it could be done in half the time by a full crew. After all, the grading of the roadbed was mostly across level land, with only a few small bridges to be built.

He walked along the edge of the organized chaos of the workers, watching as the gandydancers made their way along with the heavy steel rail between their legs, weaving from side to side, imitating the waddle of a goose as they struggled with the heavy load of the rail until reaching their goal and placing it on the ties. The term gandydancers referred to the waddle; originally meaning ganderdancer after a male goose.

As soon as they were done, the drivers began to drive the

heavy spikes in place as the rails were spaced properly by using the wooden guide jigs made for that purpose. The activity of laying rails never failed to bring about the feeling of nostalgia for George, as he had spent half his lifetime at this very job. He loved the flurry, the cries of each team of men as they communicated with each other, the steel hitting the spikes, the puff of the engine sitting back down the tracks waiting to pull forward with the next load of rails, ties, and equipment. Oh how he wished he had a steam-powered shovel for this job.

Instead, four-team hitches dragged the earth-moving equipment along, tearing the sod from its place and hauling in solid earth from another section of land that was starting to resemble the coal strip-mines of the east in Ohio, West Virginia, Pennsylvania and others, except these areas were very shallow and would soon grow back their vegetation.

As soon as a hitch seemed to lag, fresh horses were brought to play and the earth-moving continued. The hoarse cries of the drovers as they cracked their long bull whips over the backs of the teams and the stomping of the hooves just added to the cacophony that was music to Searcy's ears. He almost forgot the concern he was feeling for the two hunters' absence.

Red Elk rode hard for a quarter of an hour and then began to course back and forth, looking for signs of riders passing from two days before. It took the better part of three hours, but he finally found what he sought after. Another hour found him deep into the forest, struggling to keep on the tracks of the two riders he trailed. As night began to fall, he simply settled in to a dry camp and waited out the darkness with his horse picketed and a blanket thrown over his shoulders while eating a cold biscuit and jerky washed down with the water from his canteen. Daybreak would awaken him and as soon as the light allowed, he would resume his tracking.

Mid-afternoon the next day, Reddy paused. He was sure he had heard a shot. It came from somewhere to the north and had to be several miles away. Sound carried in those mountains, and there was no telling how far it was. Another report came and he turned a bit to the right and spurred to a run for a couple of miles before stopping to listen again. Nothing came.

Proceeding cautiously, he finally dismounted and led his mount. An hour later another shot sounded, and it seemed right under his nose! A rifle answered from further away and he heard the angry whine of a ricochet singing overhead. Reddy tied his horse in a little ravine choked with brush and pulled his rifle from the saddle sheath. He opened the breech to check for a load, and, satisfied with the readiness of the piece, started slipping off to his right toward a low promontory he could make out through the trees. He should be able to see from there.

Fifteen minutes of careful stalking later, he made the promontory. Off to his right was a copse some seventy feet below, while straight ahead across the deep gully was a ridge that looked to afford a better view of the copse. The slope before him was covered with a thick layer of leaves, with occasional growth clinging to the side. This side was too steep to navigate, while the other side was sheer cliff.

Reddy spent the next few minutes peering into the copse, trying to see any signs of life. There were none. After several minutes he caught a small sign of movement almost directly across from him. After another wait the form of a man slid into view, crawling under the outcropping of a large boulder. The man was a skinny, scurvy-looking creature pushing a Winchester lever action ahead of him. He crawled a yard, pushed the rifle ahead, and repeated the action. As he was about to reach the edge and therefore gain an unrestricted view of the shelter below, a shot rang out from somewhere on the other side of the fellow and an answering shot came from the copse. Reddy had been focused on the crawling man but caught enough of a glimpse of the return shooter to know the shooter was Joe!

That was all he needed as the little form across the gully had risen to look over the edge and was pulling the rifle to his shoulder for a shot. Reddy's own rifle came quickly up and the shot of a mere fifty yards was almost too easy. His rifle kicked against his shoulder and the head of his target snapped sideways with the impact of the leaden missile. The skinny legs stretched out, quivered a bit while the upper body strained and then the whole frame went slack. The rifle slid over the side and crashed to the floor below.

There was a thrashing on beyond the dead man and Reddy caught a brief look at a head peeking around the boulder. Seeing the dead man, the other quickly disappeared and then the sound of running through the floor of dead leaves came to the waiting Comanche. Red Elk sounded out the sound of a night bird that Joe would recognize as such and know the humanity behind it.

An answering call soon floated up from the bottom and Reddy started slipping around to his right to try to get to the ridge above Joe. The copse was beneath a prominent overhang, the presence of which had prevented the attackers from seeing down into the bottom, thus keeping the inhabitants safe from fire from above. Reddy let out a low whistle and received an immediate answer.

In a near whisper he asked, "Joe, how many are there?"

Joe came back in full voice with, "Only two. Judging by the falling rifle, you must have eliminated one of them?"

"Yep, he's no problem anymore. It sounded like the other hombre took off, but I'll check him out anyway. Whar's Bear?"

"He's down here with me, hit when they jumped us. He's in and out of consciousness, been here for nearly two days without food and only a little water from a tiny spring down here. He's been punctured in the side with a rifle ball, but I got the bleeding stopped after quite a while. They kept me too busy shooting to hold them back to bind him up right away. You have any grub with you?"

"Yep, soon as I make sure thet other varmint is gone I'll git it down to yu."

Reddy spent an hour carefully scouting the area until he was sure the second party was gone, then he made his way to the dead man. When he rolled him onto his back, Jimmy Flanders' empty eyes stared into nothing and Reddy shook his head at the sight as he closed the eyes with his left hand.

"Sorry, fella, but yu needed tu live and let live. This is what them what doesn't ends up with, a shallow grave in the middle o' nowhere."

Within minutes after that he had a fire going in the bottom of the copse and was brewing a soup of wild onions, jerky for flavor, and anything else he could find. He had run across the red flower of a Mountain Pink and dug up the radish like root for a poultice for Bear. Commonly called an Indian turnip, the root was as hot as any pepper known to man but had great healing properties when properly applied. It also would flavor the soup if he didn't put too much in it. Too much and the taste buds would simply disappear as they seemed to burn up.

Bear stirred as the two cousins lifted him to a sitting position and spooned some of the broth into his mouth. Joe checked the bandage and re-did it, this time properly. When they were done, they rigged a cover over Bear as he seemed to be in more of a sleep than passed out and left him to rest. The wound was in his side but appeared to have missed any vital organs. All they could do now was wait. Reddy left the copse to retrieve his horse and try to find those of Joe and Bear.

It was fully two hours before Reddy returned, and he had only his own horse. He sat down with Joe by the fire to hear the story of their plight.

"We had downed one buffalo that was separate from the herd, left the wagon and skinners there to dress him and came on to try to find the herd. I thought it unusual to find a lone animal, but then just passed it off as nothing important and we came on toward the trees. We jumped a bunch of elk about an hour later, and they plowed off this direction without either one of us getting a shot, but we trailed them as they came deeper into the mountains.

"Bear said he thought he saw them in this draw, out that way, and he was just starting to dismount when the rifle cracked. I don't know where he would have been hit if he hadn't been moving, but it took him the rest of the way off and I hit the dirt rolling.

"Bear slid down the bank into the ravine, scared the elk half to death; and I was being shot at on top, so I rolled down after him. I helped him up and we came down this way, not knowing it was a dead end. But at least we found some good shelter here that we could shoot from.

"Neither of us got too many shots off, because we couldn't see the shooters. Bear was doing pretty good for the first hour or so, but I could tell he was getting weaker so I made him let me examine the wound. Great Scott, he had bled a lot. I bawled him out all the time I was tying him up, dodging bullets all the time. They were shooting down into these rocks trying for a ricochet hit, but we were blessed and all of them missed us.

"I chose to shoot back once in a while when I saw movement, but didn't dare concentrate much because it seemed they must have had way more ammo than two guys would normally carry. The one was using a fifty like Bear's. Those big slugs seemed to shake the very mountain when they hit!

"I finally got a look at the one fellow and it looked like he was as big as Bear, maybe not quite so tall. I snapped a shot at him and dusted his face for him, but no harm done. Did you score when you shot?"

"Yeah, little skinny man, wasn't over thirty yards away and was lookin' at yu from thet big rock up thar." Reddy pointed and Joe turned a little pale when he saw where Reddy meant.

"It's a good thing you got here when you did. I would have been wide open for him from there!"

"Yup, so yu owe me big time, cousin. I'll pick me one of yore hosses when we get back."

"Hey, I'm not going to argue with you over that now, I just want to get Bear out of here. Do you realize we've been here two days? This hollow is getting sort of tight and I'm getting more than just hungry. How we going to do this? This big ox is going to be nearly impossible to get up out of here. I hate to put your rope around him for fear of starting the bleeding again, but I don't see any other way!"

"Wal, yore right aboot thet. I got my hoss right up thar, it looks tu be the most gradual slope down thet way, so we'll drag this moose down and then get my hoss tu pull him up. Iffn he bleeds, he bleeds, we'll jist hev tu tie it up again. We sure cain't leave him here."

They hauled the big man up the ravine a ways, then Reddy moved his horse, they put his rope around under Bear's arms and started slowly hauling him up the steep bank. Joe stayed below him, pushing and guiding him as best he could. Once they had him on the upper level, they examined the wound and re-bound it just as a precaution. Bear stirred some as they did but didn't regain consciousness.

Reddy cut two poles to make a travois, and within half an hour of hauling Bear out they had him on it behind Reddy's horse and were on their way south from the area. They figured they were at least ten or so miles from the railhead, and Reddy insisted that Joe ride because of the lack of food for the two days of their "confinement." For once, Joe didn't put up an argument.

It was late afternoon when the three trudged into the railhead camp, and within minutes Searcy had Bear on a cot and a man sent for the town doctor. Joe was quickly fed while he repeated his story. Searcy scratched his head as Joe described the one man he had caught a glimpse of, then when Reddy described the man he had killed, the supervisor exploded into angry speech, not all of which was fit for others to hear.

"Those two were the hunters I hired to supply meat. They're the two you and Bear replaced, I'm sure of it. Why they would do this is beyond me, but I'll sure as the devil find out. The big guy was named Cannon and the one you shot was Flanders. He was a scurvy little man, at best. But I say again, why?"

"Wait a minute, George," Joe spoke around a bite. "Did you say Cannon?"

"That's right, Cannon. Never gave another name, said Cannon was enough."

Joe glanced at Reddy as he swallowed the bite and then said, "Remember when Bear had that mix-up down in Salt Lake City? That was with one of the kidnappers, and his name was Cannon. You don't suppose he ended up here and recognized Bear, do you?"

"Wal, iffn he did , he ain't the one what shot him, 'cause thet warn't no fifty caliber went through Bear."

"True, but that doesn't mean they weren't both hunting Bear. We'll see what he thinks when he wakes up."

Joe finished his meal and stood, turning toward town. "Fellows, I'm going in to see Molly, then one of us needs to get back to the ranch. Reddy, do you mind if that's me? I'm not comfortable with just Dan and Skinny there in light of what just happened. I think they at least need to be warned, if nothing else."

After the night in Boomstick, spent in the hayloft of the livery after his visit with Molly, Joe was up and out before the restaurant opened up. He had grabbed some jerky the night before, and Molly had added a sandwich for him for the breakfast meal, so he straddled Reddy's horse and headed out. He would travel through the night to make the ranch as quickly as possible. The four partners of Twin Forks Ranch were all used to skipping meals when they felt the necessity. The only breaks in travel were to rest the horse. When he made the ranch he found things in turmoil because his and Bear's horses had been found by a rancher who had returned them that morning. He was still there.

"Found them about twenty miles west of here, both dragging reins and saddle sore. I loosened the girths and let 'em air out a bit, but figured you folks needed to know about it. I'm glad to find you're alright."

"I surely thank you for bringing them in. I'm just glad I got here before a search was started. What's the situation here, everything okay?"

"It is now, Joe. Do we dare take a spring wagon to bring Bear home? I know he'd rather be here to be pampered by Allie and Lucinda."

"Lucinda?"

"Oh yeah, neglected that little bit of information. We hired a cook, and a good one! She was working for old man Libbey at the hotel. I don't think he likes us now since we took his help away!"

"Hmpf, no problem there, he doesn't even like himself. I think by the time we get a wagon to Boomstick that Bear should be able to travel okay. We were both without food for a couple of days, and that had as much to do with his weakness as the wound, as far as I'm concerned. Why don't we send Skinny? With Reddy to help, he should be able to bring Bear back okay."

"That's a good idea. I'll get him out first thing tomorrow. Now, let's get the full story from you."

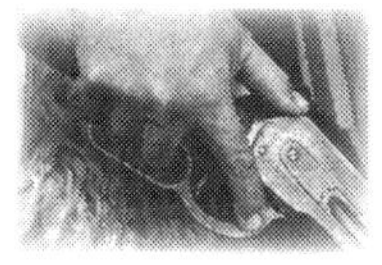

SEVEN

The telegram was a total surprise to Ted. It had come from Salt Lake City while he and Bear had been driving the harness herd to the railroad for shipment to Boomstick. His folks had sent word to Sunny Springs that they were just a few short miles out of Salt Lake City and were about to swing north as instructed to find the road to Sunny Springs with their six wagons and small herd of beef stock they had decided to use for "seed stock" when they settled into their new ranch.

Ted was amazed. He wouldn't have to leave for Texas at all, but he was also frustrated because he had wanted to be a help to the folks; it was his place, his duty, and he hadn't been allowed to fulfill it. The questions came hard and fast: How had they managed the drive without him? What had they had to leave behind because of being short-handed? And speaking of being short-handed, what help did they have with them? He was sorely tempted to forge out to the east to meet them for the final two or three days' march. When he mentioned that, both Jim and Melodi jumped in with an affirmation as to the advisability of such a task.

"You can take them straight to their new home and save them the extra twenty-five miles out of their way, Ted. That's actually fifty extra miles you'll save them from making, since it would be another twenty-five back-track." Jim Branson was very persuasive with this argument.

Melodi pitched in with her own encouragement for his joining his folks for the end of their drive. "How did they get this far without you to guide them, Ted? I thought you would be gone for months!"

"Mel darlin', I cain't imagine how they've made this drive so fast, or who they have tu drive the cattle and extra wagons! My dad musta worked some Texas magic down thar. I'll pack an' git goin' first thing after dinner. Better yet, maybe I kin git cookie tu make sumthin' I kin eat in the saddle."

"I'll do that for you; go saddle Dusty!"

He watched the little figure disappear to the house at a dead run and pushed his hat back on his forehead with a perplexed look on his face.

"Doggone, boss, I cain't figger thet girl at all. What in the blazes makes her tick? She's yore daughter; whut am I missin'?"

Branson threw his head back and guffawed loudly. "You want ME to explain either of my girls to you? You must be loco if you think I can do that. Shoot, I can't keep up with either one of them, especially the young one. A wife is confusing enough, then add a daughter just like her to the mix? Forget figuring them out, Ted, just love'em and enjoy the trip. When you finally decide to do that it gets a whole lot easier!"

Sweeny shook his head and went for his favorite mount. He would still have several hours of daylight left to travel by not eating first. Branson put a pack saddle on a small grulla dun and then went to secure a pack for the trail's requirements for his rider. They had Ted in the saddle and ready to ride in less than half an hour. Melodi stood looking up at him on the tall Dusty with a shy face that expressed inner confusion. She finally spoke with a trembling little voice that was quite unlike her.

"You be very careful, and don't you dare quit your job here to work for your folks. You can run both places, you know. I….I…."

Ted leaned down and grabbed her behind the head and pulled her close, kissing her full on the lips right in front of her dad. "I ain't aboot tu quit on yore dad, sugar. My folks will find a crew and a foreman. Yu just see to it yore here when I get back. We gotta talk."

As the stunned girl looked up at her rider, he spurred the

surprised steeldust and was gone in a flash, raising a dust cloud that engulfed her in the doing of it. She raised a tentative hand to wave and stood there frozen in place until he was out of sight. She only moved when she felt her father's arm encircle her shoulder and draw her to him.

"You better not let that one get away, sweetheart. He's true-blue and the real deal. Wild Texan or not, he's a keeper; and even with his gun rep he still isn't well-known enough to draw fame hunters after him. You understand?"

"But Daddy, what if his parents hate me for Tessa's death?"

"Honey, you just are not thinking straight. Those people are not, I repeat, not going to do that. If there's blame in their hearts, it's for the man who literally stole her life by brow-beating her into leaving her first husband and, as I understand it from Ted, was really responsible for his death in the first place."

She only looked up at her dad with a hero worship look, the one she often used to wrap him around her little finger, but this time it was genuine. Her head tilted to rest against his side as he walked her to the house.

§ § § §

The steeldust pawed restlessly at the ground atop a low hill as the rider scanned the country to the east with his field glasses. No wagons were to be seen from there.

"Dusty, we been goin' nearly two days now. We oughta be seein' sign of the folks." He descended to the road below and continued on the generally easterly direction it provided. He was sure his family would be on this road; he had described it well in his letters, but had counted on being with them to lead them to it.

It was about four hours after his nooning that he saw the dust cloud on the horizon. He picked Dusty up into a canter, and by the time he reached the cause of the cloud it had dissipated because the herd of cattle raising it had stopped. The two hours he had taken to reach them took the day to the edge of dusk. He saw a grizzled old cowpoke riding toward him, saddle gun across his lap at the ready.

The two approached each other slowly; then, as they recognized one another the horses were spurred to a quick closure. A few seconds later they clasped hands as they met silently. Ted spoke first as they broke the silence.

"Caleb Frost, you old outlaw, how did you ever talk the folks into letting a renegade like you come along?"

The old fellow spit tobacco juice to the off side and replied, "When yu need good men, yu hire good men, not some wet-behind-the-ears greenhorn. Whar yu been, yu worthless gun-slinger? We figgered tu meet up with yu days ago."

"I had no idea yu were coming 'til the telegram two days ago! I thought I'd know when the folks wanted tu leave and come tu Texas tu start the drive with them! What happened?"

"We was aboot tu send word tu yu when Tessa's old in-laws came tu yer folks an' asked iffn they could come along. They sold oot, Ted, wanted tu leave no matter whar tu. 'Boot the same feelin's as yer folks, I reckon. Jist needed new stompin' ground so's they could try 'n heal."

Caleb Frost had been foreman for the Sweenys since before the twins had been born. He was a little man, standing only five inches over five feet, slim as a rail, but hard as nails. He had taught Ted and Tessa to ride and shoot, and had been "uncle" to them for as long as they were able to talk. He and his wife had lived in their own house at the main ranch complex until she died when only in her early forties. After that, Caleb had moved into the bunkhouse with the hands to try to escape the loneliness of an empty house. He then had proceeded to invest even more time in the twins. He had grieved as deeply for Tessa as for his wife. And he had cussed Ted out soundly for not "killin' the scum what took her away! What were yu thinkin', Teddy, tell me! I oughta bust yu wide open!"

Ted had understood the old hand's outburst and was not in the least offended by it.

"I see yore still keepin' thet hoglaig low and tied down; yu still work with it ever' day?"

"Yeah Caleb, ever' day. Never know when one'll see a rat-tler."

"I know, an' he might even be walkin' upright, like back in God's garden. Too bad Adam didn't hev a Colt on him."

"C'mon, Unc, Eve musta been as pretty as Tess so he

wouldn't a been inclined tu blast the snake iffn she said 'No'."

The old fellow chuckled and nodded. "Well, we gonna set hyar all day an' leave yore folks wonderin' whar ever' one is? C'mon, let's get tu camp. Folks'll be glad tu see yu."

On their way to the wagons Ted passed by the herd and noted the different breed there. Turned to face them was a short, heavy red bull with white face and short horns. The hair on his face was curly and short. He stamped a front hoof at their approach, throwing up sod in the process as a warning not to come closer.

"What have we here, Unc? Dad get on the wrong side of a trade?"

"Yu'll think so if yu ask HIM thet. That there's a prize Hereford bull from up Missouri way. Yu'll notice several cows jist like him mixed in with thu longhorns, they're the start of a new strain yore dad's plannin' on. Longhorn tough for survival and Hereford built for more beef. Lot's more tender beef, too. Yu kin cut yore roasts with a fork."

"I'm glad to see Dad steppin' oot like thet, means he's not lost his zest for ranchin' in spite of the hard blows."

The cowboy's horse suddenly leaped into a run at the touch of spurs and Ted arrived quickly at the wagons, leaving the saddle before Dusty was even fully stopped to engulf a tall, slender, beautiful lady in a bear hug. Laura Sweeny looked anything but mid-forties as she was swept from her feet and spun in a circle by her son. She squealed like a much younger woman might have as she returned the massive hug, long auburn hair flying from the spin.

The six foot plus Jack Sweeny, built leather tough and range smart stood by with a smile the size of Texas as he watched his wife and son in their extended greeting. The two had always been close, as befitting mother and son, but the tragedy of Tessa's death had forged a bond that exceeded all that had been before. He swelled with a father's pride at the sight of his son and experienced an overflowing joy as he realized once again just how blessed he was to have this wonderful lady as wife to bless him with such a young man for an offspring. Ted had been completely honest during his last time at home when he brought the terrible news of Tessa's death. He shared his battle with drink and the subsequent finding of two wonderful friends, then, almost shyly, shared his love for Melodi Branson. When he told them of Melodi's attempts to befriend and save Tessa, his mother had cried and expressed a desire to meet "that wonderful girl."

As Ted set his mother back on her feet a smiling couple walked up from the last wagon. He recognized them with a shock as his best friend Sammy's parents, Jake and Suzan Bailey. Their son, Sammy had grown up with Ted and Tessa and had married Tessa. But he had developed a passion for cards and a gambler named Clint Shaffer had taken all his money and more. As a result, Shaffer had put Sammy in touch with men who had started him out as a rustler in order to pay the debts from his losses.

Those men had been caught in the act and all but two who had escaped were subsequently hanged on the spot, including Sammy. When Ted learned of it he had ridden in pursuit of those two because they had been the ringleaders and he held them responsible for the death of his dear friend. It took him nearly a month to track them down but he eventually found them in a little jerk-water town where many dark trail riders sought refuge from the law.

Ted had boldly walked into the saloon where they were at the time and challenged their manhood and courage. They were older, more experienced outlaws who laughed at the kid in front of them. Seconds later they were both dead, one bullet each before either one had cleared leather with a gun. The kid had downed both in a split second, backed out of the saloon with his still-smoking pistol in hand and mounted the nervous cowpony at the hitch rack, spurring it out of town at a dead run. No one pursued him for it was just another shooting scrape in a lawless town run by shady people.

When Ted arrived home he was told that Shaffer had taken Tessa and left town with her. It was learned later that she had gone with him because he threatened her in-laws with ruin if she didn't marry him. Knowing of the debts Sammy had with Shaffer, Tessa, out of her great love for the Baileys, had consented and gone with him. Ted had followed after, intending gun justice for Shaffer as well. His hunt had ended months later in Silverton, Colorado, where the final tragedy had occurred with Tessa's suicide. As Ted shook hands with Jake and hugged Suzan he scanned the rest of the camp, finding three more cowboys and a cook working busily to finish setting up.

"Dad, only four riders for the herd? How have you managed?"

"Look careful, son. You'll only find fifty head out thar," replied the old Texan. "I sold nearly ever' thing we hed so we could make this move totally clean of debts. I aim tu hev a great herd of quality beef within a year with thet new bull and them good breedin' stock o' heifers. I got a longhorn bull oot thar, too. We keep 'em as fer apart as we kin, but I figger by cross-breedin' both ways we kin git tu a good strain o' beef. Whut do you think on thet?"

"Dad, yu always did know more aboot cows than anyone else I know, so I say if yu think it'll work, it'll work!"

The rest of the daylight hours were spent with the meal and bedding the herd down for the night. They talked long into the darkness of the past few months since Ted had arranged for the purchase of the ranch in Sunny Springs Valley for his folks, each catching the others up on their lives. Ted discovered the Baileys had been approached by his folks to join them in a partnership venture and they had quickly been accepted and became as one family. It had been almost like that before when Tessa and Sammy had married; but now tragedy had cemented them even closer and the mutual desire to leave the Texas area of sorrow had finalized it.

§ § § §

The drive to Sunny Springs Valley had resumed the following morning, now six days past, and Ted had turned them north as soon as they entered the valley proper. By late afternoon they could see buildings far ahead, nestled in a bit of a natural bowl, with a very substantial stream running through the center and right beside the main cluster of buildings.

Jack's misgivings about possible flooding of the buildings soon gave way to relief when he saw that the banks of the stream were a good twenty feet lower than the ranch yard. Many years of spring run-off and the rainy season had cut it into the verdant bowl such that the buildings were always protected from high water.

A grove of willow trees mixed with beech and sycamores fairly surrounded the area of the structures and promised much shade and wind protection. When they pulled up in the area between the main house and the rest of the buildings they saw a low, rambling structure of logs and stucco attesting to the fact that expansion of the dwelling had been met in at least two stages. A low porch ran the length of the front and wrapped around both the east and west ends, with several doorways leading into the house. Further examination proved to them that each room at the front of the house had two entrances – one to the porch and one into the house. There were a total of five bedrooms, testament to the proliferation of the former tenants. Two of those bedrooms were quite large and would prove capable of housing the two couples in very substantial fashion.

The separate bunkhouse was large and roomy, with the former owner's attention to comfort for their employees showing quite clearly. Each hand would have a private room, something no Texas cowboy had ever seen at that time! Caleb would have the largest, of course. The center section of that building was a dining room and lounge where various card tables and magazine racks held prominent places.

"Ted, you didn't tell us this was an empire," said Jack, rather accusingly.

"Wasn't, Dad. As I understand it, this was the first place settled and the guy was rather puffed up with the idea of being a cattle baron. Set things up for a dynasty, but didn't know his boot heel aboot ranchin' and went under quick-like. The next settlers split the land up after he abandoned it, and now it's really one of the smaller ranches in the valley. Sunny Springs is only twenty miles to the west, and south a little. You saw the road when we turned north back a ways. Good smooth ride, even in a buckboard. What do yu think of yore new place, ever'body?"

Cries of pleasure came from all parties, even the normally quiet ranch hands. Then they set out to unload and get enough done to see them through the night. During the evening meal, Laura noticed Ted becoming melancholy, and she waited for her opportunity to talk to him alone. She finally saw him stroll off under the trees and quickly followed.

"Honey, mind if I walk with you in this heaven on earth setting?" she asked as she clasped his arm with both her hands.

"Of course not, Mom. Why would I object to a beautiful lady wanting to walk alone through the trees with me? That just isn't normal for a cowpoke like me!"

She chuckled and nodded, even though it was getting a bit too dark for one to see the nod. "You surely know your cowboys, dear, that's for sure. I remember your dad almost dragging me out for walks when he was courting me. The rest of the cowboys on my dad's place always tried to tag along just to hassle him about his courting the boss's daughter." She chuckled at the memories.

"I can't help but notice you seem a bit down in the mouth since we arrived, dear. I thought I sensed it last night when we camped, too. Would you like to share with your old Mom something that's bothering you?"

"Hmmpf. You think you have me down pat, don't yu Mom? And as far as thet goes, don't you be callin' my mom old. She's so young guys my age will be chasin' after her if Pop don't look oot after her." He gave her a little shake as they stopped beneath a big sycamore tree that overlooked the happily gurgling stream below. He sat down at the edge of the bank and bade her join him.

After a really long pause he drew a long, noisy breath and shared his thoughts with her. "Wal, dear Mother, it's this way. I'm turrible in love with Melodi, and yu'll love her too, but she's bound and determined thet you and Dad air gonna hate her, or already do, fer not savin' Tessa from herself. She's backed away from me an' won't even let me hold her hand most of thu time. I'm afraid she's killed her love fer me 'cause of her fear of you folks. I'm aboot at the end of my string now thet yore here, 'cause I figger she'll really hide from all of us from now on."

Laura leaned against her son and put her head on his shoulder and her right arm around him. "Honey, I can see where a young, impressionable girl could get that idea, but we can care for that. She hasn't killed her love for you, because if it was really love to start with, she's not able to kill it, even with fear of rejection.

"Jack and I can dispel those fears she has with just a little time together with the Bransons, and you can win her back again. If I recall your story from before, it was her who declared her love for you first, right?"

"Wal, yeah, thar in Silverton, but I knew before thet my feelin's fer her. I jist couldn't tell her knowin' we were goin' our separate ways. Mom, I'm scared she may never agree tu marry me now."

"You just leave the first part up to your dad and I, and then when you see that she's no longer frightened of us, you just walk right up to her and tell her you're getting married; don't give her time to think it over. You'll see that most women want the assurance of a man's protection and solid decision making, even if we try to manipulate you in the process! Trust me, dear, and do your darndest with her!"

This last was said just prior to a resounding kiss on the cheek and a tighter hug.

"Gosh, Mom, here I am, just a gunslingin' Texas cowboy alone under a tree in thu dark with a beautiful woman kissin' him, and it has tu be his mom! Aww, I ain't lucky at love at all. Nossir, not me!"

She broke into uncontrolled laughter as she shook him by the neck until his hat flew off and nearly rolled down the bank. As soon as he had rescued it, she pulled him to his feet by the sandy hair and steered him toward the house. "Young man, you get in there and go right to bed without your supper, you hear me?"

"Uh, Mom…we already hed supper, 'member?"

"Oh yes, so we have. Well, skip tomorrow night's, then."

The two walked slowly back, arm in arm and enjoying the gorgeous night and even better, the company.

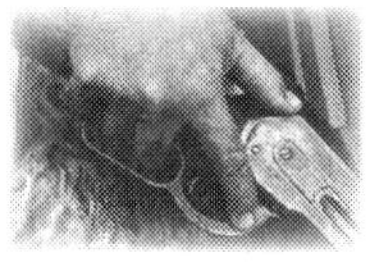

EIGHT

The newcomers were another three days getting settled in and Ted stayed the whole time to help, then persuaded them to allow him to escort them to Sunny Springs to help them get acquainted with the merchants. He also planned for them to meet the Bransons although he felt a twinge of trepidation over the possibility.

The twenty mile drive seemed to drag on forever, but by midday they could see the buildings in the distance. The Branson ranch with its shining white buildings and corrals stood out first, as though a guardian were checking the travelers for their right to pass. With rapidly beating heart, Ted signaled for them to pull into the spacious front yard of the ranch, passing under the Bar B brand on the board over the entrance.

He looked back at his family in the wagon from atop Dusty and saw the look of intense interest on his dad's face. He could tell he was impressed with the clean and well-kept look of the ranch buildings. He swelled a little with pride, because he was the foreman of such a fine-appearing establishment. This, in fact, was his home!

Jim Branson came strolling from the largest barn when he heard the rattle of trace chains and greeted all with a smile. Ted introduced him to each one, including the cowhands, and they were invited down. Jack had insisted all the hands ride in with them, feeling the herd would settle down and just rest from their journey without straying so far they couldn't be easily rounded up. The two bulls had been penned up in different corrals to keep them safe.

"Jim, I think my folks here are impressed with yore ranch; leastways it looked thet way jist now."

"Well, Ted, let's just let them speak for themselves over a cold drink and a lunch. I heard Hiram call the others to the table just a little bit ago. I wanted to finish up that last stall before knocking off. So come on in, everyone, and meet the rest of the herd over food!"

Marion Branson popped out of the door and admonished her husband, "James Branson, don't you dare refer to your family as a 'herd'! You're liable to find yourself eating out here on the porch, if you get to eat at all, you uncouth horse thief.

"Hello all, I'm Marion, boss of this outfit, no matter what that galoot there tells you."

She extended a hand to each man and hugged both of the ladies. "I can tell you are Ted's mother right away! It's those wonderful eyes, those sky blue and simply beautiful eyes. Am I right?"

"Well, you're right about me being his mother. I'm not sure about the description of my eyes, but I thank you, Marion. This other lovely lady is Suzan Bailey, the same as family to us. Her son was the husband of Ted's sister until his death."

Marion gave the same warm hug to Suzan and shared with them that Ted had shared the whole story with the Bransons, so they need not be nervous about the past; it was buried, as far as they were concerned. The three women walked arm in arm to the front door and disappeared inside. They had no sooner gone out of sight then the followers heard a whoop, and then all the female voices talking at once. When they entered they saw the women all in a cluster around Melodi, with Laura's voice now taking the lead.

"You have to be Melodi, and you're even prettier than my son described you! What a complete joy it is to meet you at last!" Melodi was engulfed in a hug to end all hugs by the older woman and tears were streaming down her cheeks unabated and plentiful. Even though Laura's face was turned the other way, Ted knew the same was going on with his mother. The two held to each other for several minutes, crying together all the while, before finally releasing each other and stepping back, only to have Laura grab Mel once again in another hug and a little moan that was a mixture of both sorrow and delight. It was as though they had gone through the actual experience of Tessa's death together in Silverton.

Laura finally stepped back again and held Melodi at arm's length while she looked her over and over. Ted piped up, "Gee, Mom, yu buyin' a hoss, or meetin' Melodi?"

"Hush, you ignorant male of the species, I'm enjoying the beauty of this wonderful girl you did such a poor job of describing to me. You only said she was pretty. I see she's more than pretty, she is simply delightful and gorgeous!"

That sentiment expressed, another hug was given, accompanied by a resounding kiss on the cheek. Melodi turned a deep shade of red as she endured yet another evaluation by the excited lady.

"You are so very kind, and if anyone here is beautiful, it's you. You can't be old enough to be Ted's mother!"

Suzan interrupted the admiration exercise by taking both by the arm and guiding them gently to the dining room, a long area with fireplaces at both ends and a table running down the middle long enough to seat a dozen people. There were six hands just finishing their noon meal, and as the guests entered they quickly rose and started out. Ted called them back and introduced them to his contingent, explaining where his folks were settling in.

"Most of you fellows were cowpokes before the boss here made yu give it up fer the easy life, so if he ever gets too bushy-tailed fer yu, check oot the folks' place. They might hev a real job fer yu. 'Course, yu'd hev tu work over thar, not like it is here."

"Hey, you ungrateful Texas ranny, if they aren't working, it's your fault, not theirs, and maybe I oughta fire your sorry carcass as foreman so we can get some real things done around here!"

Ted looked at his boss with a gleam in his eye and replied, "If yu do thet, who's gonna teach yore daughter which hosses air really thu fastest, huh?"

"Siddown, or you ain't gonna get anything to eat, and maybe

you better just hush in the process."

Any reference to a horse faster than his was a sure way to get Jim Branson to flare up and become quiet. He simply hated losing a horse race. Ted chuckled, winked at a still blushing Melodi, and did as told.

When the meal had been demolished, Jim showed them around the ranch buildings, a bit of personal pride showing as he did so. Then Ted took the family into Sunny Springs to introduce them to the merchants and establish accounts with each of them. The main mercantile was far larger than one would expect for a little town like Sunny Springs; but the owner, Harold Stout, served the entire valley and even beyond it with his well-supplied stores and fair prices. He could easily have been a banker; he kept so many credit records for his clients. Anyone could maintain a credit account there as long as they continued to prove themselves worthy.

Since Hiram wasn't a banker, it was necessary for Ted to take his party to the local bank where they would make deposits immediately.

"Man, am I glad to get that cash off my hands at last. I hated carrying all of our life's worth on the trail for two months!" Jack even showed relief on his face as he passed the bundle of cash over to the teller.

"Mister Sweeny, you could have wired the money to us; it would have been much safer," said the banker, John Sterling.

"Nothin' personal, Mister Sterling, but I don't agree. This six-gun and I hed a much better hold on thet cash than a wire strung on a pole. An' thet was only one wire. I hed a few other guns along side me on the way up hyar."

Sterling smiled and nodded; he was used to the frontier men not yet trusting the new ways. After meeting nearly everyone in town at one juncture or another, it was agreed the hands would return to the Sweeny ranch while the family spent the night with the Bransons. The cowboys, with their purchases loaded on a borrowed pack horse, started the twenty mile trek to the new home place. The Sweenys returned to the Branson ranch and spent the rest of the day talking of ranching, the trip, and whatever else came to mind.

§ § § §

Ted spent the next two weeks with his parents, helping them get established as to grazing areas, minor repairs, and the like while the cowboys schooled themselves on the ranches attributes. When he finally returned to the Bar B he was met by a somewhat contrite Melodi.

As he dismounted from Dusty she took the bridle and led the tired steed to the corral to turn him out.

"He looks tired, Teddy. You must have really pushed him today. He would normally do that twenty miles and never turn a hair."

He smiled at her admission as to his horse's stamina and replied, "Wal, he's been goin' since midnight. Dad hed one of those prize bulls o' his get loose and wander off. I tracked him down yesterday, but it took 'til nearly dark before I roped him and then grabbed a couple hours sleep before starting back with him. I couldn't believe how far thet rascal hed wandered! He ain't quite so fat as when he started oot, I'll tell yu thet. I hed no mercy on the beast, 'cause I wanted tu get back here tu see my gurl. Glad I wasn't thar when Pop saw the fat I run offa him!"

Mel blushed and poked at his chest. "And just who is YOUR girl, Mister Sweeny? I wasn't aware you had one."

She promptly found herself grabbed and kissed roundly before she could escape.

"Hey, you, a girl likes to be asked before being kissed. I never said I'd be your 'gurl'."

"Yu did so."

"Oh, really, and just when did that happen, mister cowboy with the imagination?"

"Back in Silverton, miss gurl with the absent mind. Or don't yu remember? Yu even threatened tu track me down iffn I didn't foller yu."

Melodi blushed even brighter and fled to the house, an exercise that had become more and more prevalent lately. Ted stood watching her and shaking his head. He had come to realize he would never understand women, but this wonderful girl had him more baffled than ever. His heart swelled with the memory of Melodi's expression of love for him back in Colorado and he clung to that like a bulldog to a bone.

At the supper table, Marion spoke to the group after all was done and the pies had disappeared. "I think we should have a dance for the Sweenys and the Baileys. That way the whole valley could meet them and become acquainted. Anyone disagree?"

"That's a great idea, honey! We haven't had a dance for a long time anyway, and that's the ideal reason. You gals get started on the arrangements and we'll get the dance hall ready. There's repairs need to be done before it will hold up to the stress. Been put off too long as it is." When someone mentioned dance, Jim Branson heard, "horse races" and was always ready, willing, and able to comply! He truly was hooked.

Ted spoke up, "I think the folks will love thet. Let me know when and I'll ride oot an' tell them. Mel, will yu ride with me?"

"I don't know, cowboy; maybe if you promise me we won't stop anywhere along the way for you to accost me like the last ride we made together."

Ted's face grew red while her parents both laughed aloud at his discomfort. He stalked from the room and returned to his chores at the stables.

§ § § §

The preparations took some time, and the date was established to be two weeks from then. Invitations were sent out to every rancher in the valley with encouragement to pass the word to those outside who were known to the valley people. It was certain that the old, outdated dance hall would be filled to overflowing. Ted moved the stock out of the main corral at the Bar B to accommodate visitors' animals, because the town livery would be filled for sure. The bunk house was scrubbed from top to bottom for guests and the ranch hands settled into a large tent erected for their use. The Bransons knew how to entertain and loved doing it.

During the two weeks of preparation, Ted saw Melodi sparingly because of the intense activity. Whenever he did, she had a bright smile for him and even allowed him to hold her hand while walking from the barn a couple of times. But she refused to go riding with him, a situation which frustrated him to no end.

She was both sweet and yet stand-offish at the same time. There were those times he felt she would grab him in a hug, but a thin wall always seemed in the way. Other times she was almost too sweet to be resisted. Nothing like this ever happened with a horse; you could almost always rely on their responses once you knew the animal!

The two weeks passed very rapidly because of the activity involved. The dance hall experienced renovation to both the floor and the structure on the first floor. The foundation had shown signs of weaknesses that harbored bad news for holding the weight of a hundred people engaged in active exercise such as the dances known hereabout. Grace and poise may have suffered, but enthusiasm took over and reigned supreme during the evening.

Jim made sure to have the race course measured out such that it ended in the town square for all to see the finishes, and he had his wranglers doing some last minute preparation of his favorite racers. Flash was among those placed in training, though with Melodi riding him almost daily he needed very little work, for the girl loved to ride fast. Her love for the sorrel was the stuff legends were made of and folks round about chuckled at the attempts she made to have Jim make Flame her own. He steadfastly refused, explaining to her each time it came up that she hadn't been the one to arrange the mating between the great mare, Sheba, and the stallion of the McCord ranch to the north, Flame. That union had resulted in Flash being everything people expected and more.

When there were only two days left before the event, people started drifting into town. As soon as the hotel and other rooms offered by residents were full, the Branson ranch began to find itself the center of attention. The bunkhouse filled up on Friday and more tents were erected. The town soon took on a circus atmosphere and horse races became the normal routine of each day. Branson entered several horses in the various races, holding Flash out until the "big race" was to be run. He threatened to fire Ted if he ran Dusty in that race, but the wrangler just smiled at him and paid the five dollar entry fee. The smile became a smirk when a youngster from a neighboring ranch climbed aboard

Dusty instead of Ted. The boy was a top rider and weighed little more than a hundred pounds.

Jim was furious, pacing back and forth while issuing vile threats to Sweeny all the while. Ted finally calmed him down with the comment, "Wal, Jim, err…boss, if yu wanta concede so's yu don't hev tu watch thet red devil get beat, it'll save yu a lot o' grief."

That was the final straw. Jim had forbidden Melodi to ride in the final race, "Too dangerous," he had stated. Now, he frantically searched for her in the crowd, but when he found her, she refused.

"I'm sorry, Dad, but until Ted had Jesse as a rider, I wasn't good enough. Too dangerous. Well, if Jesse's on Dusty, that means at least two horses will be rounding the turn out there at the same time and I'm frightened that I might get hurt if I'm on Flash. After all, I'm ONLY a girl!" With that, she flounced off into the crowd to the cheers of those who heard her comment. Everyone loved Jim Branson, but because of his naked passion for winning horse races they all loved to see him get beat.

As it turned out, Jesse allowed himself to get boxed in at the start and by the time he worked his way out of the situation Flash had gained too much of a lead to have Dusty catch him, even though it nearly happened. The two crossed the finish line nearly neck and neck. Branson was ecstatic until he learned Ted had bet on Flash!

"What the blazes you mean, betting on my horse? That looks like a fixed race. You did that deliberately and I NEVER would have thought that of you!"

"Boss, I knew Jesse wouldn't be able to out-fox those two rannys next to him when I saw how they were lined up, so I went and changed my bet right then. All I bet was five smackers so I would break even on the race. Now, if yu want, we kin arrange one last race jist between our two hosses, what ya think?"

"Racing's over for the day." And with that, Jim stalked off to merge into the crowd. Ted found Melodi suddenly by his side when she took his arm and snuggled in beside him. She flashed him that electrifying smile reserved only for special times and laid her head against his arm.

"Don't be too frantic over Dad's attitude. He just isn't Jim Branson at the horse races, dear. Mom always says she leaves her husband at home 'til after the races and then sends for him about an hour later. This other guy is gone by then!" She giggled at the thought and was rewarded with Ted's returning smile.

"Wal, darlin' I've come tu know yore dad during these months I've been hyar, an' I reckon yore mom knows him better'n any of us. I warn't worried none, except fer Jesse's outlook. He's probably feelin' pretty bad aboot now. Let's go find him; I reckon he took Dusty back to the ranch tu rub him down."

The two made their way back to the Bar B stables and found the despondent boy performing that very task. His eyes were bright with moisture. Both Ted and Mel spent considerable time consoling the boy and finally convinced him the world hadn't ended; that there would be other races. When he left, he was smiling and fingering the five dollars Ted had slipped into his pocket for riding for him. Five dollars was a lot of money for a fourteen-year-old in town for a dance!

Melodi commented that Ted had been very kind to Jesse to reward him in spite of the failure. Ted gently took her by the shoulders and pulled her to himself with all the intention in the world of kissing her, but his plans were thwarted when she placed her hands on his chest and held his face a mere inch from her own. Their noses were nearly touching, but Ted couldn't get any closer; she just gazed into his eyes with that "Not this time, fella" smile. He finally released her with a little shake of his head and the comment that she was going to drive him crazy some day. She replied to that by simply giving him a quick hug and going off toward the house. "It's time to get cleaned up and ready for the dance, Mister Sweeny. I'll maybe save you a dance or two if you're nice and promise to behave yourself."

"Then I guess yu won't be dancin' with me, fer I shore cain't be makin' promises I hev no intention of ever keepin'!"

He watched as she disappeared through the back door of the house and then headed for his own room to make his preparations for the evening's festivities.

Much later when Melodi stepped into the long hallway from her room she almost bumped into Laura Sweeny. "Oh Melodi, you look absolutely beautiful! Just stand there and turn around slowly and let me look at you!"

Melodi, blushing as she did so, twirled slowly for Laura's benefit. She wore white and the dress was quite lacey and full-skirted such that it flared out with the spinning. It reached her ankles in length and when she spun, the white slippers that replaced her normal riding boots showed below the hem. Laura grabbed her by the shoulders and stared deeply into her eyes.

"Dear, you are one of the absolutely loveliest young ladies I have ever seen and I love you, just totally love you. Understand, dear, I don't love you because you are so wonderful to look at, but your beauty doesn't make it any harder for me to love you. I guess you should also be told that my husband can't say enough about you. I almost think you could steal him!" she said in a teasing voice as she pinched Melodi's cheek playfully.

"Now, come with me to our room. I want to do something for you." Melodi hesitantly followed the sweet lady, stopping just inside the door.

"Come on in, dear, and close the door. We don't want probing male eyes seeing what we're doing in here. You don't know, of course, but Jack and I are a bit different from most of the Texas ranchers in that we spend some time every year somewhere in the east for time together without the rigors of the business interfering with us, sort of a honeymoon, if you will. It's usually in Saint Louis, but a few times we made it to Chicago for the time. We dine and dance and just fall in love all over again.

"When we do that, I always stock up on girly things for my husband, and, of course, for me, too. I have this perfume with me that is just wonderful and I want you to have it for tonight. Here, hold still a bit."

She placed a little of the perfume on each side of Melodi's neck and then on one wrist and instructed her to rub her wrists together. Melodi thought she would die in ecstasy at the smell of the liquid as it evaporated and rose past her nostrils. She closed her eyes as she breathed in the sweet scent.

"There, dear. Now you can knock my son off his pins for sure. You dance with him and put that tender cheek against his when you do, and I'll bet you the whole ranch he'll propose to you if you do! No man could resist you tonight, looking like you do and smelling like you do. You go out there and get him!"

"Oh, Missus Sweeny, do you…."

"It's Laura, Melodi. We are going to spend a lot of time together for the rest of our lives, and I won't have you calling me Missus like I'm some old lady."

"Okay, Laura, but do you really want me in your family? I mean…well…"

"Melodi Branson, I fell in love with you long before I met you. Ted talked of nothing else when he brought us the news of Tessa, and I could tell you had his heart lock, stock, and barrel. The more he talked, the deeper in love with you Jack and I became. Do I want you in my family? As much as I've ever wanted anything. I know my son loves you for he's told me so, as I'm sure he's told you; and that's really all I need to know."

Melodi broke into tears and fell into Laura's arms. They stayed that way for a long time as the emotionally stressed girl cried out her relief. When the tears subsided Laura held her at arms' length and smiled through her own glistening eyes at the younger ones appearance.

"Sweetheart, we need to take you back into my room and work on you a little bit. You've destroyed all your preparations from before except that beautiful dress. But, my dear, we can fix you rather quickly. Come on."

§ § § §

As the hall began to fill with people, the "band" started playing. Several area musicians were in attendance and all wanted a piece of the stage. There were three fiddle players from different ranches, and it had been said of the Sunny Springs area that every cowboy who didn't play a fiddle played the guitar. From the looks of the stage, that must have been so. After much haggling, they finally reached an agreement as to who would take turns and how long each would get to play; and the music finally got off to a peaceful start. Mayor Billy Hanks played the disastrously out-of-tune piano along with them until they kicked him off the stage. It was a good move as far as showing respect for music in general!

Ted started the night on the side, just watching all the dancers as they turned and whirled to the caller's instructions. Then when the first two-step started he located his mother and, bowing deeply, asked for a dance with her which, of course, she granted. As they made their way across the floor among the other couples, Laura spoke in his ear, "Isn't Melodi perfectly lovely in that dress? I can't believe you asked your mother to dance before her!"

"Aww, Mom, she said I hed tu promise to behave myself before she'd dance with me and I jist cain't do it. I get her in my arms and they jist naturally start squeezin' and thar's nuthin' to be done aboot it."

A squeal of delight burst unbidden from Laura and then she hid her face in his shoulder as she chuckled over her son's confession. She knew the night would not be very old before he went to Melodi.

When that dance was over, Jack claimed his wife and Ted went to Suzan Bailey for a dance. He was quite conscious of respecting the ladies of the former generation and as the night wore on he also made it a point to approach Marion Branson and Mary Hanks, among others. Ted soon proved to those who were observant that he was an experienced and smooth dancer. That quality endeared him to all the ladies present, both older and those his age, so he became a very busy young man for the evening. He had traded his boots for a pair of light dress shoes, and no ladies needed to fear having their feet trodden when they danced with him.

As the second hour approached he felt a little hand on his arm and turned to find Melodi snuggling up against him. "Well, cowboy, aren't you going to ask me to dance?"

"Wal, yu said I hed tu promise I'd behave myself and I know I jist cain't promise thet, Mel. Yore too durned pretty not tu hug a little bit."

She giggled and pulled him onto the dance floor among the swirling couples. He pulled her close but not tightly and the first few minutes were normal for them. Then Ted found Melodi snuggled against him in a closer embrace that he hadn't instigated. He put his cheek against hers and found himself nearly intoxicated by the closeness and her perfume. The softness of her hair felt wonderful to his skin and he finally spoke softly to her.

"Mel, I gotta tell yu, I'm gettin' terribly fond of you, and I don't know how I can live any longer without yu. I hev tried tu keep myself away from bein' pushy aboot things, but I hev tu ask yu right here and now: I love you more than life itself, Melodi Branson, an I jist hev tu ask yu to marry me an' live the rest o' yore life with me. Please, Mel, tell me yu will and I'll be the happiest man alive. An' I'll try my best tu be whut yu want me tu be."

He heard her gasp loudly and felt her stiffen from head to toe and knew he had "done went and done it" as old Caleb was want to say. She stopped dancing and leaned her head back, maintaining their close embrace, and smiling at him though tears.

"I'm sorry I've given you such a hard time, dear Ted. I've been wrong to do that after how I talked at Silverton and led you on. I'm sorry, dear cowboy, very sorry. Yes, I'll marry you, and the sooner the better."

Couples around them stopped dancing and watched fascinated as they kissed long and hard and then Ted escorted Melodi over to where her folks stood engaged in conversation with some other ranchers. He pulled them aside and, with serious face, spoke in a low voice.

"Boss, and Missus Boss, I hev somethin' tu ask yu. I just asked yore daughter tu marry me and she said yes, but I need tu hev yore permission first. Do I hev it?"

The hall fell into sudden silence at the war-whoop of Jim Branson. "It's about darned time you finally got around to it! I began to think I was gonna have to fire you to make something happen between you two. Of course you can marry her, and the sooner the better. When?"

"Wal, I dunno, whadaya think, Mel?"

Melodi joked as she said, "Right now, Dad."

That triggered another yell, which triggered an elbow to Jim's ribs from Marion, but then the snowball started to roll. Jim started searching through the crowd until he located the mayor and collared him.

"Billy, as mayor, you have the authority to marry folks, don't you?"

"Well, Jim, yes I do, but the parson is right over there, why not him?"

Jim soon had the parson by the arm and guided him over to Ted and Mel.

"Parson, these two want to get married right now. Will you do it?"

"Oh, Dad, I…well I…I was only teasing you."

"Were you serious when you said you'd marry Ted?"

"Oh, yes."

"Then look, we have all the folks in the valley and many from outside the valley here right now, why make them ride back here in a week for a wedding when they can attend one while they're here? Come on, Mel, why not?" Ted simply stood there looking dumbfounded at the speed with which things seemed to be progressing.

Melodi looked at her mother, then at Ted, back to Marion, and back again to Ted. Jim spoke up again, "Look honey, you have a white dress on, the parson's here, Ted doesn't have riding boots on, there's a big hog roast going on outside right now, so you see, we have all the ingredients for a big wedding. Marion, tell her that her daddy isn't crazy!"

Marion laughed and that broke the spell for Melodi. She stepped in front of Ted, took his hands, and looked wistfully into his Texas blue eyes. "Well, cowboy, I guess the jig is up for us. I started this way back in Colorado, but it looks like my daddy is going to end it right here, tonight. What do you say?"

Ted chuckled low, then, as he winked at her, said, "Wal, sweetheart, I reckon this is the first ever shotgun weddin' forced on the bride instead of the groom, so, in a way, we're makin' history. I say yes!"

Jim whooped and ran to the stage. He didn't need to call for people's attention after the whoop, so he started the announcement. "Ladies and gents, how would you all like to be invited to the wedding of my daughter to this lovesick Texas outlaw over here?"

Many exclamations to the affirmative were given so he went

on. "Well then, you are all invited to that very wedding RIGHT NOW, RIGHT HERE!!!!!! Get yourselves split into two groups with a lane down the middle leading to the stage from the front door. Charlie Manners, can you play a wedding march of sorts on that squeaky fiddle of yours?"

"Ya durn betcha, Jimmy! Ya just say when!"

People quickly lined up as requested. Jim grabbed Mel by the trembling arm and guided her to the front door, where he turned her around and prepared to march her forward to the stage. Jack grabbed Ted and ushered him to the stage, placing him to the right side of the lane between the two groups of people, and they stood there waiting.

"Who you want for a best man, son?"

"You,. Dad. Yore the best man no matter where yu are." No one but Jack noticed the little catch in Ted's voice as he said it, but it set deep feelings free as he proudly looked at his son and thought of the grief at Tessa's not being there to see. There would be much more grief released later as he thought more about it, but for now he had to be strong. Time for tears later, when he could hold Laura close and they could grieve together once again.

Old Charlie started sawing on his fiddle and Billy joined him on the piano at Branson's signal. He and Melodi started down the "aisle" as people applauded until Jim shot both sides a mean look and motioned for silence. This was going to be a proper ceremony if he had anything to say about it.

When they reached the front, where the preacher had just arrived, Mel looked at Ted and said in a low voice, "Oh Ted, should we wait until Bear could be here? I always pictured him beside you as one of us when we did this."

"So, yu thought aboot doin' this for some time, did yu? Yu shore didn't act like it little girl."

"Hey, you two, just drop it. You can visit later when you're married. And you can go see Bear on your honeymoon. That is, if you can get some time off, Sweeny," growled Jim.

That brought a deep flush to both faces and the preacher started with his ceremony to shut them all three up. Within a couple of minutes he had brought them to the part about the rings, and they suddenly realized there were no rings! Laura quickly stripped her own from her finger and as soon as Jack felt the sharp elbow of his wife, he did the same. Then the remainder of the ceremony was carried out.

The preacher turned them to the crowd and introduced them as husband and wife and the hall erupted with shouts of joy and celebration. It was at that time that someone realized there was no rice to throw, but an enterprising young cowboy had the foresight to drag a bag of oats to the front door and some were soon dipping their hands into it and heaving great quantities of the grain at Ted and Melodi. It stung.

Ted dragged Mel at a dead run from the building to escape the oats and then they were halted by some who took control and stopped the bombardment of grain in order to establish a receiving line to properly greet the new couple. Handshakes and congratulations carried long into the night, and then the dancing resumed with an even more festive note. The citizenry had both greeted their new neighbors and attended a wedding all in one fell swoop, so they carried on long enough for two dances. The sun was trying to peer over the mountain peaks to the east before the last fiddle squawked its dying last breath and was buried in its case to be silent until the next occasion sprung forth.

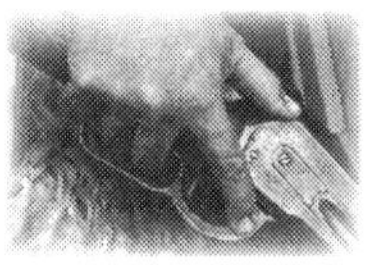

NINE

The wagon was loaded and ready for a two or three week trip and Ted was leading Dusty up to the back in preparation to tie his lead rope fast. Melodi followed with a little mare wearing her saddle when Jim Branson stopped Mel.

"You shouldn't take that little mare, Melodi. I would rather keep her here 'cause I don't think she'll take to following the wagon too well."

"Dad, she'll be fine. She does anything I ask of her. There's not another horse I'd rather take."

"Not one? Not a single, solitary one?"

"Not out of my string, Dad."

"Well, I don't think you tell the truth, young lady. I'm SURE there's a better mount that you would rather have. How about that new addition to your string?"

"New addition? Dad, I haven't bought a new horse for over a year. You surely can't mean the little colt just born to my pinto, he's only a month old. That's the only new addition I have."

"No, daughter, it isn't. Wait here, and pull your saddle off the mare while you wait. I'll get you that new addition." With that, he trotted off to the stable, disappeared through the big double doors, and emerged leading Flash.

"This is the one I was talking about. He's a lot better representative of the Branson stables, girl."

"Dad! You said the new addition to MY string. Now you

bring your favorite out. I would rather take my own horse, Dad, really."

Branson grinned the widest grin he had and pronounced to the newlyweds, "He IS yours, sweetheart; he's your wedding present from your mother and me."

Melodi let out such a scream that the normally calm Dusty started pitching and trying to pull his tie rope loose until Ted calmed him down with a gentle hand and soothing voice. He smiled as his bride wept uncontrollably while hugging her father so tightly that he began to fight for a good breath. He, too, had glistening eyes.

"Now then, Mister James Branson, new father-in-law, yu done went and done it. My new wife is gonna be more thrilled with her new hoss than she is with her new husband! I jist took a back seat fer this hyar trip. Thanks, DAD, fer nuthin'."

Jim just gazed over his daughter's head and continued to smile. No comment was forthcoming from his mouth. The two spent many minutes in the embrace, while Melodi's mother stood with her arm around Ted, silently crying at the scene before them.

"You probably don't understand us for being so sentimental this way, Ted, but we've been through a lot together; and now it's all come together so wonderfully and somewhat quickly that these tears are tears of relief and love."

"Believe me, Mother Branson, I totally understand. Remember, I was there in Silverton when Mel was first rescued. If yu'll look close, yu might just find a bit of water tryin' tu drain from my own eyes right now. I know what thet hoss means tu Jim, and this is a big sacrifice fer him."

Marion reached up and took hold of Ted's chin, turning his face down to hers and shaking him a little. "Hey, Texas cowboy, I told you before, I am Marion to you. 'Mother Branson' sounds like an old lady, and I am NOT there yet. Do… you… understand?"

She emphasized each word with an additional little shake. The tall, slender Texan grinned and nodded and then squeezed her around the shoulders. "Thet's what it'll be then, but I have tu warn yu, I might ferget myself and start flirtin' with yu if I use sech familiarity.

As the family goodbyes dwindled and both riding horses were tied to the wagon nothing was left but to launch the conveyance off down the road to the northwest. They intended to head first for Twin Forks Ranch to see Bear before just traveling in a big circle for a couple of weeks, camping alone and enjoying each other as a couple alone. Ted had a fair idea of how to find their way to the river from there, and then all they had to do was follow it north to get to the ranch. He figured a couple of days, at the least, maybe four or more at a leisurely pace.

They camped early that night in a grove of trees located in a shallow bowl that was protected from any winds. Ted built only a small fire and their evening went by quickly as they tromped the land, exploring in each direction from camp before plunking down between the fire and the tent. What a difference for Melodi between this camp and those of the previous year with the kidnappers. She snuggled into her husband's arms and gazed dreamily into the fire until they both fell asleep right where they were. Ted awoke later and pulled Melodi into the tent and covered them both with a quilt. They slept the night away without even pulling off their boots!

§ § § §

The land was unkind at this place. The wagon sat on the edge of a sharp drop-off of many feet; the river below disappeared to the right, slipping into a split between their position and the mountain on the other side. The walls on either side of the rushing water formed an impenetrable obstacle to human traffic. They were going to have to leave the river and trek off to the east for a ways. Ted used his binoculars and could see no end to the bluff on which they sat. He put the glasses down and slapped the reins to the team.

"Wal, wife, we don't hev a choice whar tu go, so hang on and I'll see if I cain't git us lost." She smacked his shoulder and kissed his cheek with a giggle that suggested she cared not whether they knew where they were going

The ridge along the river gradually drifted them east until the river was but a memory late in the afternoon. Ted stuck stubbornly to the terrain as best he could, knowing the ranch they sought was on the river. Two hours before sunset they pulled back west and found themselves traveling almost due west, at that. In another hour they sat at the edge of the drop-off overlooking Twin Forks Ranch on the opposite side of the river!

"Look at thet!" exclaimed Ted. "Two houses, two big barns, corrals aplenty, and haystacks on this side of the river! Those boys know how tu ranch!"

He drew his gun and fired three evenly spaced shots into the air to announce their presence, then proceeded to try to find a way down the steep slope. Flash and Dusty voiced their displeasure at the unannounced shots by pitching and kicking high on the ends of their lead ropes. Ted watched until a woman came out the front door of the frame house, while two men came from the closest barn to the house. They all waved a greeting.

"Yu know, Mel, we could jist leave the wagon hyar fer the night and ride down thar."

"Oh. Let's do that, dear. I so want to see Bear as soon as we can! We can lead the team over, too. Let's unhitch quickly."

They proceeded to do just that, saddling the mounts and finding their personal gear which they tied to the harness of the team. They then rode down the slope and headed for the river. As they approached the happily burbling stream, a large figure came from the log house furthest to the left. He hobbled with a crutch which barely held him up. A bushy beard of red and hair to match shone clearly in the sunlight sneaking through the trees from the west.

"There's Bear, that's him! Oh Ted, it's really him!!"

Ted was suddenly left alone in the middle of the river as Flash leaped forward at the drumming of two little heels on his sides. He chuckled and held Dusty back as the big horse wanted to race. When Melodi reached the porch she leaped directly from the saddle to the top step of the porch, stumbling a bit as she did. Then she righted herself and leaped upon the big man, either ignoring the crutch or not seeing it in her overcoming joy at the sight of her big hero. Bear was able to withstand the onslaught by grabbing the girl with one arm while dropping the crutch and grasping the open window beside him. He let out a pained grunt as her legs were thrown around his middle and found the wound.

"Hyar, gurl, ease up. I got a hole in thet thar side right whar yore leg is! What in the world air yu doin' hyar, anyway?"

"Oh Bear, aren't you glad to see me? I've missed you so much! And why do you have a hole in your side?"

"Mel, I cain't remember ever bein' so glad tu see anyone in my whole life, but please get down and let me catch my breath. Thet wound don't like this kind of attention."

"Well, answer me, how did you get a wound?"

"Supposin' we just leave thet 'til yu meet my folks over hyar. And let Ted get hyar. Say, did yu two elope?"

"No, Bear, my dear, but it wasn't all that different from eloping, at that!" she replied with a gay laugh.

Ted looped Dusty's reins over the hitch rail in front of the porch, caught Flash and did the same for him while leaving the harness reins tied to his saddle horn. He ascended the steps to carefully engulf Bear in a hug. He had noticed the crutch and heard the grunt of pain.

"Bear, tell us it isn't too bad, pard. Tell me who did it and I'll track them down!"

"Thar yu go, assumin' a wound has tu be from a person. How yu know it ain't from a hoss kickin' me?"

"Oh. Well, I guess I'm still tuned into bad people with guns causing all the trouble in the world."

"Wal, this is a gunshot, but the feller what did it is dead. Reddy cared fer him a couple of days after. Now, what happened with you two? 'Fess up."

The rest of the Twin Forks people came from the other house and the barns to climb the steps to the long front porch of the double cabin, all smiling at the newcomers. Introductions were made and then Ted explained the wedding.

"Wal, we were at a dance. I asked Mel to marry me right after I asked her daddy iffn thet was okay, and she said yes and then she did. Thet very night."

Allison squealed with joy, "So you eloped? Wonderful!"

"No ma'am, we didn't. Her daddy must not have trusted me as fer as he said, fer they went and lined up folks at the dance, walked her down thet aisle of folks, and the parson did the deed right thar and then. Was a right fine weddin', even iffn I do say so myself."

They all stood silent for a moment, then Bear turned to Melodi. "Mel, air he tellin' the truth? Did yore daddy really do thet?"

"Yes, Bear, he did. He said all the valley folks were there, so why make them ride in again when it could be over right then. He really shocked me. I never saw that side of Dad before, not even at a horse race!"

They all laughed at that, then noticed that Dan had slipped away from the group and was giving Flash a close going over. He examined the beautiful stallion from head to toe, from withers to haunches, and was stroking the fine head while they watched.

"This has to be related to Flame. And he has Sheba's lines, too. Is this the offspring Paul McCord told me about? The one they shipped Sheba north to accomplish?"

"That's him, Dan. Dad put all his hopes and dreams into Flash. I think he would have walked all the way to Arizona to accomplish that after he saw Flame and Mister McCord told him about the mare.

"You see her lines in him; that must mean you're familiar with her."

Dan got a faraway look in his eyes as he recalled the sight of the mare he had made his flight to freedom on three years before. It seemed such a long time ago.

"Yes, Melodi, I know her very well. You see, Sheba and I spent over a year together. When I had to send her back to Ira it nearly broke my heart. I could do anything I wanted with that gorgeous lady, and she always responded. There's only one horse in this world that I've seen who can match her for intelligence, endurance, and speed. Furthermore, he matches her for devotion to me, and that's something.

"Sheba acted like she and I were soul mates, and I really think we were. I bet I could call to her from a quarter of a mile away and she would still come running full out to find me!"

The last was said with a bit of choked-up emotion, for Sheba had become quite a pet and companion during Dan's fugitive years. He raised his head and called out, "Blue!" There was a commotion from behind the main house, and then hoofbeats sounded as a huge horse bounded into view. He ran to Dan and stood expectantly, tossing his head and fidgeting in anticipation before his master. Dan roughed up his forehead and ears as Ted and Melodi looked him over. They both murmured complimentary things about Blue, and that caused Dan to burst out laughing.

"Come on, you two, I know he's downright ugly; but look into his eyes and see what he really is: very intelligent. That's what I saw the first time I laid eyes on him. He proved me right, and time and time again I've thanked the good Lord for him. I never trained a horse so easily or so quickly as this old mule." The last was said with a final scrubbing of the huge ears and then a swat on the neck. "Go, Blue." Blue shook his head again and trotted off.

Ted and Melodi looked at each other with bewildered looks as Bear spoke. "He ain't nuthin' but a big dog. Yu oughta see him 'n Dan first thing in the mornin'. It's a sight tu see, the way they carry on with each other."

"Man, he's big! Dan, does he have a good gait for all-day riding?"

"Yes, Ted. We have already gone twenty hours straight with barely any rest. He's fast, as I said, enduring to the end, and smart. I never dreamed I would see such a horse, let alone own one. On second thought, I don't own him, he's my partner."

"Rider comin'!" This came from Reddy, who had just reached the porch as they proceeded back to the main house.

As the rider hit the middle of the river, Skinny commented, "That's Doug Moore, from town. He must have a telegram for someone."

The youngster of around fifteen pulled his horse to a stop by the steps and bounded down, handing the paper to Dan.

"It's from George. Someone has stolen around twenty horses. He seems to be in a real quandary over it, too. Says this could hold them up over a month without sufficient relay teams for the grading work. Wants to know if we can bring more teams or maybe help Bill Hanson with the hunt for them."

"Drat. Jist as Ted an' Mel show up. This ain't fair." Bear's growl was unpleasant to hear because of the anger behind it.

"Bear Rollins, you are going NOWHERE, got it?" responded Allison. "To start with, Ted and Melodi are far more important than any stolen horses, and secondly, YOU are far more important than any stolen horses. You aren't going anywhere until that wound is totally healed. You got that, mister!?"

Ted and Melodi looked on with astonishment as the big man towered over Allison and just nodded in obedience. Was this the same Bear Rollins they had known in Silverton? His "Yessum" came low and barely discernable to further amaze them. It left no doubt as to who was in charge at Twin Forks Ranch. The rest of the crew smiled knowingly as the mountain man meekly hobbled with them to the house.

A war council was held around the huge dining room table, and Ted and Melodi were made to feel not only welcome but a part of the family's decision-making. Dan suggested that Reddy and Joe make the trip to the railhead to see what they might be able to do to help while he and Skinny cared for the ranch. Provisions for a week, a packhorse, and relief mounts and packhorse would be taken and they would leave at first light the next day.

Dan expressed a willingness to be one of the hunters but was voted down by all the others except for Allison. She wisely remained out of the decision since she wanted Dan to remain true to himself. Dan was a part of the crew and needed to hold up his end, wife and child or not.

Ted had a hard time not volunteering to go, but his new bride at his side was a strong deterrent. Her glare in his direction did nothing to dispel that feeling! He was learning already. At the close of the council of war, Ted, Mel and Bear retired to the front porch. They found rocking chairs and parked in them as they updated each other on all the news of the past several weeks since Bear had helped drive the horses to the railroad.

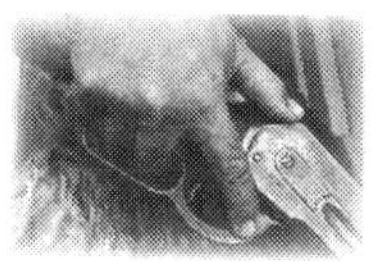

TEN

The railhead was in a turmoil of activity as the two Comanches rode in around noon on the second day. They had driven the horses hard. George Searcy, looking harried and tired greeted them with a wave and hurried to where they tied their horses.

"I am so glad to see you two! Sheriff Hanson advised me to send the telegram, though I felt we shouldn't bother you Twin Forks folks any more. You've done plenty already, but he assures me you won't mind and that you're the best trackers anywhere. Thanks for coming."

"We figger there's nuthin' better to do than track down hoss thieves, George. We might be next. 'Sides, it seems like thet's all Joe and I do any more. Must be a curse of some kind."

"It is, Reddy. It's called lawlessness and it's plagued mankind every since Adam and Eve fell for the snake's lies back in the garden! We have no idea what time of night the horses disappeared. We stopped standing guard after Cannon and his gunslinger friend were no longer seen around here. Figured they pulled up stakes for easier ground. 'Course, there' no reason to assume they did it, but that Cannon sure fits the mold of a thief."

"Reckon yore right. I hope no one has tramped around the corrals much and messed up all the tracks. We're already workin' under a handicap 'cause of the days passed."

"Come on, Reddy, let's get to it," spoke up Joe.

They worked their way around the corral, starting on the

side furthest from camp and easing in opposite directions as they coursed for signs like a bird dog in a briar patch. With each successive pass they moved farther out from the fence until Joe gave a sharp whistle. He was at least a hundred yards out on the north side.

When Reddy arrived, Joe was measuring the tracks of the ridden horses, knowing the action was probably useless. The thieves would be trading off from horse to horse as they went, never riding the same mount as before. The final count of stolen horses was twenty-two. Searcy was down to eleven teams for grading and hauling poles. He planned to work four teams in each shift of three hours except for those hauling poles from the forest. They would work a full day since the wagons pulled so much easier than the earth-moving machines.

The Indians started following the tracks as they went northwest, making slow time of it at first because of the activity close to camp. They ended up directly north of Boomstick, where the tracks veered due north. As they studied the surprising move, a light suddenly came to Reddy's eyes.

"Say, cuz', it looks tu me as though they might be followin' thet pass we used back before when we brought Flash home from those other hoss thieves. I think we oughta split up. You stay on the tracks and I'll ride fast and straight to thet little burg on the other side o' the mountains whar we found thet red hoss. It just might be they know thet old man who bought the stolen hosses before an' count on him buyin' more. What say yu?"

"I'm for it. Let's make sure the packs are split right so we both have supplies and get on with it."

The two made fast preparations for the split and then Reddy spurred his horse to a canter in the direction he had indicated. They had recovered Jim Branson's stolen horses a little over a year before and had returned to Boomstick via the route it appeared the current thieves had used to exit the area. Reddy planned to cross the mountains to the east on a more direct route in an attempt to catch those with the two-day head start.

§ § § §

As the sun began its slide to the crest of the western peaks,

Reddy topped an abrupt ridge to be greeted with sight of a green, verdant valley below. The slope before him leading down to the lower level some thousand feet below was green, plush, sprinkled with small trees among the deep grass, and sloped gradually to the floor far below. The angle was such that it was fully five miles from his vantage point to the floor. The floor of the valley was slightly rolling, with several small streams flowing through its ten miles wide and forty or more miles long depression in the mountains. If he hadn't known better he would have sworn he was looking down on Jackson's hole, but he knew it was much farther to the north.

Situated by the largest stream, some ten or twelve miles from where he sat his saddle, was a set of ranch buildings nestled among a grove of trees. With his binoculars he could just make out the layout of the place. He decided against trying to make the distance that evening and started his descent to the floor of the valley with all the intentions of camping by the small stream closest to him.

With the horses hobbled and a fire going, he started the sourdough biscuits and had bacon frying in the cast iron skillet over the fire. Naturally, the coffee was the first to find the fire and the smell was beginning to make its promise of soon-to-be-enjoyed refreshment.

With the Dutch oven now covered with coals and the bacon set to the side to keep warm until the biscuits were baked, he poured the first tin cup of coffee and settled back to wait out the baking process.

He tried to picture just how far south he was off the route he and Joe had taken to get back to Boomstick on their previous foray to rescue stolen horses a year before, then remembered they had encountered a town far to the north of there before turning south to get home. Joe would be around fifty or so miles further north before he could turn east if the thieves followed the previous path. He wasn't sure if there were any other ways through the mountains that could be easily followed.

He lifted the lid on the oven and peeked in, relishing the wonderful smell of the baking biscuits as he did so. For Red Elk, Comanche brave, to be caught off guard required a total distraction, and the hot lid plus the smell served to accomplish that very thing. As he started to slide the lid to the side a voice cut into the silence and Reddy burned his hand on the lid as he jerked to the side.

"Just hold yourself still there, Mister, and don't be moving any. You're covered from two sides."

"Do yu mind if I get back away from this here hot oven, friend? These biscuits smell mighty good, but thet lid is bodacious hot!" He stuck his burned fingers in his mouth as he said that and sucked mightily on the offended members.

"I reckon we don't mind you doing that, but keep those hands lifted away from your belt line. Carson, get his gun. Better take that pig-sticker, too, but don't get between him and me while you do it."

"I'm surmisin' yu gents air right hungry and aim tu rob me of the best biscuits north of Texas?"

"Hmmf, you ain't tasted our cook's biscuits or you wouldn't say that. Now, just stand up and move back from that fire a bit, and be slow about it. That's good right there; now turn around and let's get a look at you."

"Tarnation, Rex, this here's an Indian!" exclaimed Carson.

Reddy turned slowly around to find he was looking at two men in typical riders' garb. One was average build with a gun held in the right hand and was studying him from head to toe. A long mustache curled down in the popular handlebar style while blond, curly hair erupted from the edges of a flat-topped Stetson hat.

The other captor was a short, squat puncher with a scruffy beard and mean, squinty eyes that peered from beneath a floppy, chewed-up hat that had seen better days, but certainly not recently.

"Looks like we caught us a horse-stealin' redskin, Rex. Let's string him up right here."

"Naw, Carson, we'll take him to the old man and let him have that pleasure. Move over here, redskin, and slow-like."

"Now wait a minute, fellers. I have bills of sale for all three of my hosses, there. Always carry them."

"We ain't concerned about those horses, we're concerned

about the ones on our ranch that you came here to steal," replied Rex. "No Indian is gonna take our stock and get away with it."

"What! Whar in tarnation do yu see any hosses I might have took? Air yu stupid, or just plain blind?"

"Shut up, rustler. Everyone knows redskins are horse thieves, and you couldn't have any other reason for bein' here. We'll let my old man make the decision on your fate tomorrow. You got such a good supper cooked that we'll just settle in right here. Now lay down."

Reddy had no choice but to comply and was soon trussed up between two of the scrub trees nearby. His hands were tied together and strung to a branch some four feet off the ground while his feet were also together with a rope stretched to another tree some twenty feet away so that only his backside touched the ground. His head had nowhere to rest and once his neck tired he knew it would have to hang backwards between his arms. It was a very painful position and promised to make for a miserable night if they left him there. He lay seething at the two as they ate his meal, complaining all the while that he hadn't fixed more since there were two of them.

Once they finished the meal they tossed his utensils aside and proceeded to smoke away the evening, finally rolling into their blankets without so much as a glance at the now hurting Red Elk. His heritage was such that he steeled himself against being miserable and angry for the time being, knowing that would only increase his discomfort. He tried to relax as many muscles as possible and settled in for a long night, indeed.

§ § § §

Morning broke cold and damp, finding the Indian wet with the dew, with his body shivering uncontrollably. His arms were the worst of the lot, with the skin on his wrists rubbed raw by the rope and the muscles stretched beyond reason. His shoulders screamed with pain, while his neck felt as though it would break from the weight of his unsupported head. And speaking of his head, it ached like never before, every heartbeat coursing through the temples and on through it all. His eyes felt as though they would burst from the sockets. The smell of frying bacon still sneaked through these feelings. His captors were up.

After nearly an hour Rex came over and began to untie his trusses from the trees. He was dropped flat, and while every fiber of his being rebelled at the movement, no sound came from him. He was, after all, still a Comanche brave.

Rex kicked him and commanded he get up, which he tried valiantly to do, but it required help from the two men to accomplish it. He was marched to his horse and pushed into the saddle, where his hands were tied once again, and they led off toward the distant ranch, chuckling all the while of their "prize" for "the old man." All of Reddy's gear was left right where it had been, strewn about like a wind had situated it for him.

As they rode along, Reddy's bones began slowly to respond to the movement of the horse and he began to feel as though his muscles might actually work again some day. It was then that Carson rode up beside him and prodded him in the side with the handle of a whip. "I hope the boss is in the mood to let me sorta work on your body a bit to help it into shape. It's amazin' what good bull-whippin' can do to wake a person up." With that, he prodded even harder and pulled back to do it again. When he jammed the handle at Reddy, Reddy pulled back in the saddle and kneed his trained mount to the right which put him in reach of the bully. Reddy swung his tied hands as hard as he could to the right, smashing them into the nose of Carson and knocking him from the saddle. In the next instant he jammed the spurs to his frightened horse and the steed leaped forward, ramming Rex's horse in the right hind quarter, spinning it around in a manner that happened to place Reddy against Rex's right side, where he grabbed that worthy's forty-five from the holster and smashed it against the rider's head. Rex went down like a sack of potatoes dropped from a wheelbarrow.

Reddy whirled his horse with his knees and when the highly trained animal faced Carson there was a loud explosion and dirt flew up from between the bully's hands as he rose from the ground. The forty-five slug was well placed, in spite of the fact that Reddy was shooting with his hands tied. The next shot smashed into the holstered weapon on the downed man's side, ripping it from the shell-belt and effectively freezing him in place.

"Hombre, if yu move, yu die. Lay down right thar on yore belly and iffn yu even blink crooked, I'll kill yu. And with pleasure, yu understand?"

A nodding of the head was the only response he received, but it was with emphatic agreement to the terms. Rex began to groan and stir as Reddy dismounted and retrieved his knife from that prone form. He cut the rope from his blood-soaked wrists and flexed the fingers on his left hand, then shifted the pistol to that hand and worked on his right for a while. By the time Rex had come completely to, he found a rope around his neck that led to Carson's neck and on to Reddy's saddle horn. It left no more than ten feet of slack from Carson to the horn. The loops around their necks were very tight and abrasive because of the sisal compound of the lariat's strands. Discomfort was Reddy's goal, and he achieved it with this arrangement.

Reddy took time to build a fire and cook some side pork he found in their saddle bags, along with a pot of coffee. The riders remained seated under his horse's belly where he placed them.

"Yu stir around too much and I'll scare thet hoss so bad he'll trample yu and then drag yu by the neck. I hope yu do just thet, fer my haid hurts somethin' awful 'cause of yu two varmints. I'd love tu show yu some good old Texas cowpoke justice goin' hand in hand with some Comanche Injun revenge."

With the caffeine from the entire pot of coffee working on him, his headache was a little relieved and the food, such as it was, helped to revive him. He then smothered the fire with dirt and loaded the two hapless riders onto their horses. The rope around their necks remained tied to his saddle horn. He rode off in the direction of their ranch buildings.

"You ain't goin' to like what the old man does with you when you get there, Injun. He'll skin you alive, like every Injun should be treated."

No reply came to Rex at that comment and an hour plus change later they rode up to the front of the dilapidated main house, a log structure that showed itself to be strictly a male inhabitance. The porch was run down and the walls showed some of the chinks to be totally missing. The front door still hung on both hinges, but sagged as it did so. There was noise from inside indicating the sharing of a meal by several people.

Reddy had both men's revolvers tucked in his belt besides his own in its holster and he now drew one of those behind his belt and fired through the top of the window to the left of the door. Bedlam ensued inside and four men came boiling out of the door to pull up as they saw Rex sitting his horse beside Reddy's, the muzzle of a cocked pistol pressed to the base of his skull. It happened to be his own gun.

"Hombres, yore lookin' at the maddest redskin any of yu ever saw, and iffn any one of yu even coughs, this worthless son of yorn is gonna lose his haid. Be sure thet I'm mad 'nuff tu not care iffn I cash in over the doin' of it, but some of yu thar on the porch ain't gonna see tomorrow, fer sure. Now, take them belts off an' toss them oot hyar in the grass."

"I don't know who you are or what you think you're gonna do here, Injun, but there's a rifle aimed at your head and you won't even jerk that trigger if he puts a round in your worthless brain." This came from a scurvy-looking old man with ragged overalls, suspenders, scraggly beard, yellow, tobacco-stained teeth and hair in need of cutting for several months. In answer to his threat, the pistol leaped from another explosion and there was a grunt from inside the window as the rifle clattered to the floor inside.

"Seems tu me thet yu don't much care for this worthless son hyar. Any sudden shock tu my body an' this thing in my hand goes off. 'Course, from whut I've seen the last few hours, he ain't worth carin' fer.

"Men, these two captured me oot hyar on the range, ate my food I hed ready fer my supper, tied me up in a most uncomfortable manner, accused me of hoss stealin' even though I have bills of sale fer all three of my hosses, and threatened tu scalp me alive jist 'cause I'm Injun. I'm a pretty unhappy feller right now, and y'all air gonna pay fer it.

"Any worthless, no-good scum thet would raise a pup like this hyar Rex don't deserve no pity, an' I don't plan on showin' any. My haid still aches like the very blazes 'cause o' him and this other near daid man. He's near daid 'cause I aim tu kill him, slow-like."

Carson blanched white at that statement and the four on the porch looked at one another in a near panic. Then there came a groan from inside. The man inside with the rifle must still be alive. Reddy cocked the gun in his hand and commanded the men to undress.

"Take it down tu yore underwear, men, and pronto."

There were soon four men in long underwear self-consciously tossing their outer-wear out to where their guns lay. Reddy then proceeded to place them back to back in pairs with their backs against the posts that held up the porch roof. Well, they almost held it up, things surely needed attention here. Then he supervised their tying each other with careful inspection of each job. When those doing the tying were done he proceeded to finish the trussing job on his own.

Then he went inside to check out the wounded man, advancing carefully until he had the rifle and the fellow's pistol in hand. The old duffer had a head wound, a nasty spot above his left ear where the bullet had actually bounced off the rifle and bashed him in the skull. He was dazed but would live, and Reddy dragged him out to tie him up with the others as well as tying Rex and Carson. He tied them roughly, and he tied them tight, very tight. He then proceeded to cut the clothes from Rex and Carson with the razor-sharp knife he always carried, leaving them in the same outfits as the others.

Tossing the clothes all in a pile with the guns, he proceeded to disable every weapon with a rock he found in the yard. He bashed and smashed the firing mechanisms on each and every gun he could find, both there and in the house. He entered the house and soon re-emerged with a lantern. He poured the coal oil from the lantern onto the pile of clothes and weapons and then lighted the pile on fire. Strangely, all the men just watched without comment. They seemed to sense the fury with which their guest was operating.

As soon as the fire was sending personal items up in smoke, Reddy strode to the outbuildings. He searched the corrals and barn, finding evidence there that really incensed him even morc. He returned to the house.

Drawing the knife, he straddled Carson, grabbed him by the hair and jerked hard to raise his head from his chest. He placed the blade against the hairline just at the top of the forehead and drew it slowly across, leaving a tiny red line of blood.

"So, yu wanted tu scalp this redskin 'cause every redskin is a hoss thief, huh? Ever' last hoss I found down thar but two has hed thar brand worked over within the last couple o' days, mister. Now, give me a few hundred good reasons why I shouldn't scalp yu alive right now."

With each word he pulled harder on the hair until Carson's head was about to leave his neck. Then Reddy gave a sudden slash of the blade and severed the handful of hair in his hand. With that action done, he pulled Rex and Carson over to the tree where the horses stood. He tied their feet together with a rope and pulled them up to the lowest limb, where he tossed the rope over it, dallied it around his saddle horn and pulled them up.

"Thar, now yu can feel the headache like yu gave me last night."

He then went to each and every man there and gave them "haircut" with the knife, leaving them with patches of white scalp showing between the unkempt strands of greasy hair common to all but Rex. Rex had the curly blond hair that he treasured and kept somewhat cared for. Reddy completely shaved his head with the knife, then when he was done, he scrounged around in the house until he found some horse liniment which he then painted on the fellow's scalp. Horse liniment burns like crazy on tender skin and Rex squirmed under the cruel treatment, maybe as much for the dyeing effect the compound would have on his skin as much as for the pain. His pale, light scalp would take months to return to its previous color. Since his hat had been burned with the clothes, there was no immediate relief for the potential sunburn he would experience.

Then Reddy remembered he was hungry. He entered the house once again and located the meal the others had been about to eat. He went out to the porch with his repast and sat down to enjoy it among the men. Finishing, he returned to the kitchen and found half an apple pie. He eagerly grabbed it up and parked himself back on the porch steps. Using his big knife with which to eat it, he slurped and moaned with pleasure as he devoured the entire thing. When he was done he took the pie plate over to "Dad," as he called him, smeared the leavings all over his face and then pitched the plate out into the yard.

"Reckon yu'll enjoy the flies what finds thet pie stuff on yu. Think aboot whether or not yu wanna teach yore pup tu have better manners fer Injuns after this."

Once Reddy had committed all the cruel mischief he could think of, he tightened the cinch on his mount and climbed aboard. One of the men cried out, "Hey, you can't just leave us like this!"

"Seriously? Hmmf, I dunno why not. Yore little white haired pup thar intended tu hang me. Yore lucky I'm a civilized Injun, mister. I oughtta kill ever' blamed one of yu an' burn the place down around yu."

He turned east and clattered out of the place, stirring dust which drifted over the captured men to add insult to injury.

§ § § §

As the clock in the window of the general store found five o'clock John Goodman strode out of that establishment with the intention of riding straight home to his nearby ranch. A dusty rider trotted his horses up to the hitch-rail and dismounted, then approached him.

"'Scuse me, sir, but would yu be a local feller?"

"Yes I am, cowboy. What can I do for you?"

"Wal, it's more what I kin do fer yu. Yu a rancher here 'bouts?"

"You would be right about that, Tex."

"Say, yore right sharp. How in the world would yu ever guess whar I was from?"

That was said with a chuckle and the two met in a firm handshake.

"Lucky guess, fellow. I would also guess Comanche if I had to hazard another guess."

"Say, I cain't get nuthin by yu, kin I?"

"Another lucky guess. What can you do for me?"

That brought a chuckle for Reddy and he motioned to the

bench along the wall of the store. They sat down and he started in with his story. Reddy left nothing out and had the rancher howling with glee before thc story was finished.

"You…you actually PAINTED Rex's head with horse liniment? Oh, that is choice. That's too rich to be real! The valley is going to love this! He is the proudest peacock any of us have ever seen and thinks all the women around here just have to want him."

"Wal, if they like dark brown skin 'stead o' hair, they'll all flock after him. Now, the main thing I need tu tell yu: I looked all the hosses in their corral over real close like, and all but one have had their brands altered within the last two days. They're all fresh and will take more time tu heal. Some of the old brands I could make out were a flyin' W and a bar X slanted. Those boys air stealin' hosses, sir."

"That's not all they're doing, they're stealing MY horses; the bar X slanted is MY brand, cowboy. I'll recognize my horses when I go out there today, you can bet on that! Looks like the circuit judges are going to have to offer a few hangings around here.

"Thanks, cowboy. I'll grab my men and get out there as soon as I can. We owe you a real thanks. I'm glad you happened along, even though it cost you some major discomfort. In fact, I could use another hand if you know cows like I think you do. Want a job? Forty and found."

"I surely thank yu, sir, but I came here tryin' tu track down different hoss thieves than these. We lost over twenty haid o' harness hosses over west o' hyar. My three pardners and I been helpin' the railroad builders over thar, so they have me 'n my other Injun pardner, a cousin, trackin' them. We came through that mountain range a year ago on the same type of job and I figgered maybe I could save some time and maybe catch up with them. They had a two-day haid start, yu see."

"I wonder if they might be selling their stolen herds the same place as our good friends over here? I think you should go back with us and maybe… uhh… kind of 'help' question those boys about that. What do you say? I'll supply you, then, before you move on. It isn't too likely you'll regain your two days, but you might find out where to look for the stock."

"Yu know, thet just might be a good idea. By the way, I'm Reddy, short fer Red Elk. I'm part owner of the Twin Forks Ranch aboot a hundred miles west o' hyar. We're strictly a hoss ranch. I know cattle, sir, but I don't miss punchin' those cantankerous critters one little bit. Nossir, not one little bit! My condolences to yu fer yore ownin' the beasts. The onliest good cow is on a spit over a fire. With the hide off, o' course. I always allowed as tu how God never made the cow until Adam messed up an' then He made the cow as part o' mans' punishment, along with the thorns n' such."

The rancher laughed aloud at that, held out his hand and introduced himself. "I'm John Goodman, Reddy, and I'm right happy to meet you. And while I don't exactly share your opinion of cows, I surely understand it. Let's go get my boys and ride west. I don't want those men getting loose and escaping."

"No chance o' thet, John. When a Comanche ties a man up, he's tied up 'til help comes along. Those boys will still be thar. They might be a bit cold as soon as the sun goes down, but they'll be thar."

The two mounted up and rode south out of town, arriving at the Goodman ranch half an hour later. Goodman rousted up his hands who were around and the mounted posse was soon on its way west. Dusk was well underway when they rode up to the ramshackle outbuildings, and John dismounted to look over the brands Red Elk had mentioned. He and his hands examined the horses closely, roping some in order to do so, and lighted a lantern they found in the barn in order to see better the crude jobs of brand changing. Then they stalked to the house.

"Who's there? Get up here and get us loose; we been robbed by a tribe of Apaches! We're lucky the savages didn't scalp us! Musta been twenty or more of the varmints!"

"Hello there, Norm. Looks like they nailed you down for sure. Real big bunch of them, huh?"

"Said so didn't I? Now get us outta here! And get my boy down over there first. He's been hangin' there for hours. I'm feered he's gonna bust a head from bein' that way."

Reddy stalked over to the two hanging by their feet and

pulled his knife. A cry came from one of the men, "Hey, don't cut that rope, buddy, I just got that when those Indians took it from me. It's brand new last week!" THUD!

Reddy had chuckled deep in his chest and slashed the rope, stepping back as the two hapless and helpless bodies of the two plunked to the ground. Both grunted and moaned upon impact, then whimpered when they saw who had released them. He just stood there twisting the knife around and around in his hand with a big, evil smile on his face that showed in the lamplight.

"So, Norman, my good friend, how many of those red devils were there? 'Round twenty or more, I think you said?"

About the time John Goodman asked the question, the old fellow saw Reddy and flushed deep red.

"Never mind what I said, shoot that worthless robber! He's one of the bunch."

"Say, Norman, my friend, just what is this pile of ashes here? And where are all your clothes? You been runnin' around out here without anything but your long johns on? What kind of ranch you runnin', anyway?"

"JUST GET US LOOSE!" And with that he burst into a long string of profanity aimed at the rancher, his hands, redskins in general, and maybe even the horses they rode in on. When he was done, Goodman got down to business.

"Here's the way it is, neighbor. You got horses with burned brands out in your corral. Some of them were mine until this week. Others were property of other neighbors here in the valley until recently. We want to know why they are in your corral and why the brands have been changed?"

Silence hovered over the place like a blanket for a long time, then the rancher walked over to the old man and took him roughly by the hair that remained on his head. Goodman couldn't help a chuckle as he surveyed the "haircut" the fellow had experienced. Bending the man's head back so he could stare him in the eye, he said, "Norman, neighbor, thief, dirty old man, here's how this is going to happen. We should hang all of you for being horse thieves. No one would fault us for it, you know. But I have a more merciful idea; you and your other thieves here are going to walk to town just like you are in the morning. That's going to take you at least four hours, and believe me, there are going to be some sore feet and legs in this bunch.

"Now, any man of you who prefers not to do that can choose to hang instead. Once we get you to town, you'll be locked up and can wait for a judge to come in from the territorial capital. I suspect the lot of you will be learning a new trade soon, that of making little rocks out of big ones. Don't object, Norm, unless you are one that will choose the rope and that tree over there.

"Well, anyone prefer that?...Didn't think so. Men, fix what food you can find from inside and set up camp. I want four of you to stay here and herd these outlaws into town tomorrow. You'll get an extra day off with pay for your pain. Who wants the job?"

As soon as he had his volunteers he looked at Reddy. "Want to sleep in a bed tonight, friend? With a good meal inside you?"

"Now, John, thet's exactly whut I want. Let's go."

The men staying proceeded to establish their watch and camp while the rest mounted and rode east toward the Goodman ranch. Reddy looked back to see Carson and Rex being tied to the one remaining porch post. He rode up beside Goodman and said, "I bet those two won't make the mistake of goin' after another thievin' redskin, John. Those twenty or so 'Apaches' musta been real nasty fellers."

Goodman broke into laughter along with his men and the entourage laughed and visited the rest of the long ride home. Once they arrived, John introduced Reddy to his wife and daughter, then the cook, and Reddy felt as though he might just be in paradise as he saw that individual begin to break out food that was piping hot. The cook had heard the three shots fired from several miles away. Sound carried far in the night air at those altitudes.

After they had consumed the meal, he was shown to his room in the main house and John asked him, "What are your plans, now? You're welcome to stay as long as you like."

"I surely thank yu for thet, John, but I gotta get on and try tu find my cousin. He's somewhere north o' hyar and may need help drivin' those hosses home."

Goodman noted that there was no doubt in the Indian's mind that his cousin would find the stolen horses. He smiled as he watched Reddy stride down the hall to the assigned room. He put his arm over his wife's shoulder and commented, "We could use a few more men of that stripe around this valley, dear. In fact, we could use a LOT more men like that."

§ § § §

Morning found Reddy saddling up after a huge breakfast. His horses had enjoyed a good bait of oats the night before and were frisky as they were prepared for the day's duties. Goodman had insisted on supplying Reddy with several days' food for the ride, and the pack horse was loaded last. Reddy swung his leg over the saddle and reached a hand down to the kindly rancher.

"John Goodman, its good tu know yu. If ever yu get over west, look up the Twin Forks Ranch clear on the other side o' the Sawtooths. Boomstick will be the first burg yu get to; anyone thar can tell yu how tu find us. Ride safe, and thanks again for the hospitality."

"Ride safe yourself, Red Elk. We owe you a real debt for cornering those thieving rustlers. They've been going at it for way too long, and now we know who was doing that. We've tried to solve the problem for six months or better, and you do it in a day! Take care, my friend, and watch out for those twenty Apaches!"

Reddy burst out in a loud guffaw and spurred his horse out of the yard, turning to wave as he hit the road where it turned north.

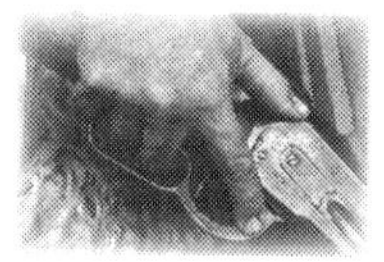

ELEVEN

Joe looked at the old hostler in exasperation as he tried to get an answer out of him. This was the same old fellow he and Red Elk had hornswaggled out of the Bransons' red stallion, Flash, a year before. The fellow bought anything he could make a buck on and cared not where it came from. Joe simply wanted to know if the stolen horses had come through this little town, but the hostler wanted nothing to do with the situation. Joe felt the old man remembered him and that had something to do with the closed mouth approach with which he was met.

Joe finally gave up and led his horse up the dusty street to the saloon for lunch. It was the only eating establishment in the little town. During his lunch he quizzed the bartender as to any small herds of horses coming through.

"Naw, not lately. I see every horse, dog, man, woman, buckboard or freight wagon that comes through, and I would have noticed that many horses. If I'm not wrong, ain't you one of the fellers what hornswaggled old Ezra down at the livery out of the red horse he had bought?"

Joe chuckled and nodded.

"I thought you looked familiar. Say, that was the greatest thing this town ever did see! That old reprobate ain't lived it down yet! Best part is, he forgets you two fellers left him one of the stolen horses and claims you did him out of a year's wages! Don't think we don't love settin' the old grump straight. That was sweet."

"We just needed the red stud back; he's a great horse and is producing some wonderful colts back home. Do you think you would remember my cousin who was with me that day? I need to leave word for him in case he comes this way."

"I seldom forget a face. 'Course, it ain't like we see that many different people come through here. I'll be glad to hold a message for him. You gonna write it out or use smoke signals for the chief?" He burst out laughing at that sally as he mopped an already clean bar.

Joe smiled tolerantly and asked for pen and paper. Upon receipt of same he wrote quickly and sealed the note in an envelope provided by the jovial bartender. If Reddy came this way, he would no doubt stop here and inquire about Joe. If and when he did, he would find that Joe was giving up the trail and heading home. The horses were gone and there would be no finding them or the men responsible. They had gotten way too much of a head start and common sense told him to break off the chase.

As soon as Joe was finished with his meal, he moved to the street and led his horses down the street to the general store for supplies. A half hour later he rode west out of town the way he had come. It figured to be about three days' ride back to Boomstick. That meant three days before he could see Molly Clements, and those three days would seem longer than most.

§ § § §

"Now we got cash to operate with, John. Didn't I tell yu it would be easy?"

"Yes, Cannon, you told me. How long do you plan to take to find this Rollins character?"

"Don't matter. I kin wait as long as it takes tu skin thet skunk. Yu want out, get out, but the money fer the gurl will all be mine then. Don't matter none tu me no more; I'm gettin' kinda tired o' you anyway."

"Tired or not, you promised me a good stake, and I plan to get it no matter what you do about Rollins. I just don't plan to wait too long around here. The climate's not to conducive to our good health."

"You never mind that. We got cash, we got supplies, we got whiskey, and we got time. Them's all we need fer now. Rollins will show up soon. Jimmy 'bout did him in before, but the little feller got buck fever, he did."

"You understand I don't plan to camp out when we get to Boomstick, don't you? I'll still have my room at the hotel and I'll want some cash for that."

"Yu wanna spend money on fancy rooms, thet's yore problem. We'll divvy up what's left o' the horse trade soon as we set up camp tonight. We're still a day outta Boomstick."

The two finished up the daylight hours only ten miles out of Boomstick, and Smoots relished the thought of a soft bed for the next night. He would need to be on the watch for the pushy lawman, though, in case he had observed that John had been missing for a time.

§ § § §

Reddy couldn't help but chuckle as he rode into the nondescript little town in search of Joe. It had taken him four days to find his way through the mountains south of the place and another two to find the town. He rode up to the livery remembering the fear he and Joe had put into the heart of old Ezra the stableman. He actually felt just a little guilty about it, but the sensation quickly passed when the old fellow came out of the door cussing him.

"What in tarnation's goin' on 'round here? All I have any more is bad dreams. You get your worthless red carcass outta here, you hear me? I don't want your kind here. Two of yore kind hornswaggled me outta the best horse I ever had, an' you ain't welcome, cause yore probably kin to them!"

Reddy exploded into mirth at that and after several minutes of trying to get himself under control he choked out, "Shucks, Ezra, I'm one of them what did thet!"

He whirled the horses around and trotted up the street before the old fellow could answer or get his shotgun. Reddy had traveled all that day with no meal after breakfast, so he tied up at the saloon and went in for anything and everything he could have them scrape up. The bartender spotted him as soon as he came through the door and reached under the bar. Reddy tensed up, wondering what the man was reaching for.

"Joe was in here over a week ago, left this for you. You ARE Red Elk, ain't you? I remember you 'cause of old Ezra."

Reddy took the envelope from him and nodded, not feeling safe to speak lest he break into full laughter again. He slipped a thumb into the fold and tore the thing open. When he had read it, he wadded it up, gave a grunt of disappointment, and ordered food.

"Yu say it was over a week ago?"

"Yep. 'Round a week last Wednesday it was."

"And what's today?"

"This here's Saturday. I'll soon be seein' customers from the outlying ranches hittin' town fer the weekend."

"Wal, I got several hours o' daylight left, so soon's I get me wrapped around that steak comin,' I'll be headin' west. Much obliged fer the letter. I got a question fer yu; does old Ezra eat hyar?"

"Sometimes."

"Good. Hyar's ten dollars; buy him thet many meals an' tell him it's from the worthless redskins 'round hyar."

"Man, Red Elk, that'll feed that old man for a month! You sure you wanta do this?"

"Yeah, it's worth it fer the laugh we got from him. I don't wanta leave him with a wounded pride."

The meal came through the door to the kitchen just then and Reddy fell to over it. As soon as it was consumed he rose, shifted his belt, and stalked out with a wave and a word of good-bye. A few minutes later he was on his way out of town on the road headed west.

§ § § §

As Joe rode into Boomstick on Wednesday morning he felt the urge to stop and see Molly before riding out to the railhead camp to report to George Searcy. Realizing he was trail-worn and grungy, he rode on by, quenching the desire to see her first.

On arrival at the camp he dropped the reins and entered the headquarters tent only to find it empty. He retraced his steps and began a search for the superintendent. Half an hour later he was told that Searcy was at the end of the line trying to solve an engineering problem that had arisen. He wearily climbed back in the saddle and, leaving the extra saddle horse and pack horse there, proceeded to ride along the tracks. He was amazed at how far the rails had gotten during his absence! If the land was level and the grading therefore going fast they could lay five miles of track a day. With the rolling terrain here, the grading was much slower, especially with the fewer work horses. The heavy equipment tired the teams much faster than other work so they needed to be switched much more often. When he asked a worker how far it was to the end and got his answer he turned back. It was twenty miles to the end of the tracks. Searcy could wait. For now, he wanted nothing more than a bath and to see Molly.

Riding through town toward the Clements' house he noticed the gunman, John Smoots, sitting on the porch of the hotel cleaning a gun. He had targeted the gunman in his mind as being a likely suspect in the theft of the horses simply because he was a known cohort of Cannon and Cannon had been one of those shooting at him and Bear before. He was sure Cannon was one of the thieves involved and therefore put Smoots with him.

Joe pulled up before the porch and sat there just looking at Smoots for a bit before speaking. "You hit any more horses that weren't yours recently, Mister?"

"'Pears to me that isn't any of your business, nosey man. Move along, I don't like looking at your ugly face."

"Too bad. I'll set here as long as I like. It's a free country. Where you been the last few days? Take a ride in the mountains to the east?"

"None of your business, nosey man. I said move on."

"I'll move when I please, and right now, I don't please. You want to push it?"

"I just might do that. Which gun you want me to notch for you, the left or the right?"

"I'd say neither one, Mister Smoots. Joe, ride on; I'll handle this coyote. Smoots, now I'm askin' you, where you been the last three days?"

The two turned their heads to the corner of the building

where Bill Hanson stood resting the stock of his double barrel against his thigh. It was pointed slightly up, but at a level that could easily drop to the necessary height in a split second. Smoots glared at him in an obvious fury at being cornered where he had no chance for an even break. His fast gun was of no use to him here.

"None of your business, either, lawman. My whereabouts is my own business."

"Well, maybe yes, maybe no. Joe, I asked you to move along. No, I'm tellin' you again, Molly's probably waitin' for you."

Joe nodded and turned his horse, watching Smoots all the while. He trotted off to the north, found the side street he needed and turned down it. As he turned, he spun his horse in a complete circle, glaring back at Smoots as he did so. The gunman couldn't fail to see the move; it was a direct challenge to him. That was unlike Joe, but he had garnered an intense dislike for the man.

Bill Hanson strolled to the chair beside Smoots and sat down. The shotgun lay across his lap at a very convenient angle, suggesting an intentional positioning by the lawman.

"Now mister gunman, I hope you understand that I can make your business into MY business. Shoot, I can even give you a fine suite in my own hotel for a couple of nights if I want. Don't need a reason, just a suspicion."

"And what would that suspicion be, lawdog?"

"Horse rustlin' gunman, horse rustlin'. Been a few missin' lately, and you were gone for a few days. Where's your partner, that guy called Cannon?"

"The big mountain man? He's no partner of mine. We just happened to come in on the same train."

"That you did, that you did. You know, I just happen to know that train had no passenger cars on it. And there was another fella with the two of you, a skinny little fella, not very clean. Whatever happened to him, by the way?"

"How would I know? I hadn't been appointed his keeper. Don't know anything about him OR Cannon, so why don't you just move on?"

"When I'm ready. Not before. Remember, this is MY town. Don't be forgettin' that. Not only that, this is also MY territory. Anything happens around here, I get involved. I'm now involved with questioning YOU. Now where you been the last few days?"

"Rode out for awhile. Got tired of the smell in this town and needed a break. That suit you? It might as well; it's all you're gettin'."

"Okay, Mister Smoots. I'll take that for now, but you better keep those hoglegs holstered unless you're cleanin' them. You use one of them in MY town and I'll kill you, whether it's an even break or not. Don't forget that."

Smoots' hand twitched as he watched Hanson stand up, stretch, and walk by him to proceed down the walk to the saloon. He had a strong urge to just shoot the man in the back and move on. No one challenged John Smoots that way and lived. He decided to wait until later for his vengeance.

John had no way of knowing he was watched from across the street. Dan Kade had come to Boomstick to check on his partners and had seen Joe issue his challenge to the gunman. Knowing Joe's easygoing disposition, Dan had felt the need to watch carefully as the incident took form. When Bill had interfered he had relaxed a bit until the marshal showed his obvious contempt for the man by turning his back on him. It was then Dan had removed the thong from the hammer of his gun. Smoots only watched the retreating back of Hanson for a few steps, however, and resumed cleaning the gun he had been working on before Joe's appearance.

Dan followed Joe's route to Clements' and found Joe's horse tied to the fence around the front yard. He went through the gate and climbed the steps to the front porch, hesitating as he heard the gay laughter of Molly from within. Maybe he should come back another time. Just as he was about to turn away from the door it opened and Molly's mother came out.

"Hi, Dan Kade, what are you doing here?"

"Hi, Missus Clements. I was just looking for Joe and figured I'd find him here."

"Ha! Where else would you find the redskin renegade, Danny boy? He practically lives here when he gets over this way. I don't think you people let him out of your sight often enough; he always seems starved for attention when he gets to Boomstick!" The last was followed by a loud cackle of joy as she grabbed the right arm of Dan and drew him along with her.

"Here, walk me to the store, handsome stranger, and I'll tell you what Joe told us when he first came in. It seems they lost the trail somewhere east and north of here after he and Reddy split up. Reddy rode fast and direct to try and find them where he and Joe had recovered those horses last time. It didn't work, so Joe left word for Reddy and came back here.

"You know, Dan, I think he's got a pretty strong case on my daughter. He can't stay away."

"Well, Mother Clements, what is your outlook on that? Do you approve of Joe?"

"Hmmff, does a horse wear a saddle? Of course I approve of Joe Five Ponies. I've never met a nicer, more polite, and might I say, handsome, fellow anywhere. What is your outlook on their relationship?"

Dan chuckled at her enthusiasm and replied, "We all think Joe is a goner. He has a faraway look so often back at the ranch, and that just isn't like him. Joe has always been the one to think things through first, never acts too quickly on anything, and is the one we consider the main person to pay attention to when decisions are in front of us that could take us either way when they're made. He's our mister steady."

"That doesn't surprise me a bit, Dan. On a more serious note, you have been treading on dangerous ground, dear man, dangerous ground indeed. I must be the one to warn you and therefore save you from physical ruin."

"Uuuuhh, what in the world are you talking about?"

"You have been calling me Mother Clements, young man, and if you don't start calling me Ann, I'm going to take a skillet to you. Mother ANYTHING sounds way too old for me, so straighten up, Dan Kade, or sweet Allison is going to be raising that cute youngster alone!"

"Oooohhboy. I'm sure not ready to leave yet, ANN, so I'll try to do better. It's just that my parents taught me to always respect my…never mind, I didn't start to say ANYTHING…Ann."

She burst out with a gay, happy laugh at that and clutched his arm close to her, laying her head against his shoulder for an instant.

"Now, there's the store, so maybe we better not be so cozy; my husband might not like for me to be in the close company of such a handsome young escort. Seriously, Dan, you and Allie really should get to Boomstick more often. We love to have you visit."

"We keep saying that, but you know how things can get in the way. Thanks for the invite, though. I'll wait at the diner for Joe. Maybe I'll even go back and get his horse and bring it here so I know he'll find me."

"Oh," she said delightedly, "that would be great! He'll wonder if HE left it here! He gets so lost in my daughter's eyes he doesn't know which way is up. DO IT, Dan, do it!"

He laughed and retraced his steps, intending to do just that, but when he turned down the street leading to the house he ran into Joe leading his horse around the corner.

"Dan! What are you doing here? Did our guests leave?"

"No, in fact, they are coming to Boomstick next week for a few days just to see the railhead progress. I came to see what I could find out about you and Reddy. Allison and Bear both thought I should, so here I am."

Just then John Smoots stepped in front of Joe, forcing him to stop. Joe dropped the reins and stepped out of line from his horse and Dan.

"Well, well. What have we here? You're finally somewhere without your lawdog and his shotgun. You still feel lucky, Indian?"

Dan stepped between them and crouched, hand poised for a draw. "He might not, but I do. Where would you like the last bullet you ever feel hit you, dead man?"

As he said that he drew, the revolver coming level at a full cock and then ending back in his holster with the hammer back at rest before Smoots ever flinched. Smoots swallowed hard. He had never seen such dexterity of hand with a gun before, and he had seen the best. Or so he had thought. He had no knowledge of Dan Kade, so couldn't be aware of the speed and accuracy Dan had achieved with the instruction of Red Elk. Kade had never stopped practicing daily with his draw, shooting every other day to keep sharp. Too much had depended on that skill in the past, and perhaps the only man in the area to equal Dan's skill would be Ted Sweeny, the former Texas gunslinger. Fortunately for the law thereabouts, both men were honest ranchers.

Dan stood looking Smoots in the eye and silently challenged him to draw. In the past, Dan had used his skill in similar manner to spare the life of would-be gunslingers, demonstrating his speed and dexterity in a manner that convinced the opponent to back away from the confrontation. One such event had happened when he first met Allison McCord and her family. Dan had faced down a bully by the name of Harvey Croft by first cleaning the man's pistol and then drawing and dry-firing it several times before returning it to its owner. The result was a cowed enemy.

John Smoots was not burdened by an ego that forced him to stay and fight when he did not have the odds in his favor, so he simply turned and walked wordlessly away. Dan turned to Joe and asked, "What is all this about, Joe?"

"I accused the cheap gunman of horse stealing. He didn't like it. Bill Hanson broke up the first time we met today, then you came along to baby-sit me this time. I guess I'll not be whopping on the man again soon. I think he's in cahoots with that man, Cannon, who's apparently after Bear. The two were seen together a lot before the horses were stolen."

"So what's next, Joe? Is Searcy able to get along without the horses? How many did he lose?"

"Twenty. I guess it really has slowed him down since the grading is so tedious in this rolling terrain. Why are you here, again?"

"We wondered why you two were still out, so I volunteered to come check up on you. Bear insists he's ready for full duty, but Allie and Lucinda have him corralled. Ted and Melodi are still there, but Ted is awfully interested in the railroad and the rustling, so I look for him to stick around a while. When are you coming back?"

"I'll ride out today, as soon as I switch my saddle to my other horse. There's nothing to hold me here now; I can see George on our way back. They tell me the line is twenty miles out now."

"I passed the end of the tracks on my way here. Another ten miles and they'll be just north of the McCord ranch buildings. They'll be close enough for Paul to load horses less than five miles from his headquarters. He's going to build corrals there and Searcy is putting in a spur so cars can sit there and not hold up the normal trains going through. I tell you, Joe, George Searcy is fulfilling all the promises he made and more. I just wish we were going to be closer, but you can't have everything."

"What do you think Cogswell would say to a siding at his place? He'll need to load produce somewhere; and if he can avoid hauling to Twin Forks, that would be a plus. That would only save us five miles or so, but that's still five miles!"

"Maybe you can head up that way tomorrow and see what he thinks. It'd be a good time to check out our north herd, too. See if that old grizzly is behaving himself at the same time."

"Good idea. I might as well; probably couldn't sleep good in a bed anyway. It's been too long, so why bother now?"

Dan chuckled as he helped by tightening the latigos while Joe slipped the bit into his other mount's mouth. They were soon riding west out of Boomstick along the new tracks. They would see Searcy yet that evening.

§ § § §

The Twin Forks Ranch supper table was humming with conversation two days later as the members discussed the latest news from the U.P. spur headed for the town of Twin Forks. George Searcy had agreed to a siding at the Cogswell farm but had also suggested a deal the ranchers felt they couldn't refuse.

"You fellows do the grading," he had offered, "and I'll lay tracks as far as your grading goes. You grade right up to your front door and you'll have tracks there."

As they discussed it, the decision was made to grade all the way to a place two miles north, where their hay fields were. Joe was to ride north the next day and talk to Cogswell about a siding at his place, as well as to check out the north herd. It had been too long since any of them had been that way to see to the horses. Dan's trip to hire Lucinda had not allowed him time for the horses.

"Joe, are you going to get into Twin Forks at all?" asked Skinny. "I need more powder and balls for my thirty-six caliber."

"What?" Reddy perked up immediately. "You been practicin' thet much, button?"

"Yeah, I have, and I keep tellin' you, I ain't no button no more Reddy!"

"Aww, I don't mean nuthin' by it, Skinny, but yu gotta take the hasslin' long as yore still a youngster. It jist gits yu ready tu be a man."

"I seem to remember a fifteen year old hitting a Texas cowboy in the nose for that very thing some time back, cousin," spoke up Joe. "Said he was already a man and would prove it right then and there."

"He really did that, Joe? What happened?" asked Skinny.

"It seems to me, if I remember it right, that the fifteen-year-old had to be helped to his bunk that night. Was really beat up, as I recall. It took several days for the one eye to open up."

Reddy glared at his cousin and fell silent; Skinny had to look away to hide his smile.

The plans for the grading were completed over the next few hours, and Ted and Melodi joined in with their suggestions as though they were part of the Twin Forks crew. The few days there had been more than a honeymoon; they had resulted in the forming of family bonds with all of the Twin Forks crew.

The couple had spent much time walking hand in hand back up the narrow valley behind the ranch house, exploring all around that section of the mountains and sometimes staying out all day. Lucinda had packed lunches for them each time they asked, and the days had been especially blissful.

The narrowness of the valley back there made for hard going until they were back in nearly half a mile, then it widened out into a broader area that teemed with small game. To the north was a slope of the mighty mountain that towered over them. The side was strewn with cedars and pines that occasionally saw success at growing large enough to provide shelter for some of the elk that slipped in from time to time.

The small, burbling stream flowed over rocks in a rather mad rush because of the drop in the terrain there, whirling in small pools that contained trout, rock bass and other water creatures. Ted amused them both by catching small, green frogs and watching them hop away when he released them.

When they looked up at the mountain top to the north they had to lean their heads back at an uncomfortable angle; but the mountain to the south was not as steep, so they would climb it from time to time on their jaunts. The side was strewn with boulders from the size of a man to that of a house, while the north slope was relatively clear of such objects. When a puffy white cloud of any size drifted over the tops of the mountains the valley became quite dark because of the narrowness, and the two always plopped down to rest and await the return of the sun's warmth.

The occasional eagle's cry would echo in their ears as those keepers of the air soared high in the currents of air. When watched closely, they could be observed diving at breakneck speeds to grasp some unseen prey. Each time one was successful Melodi would cry out in alarm and Ted would remind her that God had provided for the eagle's well-being by furnishing the game it had just captured.

"It's the way nature was designed, darlin'. It's just like you and me eatin' deer meat. Shore, we don't pull our steaks off while it's alive like the eagles do, but the deer is daid just the same."

"Don't tell me that, Ted Sweeny. I just don't like to see anything hurt."

"Wal, not tu prolong yore pain, love, but did yu know some Indian tribes actually pray to the game they jist killed and thank it fer givin' its life fer their benefit?"

"Really? I never heard that. You're just making that up."

"Nope, it's true. We'll ask Reddy n' Joe; they'll know aboot it even iffn their tribes don't do it."

They made their way slowly back to the house late in the afternoon and settled into chairs on the porch just in time to observe Dan and Joe riding across the river. Night found them sitting together on the front porch steps, with Mel leaning back against Ted much in the manner that Dan and Allie had done some three years before as they planned the building of that same house. Life seemed good.

They were still there when Reddy rode in a little after daybreak, and he tiptoed by as he chuckled tiredly at the sleeping couple. The ride had been hard through the night and his horses were more weary then he, but he had felt the need to be at the ranch as soon as possible. He wished to hear Joe's thoughts concerning the results of their fruitless hunt.

When Allison slipped into the kitchen and started the coffee pot to heating on the stove she found the sleepy Comanche with his head down on the table, softly breathing the breath of deep sleep. She smiled and gently raised her friend's head to place a folded towel under it, shoulders silently shaking at the half open eye he turned her way as she did so, and even more so as those eyes closed instantly to return to the slumber at hand. This adopted brother was a neverending delight to Allison and Dan with his mischievous ways and dedication to their well-being.

"Sleep on, Reddy, the fellows will soon take that away from you. They have no mercy and will need to hear your story of the chase," she whispered fondly.

§ § § §

"Joe already left, Reddy. He ate breakfast right beside you, packed up his saddle bags right behind you, and rode off to check the north herd and then go see Cogswell. He said he probably couldn't have done that around a white man, but most Comanches were sound sleepers. Bear and I agreed, since you WERE making sounds, loud ones that sounded like snoring."

"I ain't believin' yu, Dan Kade. Yore lyin' tu me. Yu been sneakin' 'round hyar like a bunch of desperate cavalry men so's tu not draw the ire of the chief!"

"Chief? Where?"

That comment drew a towel flying through the air at Dan, who caught it and threw it to Allie. While this was happening,

Joe was already far to the north on his quest for the herd. He was about to check out the main herd when the steeldust he was riding snorted and began to dance-step, shaking his head up and down with obvious agitation at something.

Joe began scanning around as he pulled the fractious horse to a stop. It still insisted on fidgeting nervously. He followed the direction his mount was looking and saw, far off and upwind, a reddish form nestled up against the beginning of a sharp rise of rocks. He forced the steed in that direction, dismounting several yards from the object.

Pulling forcefully on the reins to drag the recalcitrant animal with him he soon identified the reason for the gelding's reluctance. Lying before him was a sorrel colt, its dead carcass missing much of the body as a result of wild animals having eaten from it.

He tied the horse to a bush and carefully inspected the corpse. He found the colt had a broken neck, the sign of a bear kill. This was the fourth in three weeks! Joe's response was immediate; he started back-tracking his own route, leaving signs leading to the colt for the others should they come looking for him. He then returned to the body, and mounting up, tried tracking the killer. He was sure the bear would return to the kill at night, but Joe wished to know the general direction of its approach.

Hours later, as the subtle fingers of dusk began to massage away the burning of the daylight, they found Joe removing his saddle bags and blanket roll and attaching a note to the saddle horn with a leather thong.. All four of the partners carried the necessary items for various ways of communication. His note said simply, "Another bear kill, I'll get him." He then tied the reins together, looped them around the horn, and slapped the steed sharply on the rump to start him home.

Most fully domesticated horses prefer their hay and oats at the mangers of their home stables, and Joe knew this one was no different. He would meander along the way, but would wander in before dark. Joe then chose a spot about fifty yards downwind and settled in for the night, hoping for bright moonlight for good shooting.

Morning found Joe wrapped in his blanket with a chilly covering of dew over him. The bear hadn't returned and he was disappointed; this was going to take longer than he wanted. "Oh well," he thought, "there's jerky and biscuits in my bags and a couple of days' other needs besides. It's time I stayed and got this character."

With that, he gathered up his gear, double checked his rifle and trudged off, following the tracks he had finally found. He knew the fellow would not wander far from the local area, for grizzlies typically roamed the same territory most of the time, especially if there was easy food for the taking. Their four colts were as easy as it gets.

The area where Joe had found the colt was smack up against the mountain and was right at the mouth of a narrow rift between two of them. The faint tracks he found led into the rift beside the small stream that flowed in the center of it. He felt this might just turn into a waiting game, but was more than ready for it; the loss of colts was too much.

While both Joe and Reddy had become a close part of the white culture they were both still proud of their Comanche heritage and clung tenaciously to the great, incomparable skills of those wonderful hunters and survivors, their blood relatives. Neither had ever regretted their background and tribe.

Known for their tracking and hunting skills as well as their brilliant military strategies, the Comanches were easily among the best of the best at dealing with the mountain wilderness.

This was an area where neither Joe, nor any of the others for that matter, had ventured from the level of the valley's expanse to explore deeper into the mountains. He found himself following a happily frolicking stream only a few feet wide, with the very smallest of occasional pools no deeper than a couple of feet. He could see small trout in most of those pools and knew he would eat well. Close examination showed him the mountain sides sloping away at angles which would allow him to climb several hundred feet before encountering the need to stop.

Feeling sure the grizzly would be returning down this stream he determined to climb the north slope and establish a dry camp during the day and wait out the furry marauder for as long as it took to get him.

He started up the slope via a winding route, spotted a ledge some four or five hundred feet up and aimed for it. It was much higher than he wanted, because an accurate shot from his saddle gun would be next to impossible with that much drop to compensate for. He wished for Bear Rollins' big Sharps fifty at the moment, but his short-barreled forty-four would have to do.

Reaching the ledge he saw it was only six feet from front to back and barely ten wide. There were stones by the front that stuck up and afforded both some protection from the winds and also from the sharp eyes of his quarry. He set about gathering wood for his night fire; he knew the night temperatures would require one. With that task complete he broke out his fishing line from the saddlebags, cut and rigged a small pole and, keeping the rifle at hand, descended once more to the stream. Trout for supper sounded fine.

§ § § §

The third day was well on its way to closure, and Joe had been nearly two miles farther up the stream in search of signs, but the bear was nowhere to be found. He returned to his mountain-side ledge to prepare for the night, gathering wood as he went, stopping to procure two small trout on his way. He wanted very much to strip and bathe but was uncomfortable with the thought of doing so; as soon as he hit the cold water without his rifle that cantankerous old griz' was sure to show! Of course, he chuckled to himself, that was one sure way to find the ornery cuss!

The night was unusually dark and the lights from his tiny fire flickered, danced, and glimmered off the smooth granite wall behind the ledge. They revealed a solitary figure of a man hunched against the cold while wrapped in both a blanket and deep thought. It was a night of deep introspection for Joe Five Ponies.

As a five-year-old son of a Comanche chieftain, Five Ponies had benefited from his father's wisdom and foresight when it became obvious the numbers of white-eyes loomed as a far superior force. His father had possessed the courage to lay down his arms and turn to the different lifestyle. They had somehow escaped the many horror stories accompanying such a surrender and had settled into a peaceful life.

The result of that change was his children's attending the nearby mission school. All four children took to the schooling like a bear to a honey tree. There was a minor ruckus or two with some of the Army brats until the pure athletic ability and strength coupled with the determined effort to protect his two older sisters proved to them the pain involved in picking on the "new redskins" just wasn't worth it. When the bullies started to harass the girls the younger boy promptly took quick and efficient control of what proved to be a short scrap by grabbing the two ten-year-olds by the hair and bashing their heads together with a bone-jarring crash just prior to kicking the one still standing in the stomach and then smashing a small but very hard knee into the nose of that worthy. It was over almost before it started.

As these past times floated through his idle memories, a sonorous chuckle rose from his chest. He recalled those early years and remembered it was the bigger lad with the crushed and bleeding nose who had tagged him with the name that followed him yet today.

"Okay Joe, you win, you win. Who taught you to fight like that?"

Joe remembered just looking back at the surrendered boy silently until the lad turned and walked away.

As he allowed the memories to march through his mind, the natural course of thought came to the evaluation process of what had been accomplished and what might be next.

There dwelt in his past the fond thoughts of his journey with that irascible cousin, Red Elk, and the mischievous capers that individual had cooked up in his ever-active mind. Memories of some of those brought more deep chuckles for a bit.

As the fire begged for more fuel, his thoughts turned to the family he really had never gotten to know as most others knew their families. His father, the chieftain, had seemed a wonderfully warm person, loving his children through all the skinned places and squabbles present in any family, whether red or white, while teaching even Joe's sisters the rudiments of hunting and tracking – necessary skills for survival for the Comanche.

The strength of his mother's presence as a stabilizing force came flooding to him and for a few moments the dark eyes of the Comanche brave glistened with moisture as he truly missed the complete childhood he had never realized. The truth of his father's sacrifice for his children hit him with renewed force. He knew without doubt that his mother and father had loved them and therefore had missed much of the joy connected with raising their own children! He shuddered with the thought that trails once ridden were behind forever and need not be covered again. It was not easy, sometimes, to look back.

It was only natural that his thoughts then turned to the romances slowly receding into the dimmer regions of his past. It had been claimed many times by some that Joe preferred white girls over his own race, but truth be told, it had been simply that they far outnumbered the available Indian girls in the trails he had frequented and traveled.

Never before Twin Forks had Joe stayed in one place more than a few months. His partnering with Reddy, Dan, and Bear had taken his life to new heights of satisfaction and peace, even though they had always been on the move until buying the ranch. Now, having been settled at the ranch for close to three years, he felt as though he actually had a family life.

He smiled as he thought of the three men who had stood with him through times both good and bad and had proven just how trustworthy true friends could be. Add Allison Kade to the mix and that, rather than adding more contentment, held complete peace just a hair's breadth away.

Why wouldn't the presence of that lovely and lovable wife of Dan's only serve to cement totality to the scene? Allie showed a sister's love to all three of Dan's partners, as well as to Skinny Robins, the youngster they had hired to help with barn chores, as Reddy referred to them.

But, the presence of Allie was a tiny bit unsettling which completely baffled Joe. He gazed upward into the dark blue of the night and his sharp ears listened to all the little night sounds of the tiny creatures on the mountainside who were busily foraging for their night's subsistence. Those bright stars winking back at him maintained their positions like they had been assigned their place by the Great Creator and were forbidden to change. He knew this to be true. In fact, he and his people had known this even before the white missionaries came along to teach them of a God and to give Him a name. The mission school had only confirmed in him the solidity of his previous belief and of the fact that there was, indeed, a Great Spirit.

As he thought through the effect Allison had on him, his reaction was to then drift to the picture in his mind of a lovely face with snapping, dusky eyes and a mischievous countenance bolstered by an intelligence and love of life that injected energy and vitality into the very air around her. He smiled as the petite but well-rounded figure of little Molly Clements quickly crowded all else from his mind.

"What a delightful little package of loveliness and sweetness she is!" he expressed aloud to the stars.

The sweet memory of Molly's kiss the last time he had parted from her pushed aside all else. She had been standing on the top step of the porch of the Clements' home and had placed a firm but gentle hand behind his head and pulled him to her. Her soft lips had lingered long and sweet on his until she slid her cheek alongside his, hesitating long enough to draw a deep breath before quickly pulling away to turn and run into the house. Joe was sure he had seen a tear running down that silken cheek as she turned away.

He suddenly realized where he was now and that he was holding his breath. He drew air into trembling lungs and felt the trip-hammer beat of his heart as it seemed to be attempting to free itself from his chest. Even though he was nearly two days' ride from her, little Molly Clements might as well have been there beside him! Then he was startled by the sound of his own deep, rich voice as he spoke aloud to the night. "I love her! I really, completely and hopelessly love that precious little woman," he told the world around him and himself. With poignant realization of the truth of the matter that this was the first and only time in his twenty-plus years he had ever thought of making such a confession, he knew his life's direction had just taken on a new path, a path that was to forever include Molly if she would have him. As soon as this killer of colts was done in he would head to Boomstick town and try to claim a bride!

It seemed the night grew warmer as he mentally and emotionally left the ledge and allowed the fire to fend for itself. It slowly died; and when the eastern sky began at last to empty its cloak of darkness into the west, he sat, still awake and lost in his musings. He had spent the night planning, dreaming, and imagining a wonderfully full future with the girl he now confessed to himself that he loved.

It was two years since he had first seen the dusky-eyed, dark-haired girl on the boardwalk of Boomstick and thought she was the prettiest girl he had ever seen. Joe chuckled at the memory, as he could still feel Reddy's strong hand clutching his arm with a firm shake. "Hey, wake up, cousin! You ain't got time to be makin' up to the white gurls in this town! Ya wanna get us red-skins rid outta town on a rail?"

Red Elk. What a lovable, irascible character. They had been inseparable ever since finding one another on a ranch down in Texas and learning they were cousins. They were sixteen or so at the time. Neither knew for sure just how old they really were except for the number of seasons of the moon behind them. Both could track a rattlesnake over bare rock, both were more than just proficient with both rifle and pistol, but the thing that held them closest to each other was their common love for horses.

As his thoughts turned to Reddy, they also embraced the picture of Bear Rollins and Dan and Allison Kade. He suddenly felt a wonderful swelling of his chest as the richness of his life because of his friends cascaded all through his being.

Then he decided: if he failed to get the bear today he was going home to Twin Forks Ranch and inform his "family" of his decision to ask Molly to be his wife! Then he would saddle up a tough little mustang and head for Boomstick town for that very purpose! He felt wonderfully exhilarated!

The Indian heritage and background of his life made impatience a totally foreign emotion to this Comanche brave turned wrangler, but it was not easily held at bay this time. It was as though the stoic brave had suddenly undergone a transformation that sent the calmness, so much a part of him, to flight. Now the day was going to be much longer.

§ § § §

Mid-morning arrived with still no sign of the grizzly, when a different "Bear" showed up at the entrance to the hollow. Joe caught a brief glimpse of movement and concentrated his focus on the area in question. After a bit the buckskin-clad figure of Rollins showed briefly as he slipped along the stream.

Joe let out a shrill whistle that copied the eagle's call, then quickly repeated it. The big man stopped in his tracks and began to scan the sky. Seeing no eagle, he quickly concentrated his examination on the mountain, and when the third cry came he spotted Joe standing on his ledge, hat held high and waving. Ten minutes later the two clasped hands and Bear handed Joe a canvas bag filled with cold biscuits and venison roast.

"You really know how to soften a guy up; I was actually getting tired of trout."

"I see there's lots of 'em in thet stream; nearly stopped tu ketch a batch fer myself. We figgered yu'd be gittin' hungry. When yu comin' home?"

"Well, Bear, I decided this morning that even if I don't see that old silver-tip today I'm going to call it quits. I have something really important to care for and I want to get cracking on it."

"Wal, Joe, my fine feathered friend, ya might just as well pack up an' light a shuck outta hyar right now, 'cause ya ain't a gonna see thet griz' today."

"And just how do you know that?"

"Wal, in thinkin' on it a bit, whut I said ain't 'zactly true, either… whut I shoulda said was, yore gonna see him, but only whilst he's sleepin right sound from a dose of Sharps fifty.

"He musta hed 'nuther way 'round back ta the valley 'cause when I rode 'round the point down 'bout half a mile from the kill yu found , thar he was, chompin' on another fine filly colt!

"He stood an' challenged my right tu be thar and jist naturally tried tu face down the wrong Sharps fifty. I put the first one right in the old warrior's heart an' jist fer good measure, follered thet with another jist tu be sure he was gonna be plumb peaceful-like whilst I butchered him. Got some good-lookin' steaks outta the rascal iffn he ain't too tough tu cook! Got some age on 'im."

"Man, Bear, I'm so glad you were bringing me some supplies when you were. I hate knowing we lost yet another colt to him, but at least he's history and I can forget trout for a while."

The two partners made the hour hike to the bear's location and proceeded to finish butchering him out. They rolled all the good cuts of meat into the hide and then spent the better part of an hour retrieving Bear's horse from where he had tethered it and trying to get it to allow them to load the bear's remains onto the saddle to tie down.

They were finally successful and, dragging a very upset mount with them, they trekked southward in the direction of Twin Forks Ranch. After a couple of miles, Bear spoke up.

"Yu said yu hed somethin' important tu take care of, Joe. Mind iffn I ask what?"

"No, I don't mind, but I think I'll wait until we get back so we can all be together and I'll only have to go over it once. You mind?"

"Nossir, not atall. Makes good sense tu me."

Several hours later the two stood on the east bank of the Twin Forks River, directly across from the ranch buildings. Dusk was starting to seriously consider beginning its daily invasion of the daylight as Joe pulled his pistol and fired two shots into the ground. He was rewarded by the sight of Reddy emerging from the barn with a wave and then disappearing back into the building. It was but a minute or two until he reappeared astride bareback, leading two other horses. They would cross the river with dry feet!

A late supper was in order that evening, because Allison hadn't known whether or not the two would even return that day. Because of this she had Lucinda wait longer than usual before starting preparations. Dan pitched in to help, then Bear, then Reddy, and soon all were crowding each other in the kitchen as the meal was prepared. Fresh bear steaks would be the treat of the day!

Once the table was set and then laden with steaming food

and little Ira was captured and secured into the high chair Bear had fashioned for him they quieted while Dan said grace and then they all dug in.

When work-hardened, hungry men and women sit down to an evening meal there is seldom much conversation except for, "Please pass the meat" or, "I'd like more gravy, please," and the meal passes quickly.

Allison started to rise to get the coffee and pie when Joe spoke. "Allie, could you wait a bit? I have something very important to discuss. It won't take long, I promise."

She relaxed and he continued. "I need some advice. I would like to build another cabin here somewhere in our immediate area but still far enough back for some privacy. First, would any of you object to that; and second, if not, where would you suggest?"

There ensued a long, pregnant silence before Allison replied, "Of course no one would object, Joe, how could we?"

Joe looked from face to face of each of his three partners for their reactions, finding blank looks on each one.

"Joe, if you want a cabin, we'll build you a cabin. As to where, we'll need to look the place over a bit. Right guys?" was Dan's delayed answer.

Both Bear and Reddy nodded in agreement and then Bear spoke. "Straight back from the house hyar, bout fifty yards or so, is a nice, flat shelf thet borders the crick. Looks tu me tu be a ideal place fer a cabin. Plenty of room an' has a small grove of trees twixt hyar and thar."

Reddy looked fondly at his cousin and finally voiced the question in each one's mind, even though he expressed it in a much different manner. "Cousin, ain't Bear and I bathin' often enough for you? Whut for you want a cabin?"

"Back up on the side of that mountain I had a lot of time to think; and it changed me forever, because I got a good look deep into my heart. I realized that I don't want to go any longer in my life without the joy of family. I mean, you people are my family, and you always will be, but I want more.

"I am hopelessly, deeply, and wonderfully in love with Molly Clements and I plan to ride over there as soon as I can get away and ask her to marry me."

Allison let out a high-pitched squeal and leaped out of her chair to run and climb into Joe's lap and proceeded to smother him with hugs and kisses until he begged for mercy. The rest just sat rather dumbfounded at the news and at her reaction. All but Dan, that is. He tried unsuccessfully to hold back the contented chuckles that came from deep within as he watched his lovely wife show her excitement at their "brother's" news. He knew Allison loved Joe just as he did and also realized this meant another woman around to bolster Allie's day with even more female companionship besides Lucinda. He couldn't be more pleased.

At Joe's cries of protest, when he could finally get them out, she calmed down and plopped back into her chair. Joe's next comment turned her red as he said, "Gosh, Allie, I won't need to propose to Molly if you keep that up. I'll just marry you!"

The rest burst into laughter so loud it got Ira to yelling and banging a spoon on his tray. Allison jumped from her seat and started on her way to the kitchen to escape. Just as she neared Reddy's place he spoke out. "I sure cain't figger my cousin's fascination with these white wimmen. Why cain't he jist settle for a sweet little Comanche gurl what would treat him like his papa was?"

It just so happened that Allie had arrived directly behind Reddy's chair as he said this and she stopped, grabbed his coal-black hair and jerked hard on it. His head hit the high back of the chair with a thud and he suddenly found himself looking straight at the ceiling, with a lovely face descending slowly until it was a mere two inches from his. The firm grip on his hair held him captive.

"Now, mister Comanche brave turned half white with the big mouth, just what is so terribly bad about Joe loving a white girl instead of an Indian? Just where, my redskin friend, do we paleface women fall so far short on wifing?"

With each emphasis on a word, she banged Reddy's head against the back of the chair with a solid thump. His eyes seemed about to cross because the bright green eyes of Allison McCord Kade came continuously closer until her nose was touching his forehead. Lucinda was having a hard time not exploding aloud with laughter and cheers.

"Uhhhh… wal, I …I wasn't sayin' yu all fall short. Jist seems tu me thet, wal, thet …Aw, doggone it Allie, I dunno whut I meant, jist leggo my hair. Yore startin' tu cause considerable pain hyar!"

"Just you remember, redskin, that we women, no matter what color skin, are in charge. Got it?"

Then with a final thump of his head she planted a big, sloppy kiss on his forehead and continued her way to the kitchen, much to Red Elk's relief! The rest of them shook with silent laughter at Reddy's discomfort. Then they all lost their control, bursting into laughter that once again caused little Ira to renew his cacophony with both voice and spoon. Reddy's total love and devotion to Dan and Allison was well known to all of them and in fact, shared by all.

The reputation of the four partners of the Twin Forks Ranch had become well known far and wide as a solid unit of an inseparable quartet to be called upon in time of need. Also, it was widely known that if you caused trouble to one, you had trouble with all.

Allison called back to Joe from her stove, where she was cutting a pie. "Don't you pay any attention to that renegade cousin of yours, Joe; Molly Clements is a great catch."

Joe smiled as she plopped a quarter of a pie down on his plate and a small piece on that of Red Elk.

"Aww, Allie, now thet's goin' too blamed far! Yu cain't do thet! He don't deserve a bigger piece 'cause he's in love! Thet ain't fair!"

"He didn't get the bigger piece because he's in love, he got it because he's in love with a WHITE girl! And I can too do it. I'm the cook, remember?"

Reddy just shook his head in final surrender and turned to the piece he had in front of him, muttering all the while.

§ § § §

As the tired, but tough little mustang carried Joe down the nearly deserted main street of Boomstick, he was noticeably drooping. Joe had pushed him pretty hard to make the journey's end before dark and the little guy had responded by hanging tough, the mark of the mustang strain.

Joe turned him into the livery stable, unsaddled and rubbed him down and then found an empty box stall for him. He climbed to the hay loft and forked down a good amount of rich alfalfa, with which he then filled the manger in the stall. Then he visited the grain bin and procured a small bucket of oats for the mount. By the time he left the stable the mustang was eagerly munching away.

In his eagerness to see Molly, Joe forsook any thoughts of turning in to the still-open restaurant. Turning down the side street leading to the Clements' house, his stiffness seemed to disappear and his steps quickened. After all, it had been three weeks since he had last seen Molly, much too long!

Hopping over the little gate through the picket fence separating the yard from the street instead of opening it, he gained the porch with a leap that cleared all three steps and rapped his knuckles against the door. A little squeal came from the direction of the kitchen and rapid but light footsteps beat a tattoo across the wooden floor.

The door flew open and a pretty, petite whirling dervish assailed the tired Comanche by throwing strong, brown arms around his neck while she smothered his face with kisses. Joe hung onto her firm little form for a bit, lifting her from the floor before reluctantly setting her down.

"Hi, Molly girl. Glad to see me? Or were you expecting one of your other suitors?"

It was a game they always played, his teasing her about having many young men of the area chasing after her. While it was true, she paid no attention to any but him. Those strong little hands slipped from around his neck and firmly grabbed him by both ears. It was her way of reacting each time he displeased her, and one would have thought Joe would cease the teasing or lose at least one ear, for she shook him violently several times before answering.

"You worthless redskin, I don't know why I put up with you! I ought to have one of those handsome young men in town shoot your worthless hide, skin you, and make a rug or a purse out of it and feed the rest to the hogs!"

Molly Clements was a whopping four inches over five feet, with a well-formed, strong little body topped by a very pretty face. A little pug nose perched over a nearly permanent smile showing sparkling white teeth behind soft, red lips, and her hair was a soft brown with a hint of auburn when the sun hit it. That hair framed a pair of dusky, dark eyes that always sparkled with delightful, mischievous energy.

As Allison Kade had put it, "She is a great catch."

When Molly took his hand and attempted to pull Joe into the house, he resisted. "Molly, I rode hard to get here today – got a real late start and about ruined my mustang to make it. I need to talk to you, and I have to get it off my chest as quickly as possible. Can we sit out here on the porch swing?"

His suddenly serious demeanor halted her, and she just stood rooted to the spot for a few seconds. Then, with trepidation, she allowed him to pull her to the swing. Joe was never this somber and absolutely never in a rush!

They sat for a bit, Joe drawing several deep breaths, which she heard and which unnerved her even more, before casting a very serious look her way and visibly swallowing hard. Something was not right here, she thought. He was totally out of character! This was NOT her calm and cool Indian.

"Molly," he began, "I can't do this any longer. It's just impossible for me to continue a long-distance relationship with you. I sit over there knowing there's at least a dozen men wanting you for their own. I worry about that. Then I think of the long ride here to see you, knowing I have to ride back, and I just can't do it any longer."

Her heart dropped, tears formed in those dark eyes, and breath came only with an effort. A little sob shook her from within as Joe spoke again, oblivious to her misery.

"Molly, I need you near me. We have cleared an area back from the main house, Dan and Allie's house, where we can build a good-sized cabin.

"Molly, dear Molly, I love you so much and I just don't want to go on like this, I want to marry you and always have you with me."

Molly's face took on a look that was a mixture of horror and ecstasy as the plunge from one to the other became way too much for her heart. She uttered a mournful cry, started pounding his chest with both fists and then jumped up and ran into the house without a word. Joe sat there dumbfounded.

He could hear a sobbing conversation from Molly and a low murmur of reply from her mother, and after a few of these exchanges he could hear another set of footsteps coming across the floor. Here came the reckoning!

Ann Clements was in her early forties and still a youthful and attractive lady who stood another three inches taller than her daughter. She came at Joe with a determined step and he quickly stood. When she got close she demonstrated a unique trait shared with her daughter as she grabbed Joe by the ears and pulled his face to hers with a resulting resounding thunk as their foreheads came together. She shook him, just as her Molly had.

"Now look here, you big, handsome renegade redskin, you nearly broke my poor Molly's heart before getting around to your purpose! I ought to skin you instead of kissing you!" She then kissed him soundly on the cheek and drew back, beaming.

Joe let a loud sigh escape and wiped the sweat from his still-stinging brow. "Mother Clements, I know for sure that Molly is yours! You both nearly tore my ears off, and you both want to skin me! Are you sure you're not Comanche?"

She stepped against him with a hug that spoke volumes as to her love and acceptance for this man who had won her daughter's heart. "Molly's freshening up from the tears YOU caused and will be back out shortly. Joe, I can't tell you how happy you have made me."

"Thank you, Mother Clements, thank you. Are you telling me Molly is going to say yes?"

"I'll let her be the one to answer that. Understand one thing, Joe Five Ponies…if you continue to call me 'Mother Clements' I intend to make your life miserable. It makes me sound eighty years old! I had to straighten your partner, Dan, out on this some weeks ago!"

He chuckled nervously and nodded his acknowledgement of

her comment and then asked, "Advice taken, but what do I call you, then?"

"My parents named me Ann. My husband calls me dear, or sweetheart, or honey; but I think those unadvisable in the interest of keeping peace in the family."

Joe shook his head in amusement at the sweet lady's sense of humor and then gave her another hug and stepped back to listen for footsteps from inside. When he had released his future mother-in-law he returned to the swing to await his fate. Ann returned to her kitchen.

It was fully half an hour before Joe suddenly sensed a physical presence on the porch and, looking quickly to his right, he found Molly standing in the doorway just gazing at him. Upon seeing she had been discovered she came to him and plopped down beside him, obviously still somewhat shaken.

"Joe Five Ponies, you nearly broke my heart the way you started out! It sounded like you were saying goodbye!" She shuddered physically at the thought.

"I am so sorry, Molly, I wasn't thinking of how it must have sounded. But dear little one, since you've not given me an answer yet, let me do it properly in the accepted manner of the white man."

He then knelt before her, took her hand in both of his and asked, "Molly Clements, will you be my wife, my lover, and my lifetime companion?"

She hesitated a moment, drawing a deep breath, then, at a loss for words, simply nodded and fell weeping into his arms. The porch swing would be occupied well into the darkness of the night that day as the two made their plans for a life together.

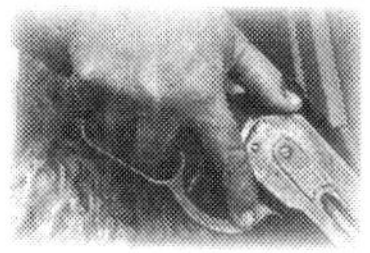

TWELVE

"I'm really feeling good about the deal with Hiram Cogswell, people, but I wonder if we shouldn't make contact with him a little more often for a while just to keep relations open and current?" Dan pulled his boots off the porch railing and let the tipped back chair thump to the floor. He looked at the others as they nodded agreement, hoping one of them would volunteer to go north to see the man. Dan felt as though Hiram should get to know all the partners.

"Yu tryin' tu get outta the next hayin'?"

"No, Reddy, I'm not. What I'm really thinking is that he should get to know each one of us so we have a complete trust between us. Plus, the railroad should be getting close to him by now and I want him to be sure we're backing it, but not at his expense."

"Wal, I get yore drift, Danny boy, an' I'll be goin' his way tomorrow if yu like. I kin use a couple days away from this moonstruck cousin o' mine an' thet crazy young'un tryin' tu outshoot me ever' blasted day. I swear Skinny is gonna wear thet old shootin' iron oot afore too long."

Dan laughed and said, "Hey, Indian, you started him at it, now take your medicine."

"Yeah, I did, but I never figgered he'd wanta live with the thing in his hand or sleep with it."

A chuckle was the only answer he received as Dan rose and went into the house, returning a couple of minutes later with a cup of coffee in each hand. The two sat there alone with their thoughts as twilight made its way over the ranch and the sun slipped away behind them. The sounds of frogs down at the river reached their ears, along with the occasional stamping of a hoof from the corrals. The grinding of grass between teeth could be detected from along the side of the house as Blue worked at finishing his daily lawn-mowing exercise. The sounds of the night birds soon slipped their harmony into the music of the night, and the two wranglers sat together on the porch much as they had beside campfires since fate had put them together on a lonely canyon rim several years before. Theirs was a closeness of brothers, developed through hardship, trials, and eventual success through mutual dedication to purpose and the hard work that accompanied it.

§ § § §

Morning found Red Elk saddling a horse as the call to breakfast rang out with Lucinda pounding the Apache drum she had acquired from some unknown source for just that purpose. She said it made her feel more at home to be able to declare herself on the warpath with the wranglers, especially Red Elk. Their constant feuding was a source of continuous amusement to the rest.

It was noteworthy, however, that when Reddy rode out he had a goodly supply of prepared food that had come from the portly cook behind his saddle. Lucinda always made sure of "her riders" having plenty of trail supplies when they departed.

The view from the top of a rise four hours later revealed the plowed and planted fields of Hiram Cogswell's farm. The buildings still reflected the sun from the yellow, peeled logs Hiram and sons had used for the buildings that very spring. As Reddy surveyed the surrounding area, he caught sight of activity far to the east. He pulled the glasses from his saddle bags and raised them to his eyes. Just as he had thought, the rail-laying crew was there in force and the twin ribbons of steel were relentlessly creeping ever closer to the town of Twin Forks.

As he scanned back to the farm buildings he noted there were many wagons and saddle horses present. A crowd was gathered in front of the house and there appeared to be much turmoil present. He spurred his mustang down the rise and headed for the place.

As he rode up, Reddy noted there was a distinct separation of two factors in those present. He rode his horse directly between the two groups. Paying no attention to anyone in particular, he dismounted and turned to those who wore the garb that made them obvious farmers. The others were cowmen and numbered more than the farmers by about two to one.

"I'm Red Elk of the Twin Forks Ranch and lookin' fer Mister Cogswell."

A burly man in bib overalls stepped forward and said, "I'm Cogswell. What can I do for you?"

"Wal, Mister Cogswell, us fellers down at the ranch was wonderin' if yu was comin' along okay, so I just volunteered tu slip up this way and check up on thet. Looks like yu got others what is wonderin' the same thing."

Cogswell smile wryly and held out his hand. "You could say that. These men here by me are farmers who have been talking about organizing into a common pool for the purpose of marketing our crops more effectively. Those men over there are cattlemen who, for some reason they can't explain, are opposed to the idea."

A rider stepped forth who was a couple of inches taller than Reddy and took a threatening stance a foot from him. He put his fisted hands on his hips and spoke forcefully, "That's right, Injun. We don't want no farmers organizin' so they can take over this area. It just ain't gonna happen. Now, what's a redskin got to do with this?"

The Texas drawl got even slower as Reddy looked the bigger man in the eye and replied, "Wal, mister whoever you air, this redskin happens tu own a quarter share in the Twin Forks Ranch, which Mister Cogswell hyar is presently a part of, but only for the time being. This hyar redskin is also not pleasantly disposed tu havin' some big ugly hunk o' meat like yourself standin' so close tu him in such a bluff as yore puttin' up right now. So, blowhard rancher, yu either back off or take a forty-five in the guts."

The rest of the ranch crowd reached for guns but stopped when the leader doubled over gasping for breath when the barrel of a Colt rammed into him just below the belt buckle. The sound of the hammer clicking to full cock was heard as the big man sunk to his knees while holding his stomach in misery.

"I don't want yu gents tu think I plan any harm tu any of yu, but this hyar gatherin' is obviously agin proper freedom of this hyar territory. I don't like big shots like this man who think they kin push littler folks around, so iffn I see one hand even touch a gun I'll kill thet man first.

"Now then, anyone besides this galoot want tu challenge this renegade injun? I don't wanna seem like a troublemaker, but I jist don't like this feller. I git tired o' people thinking they kin push smaller folks around jist 'cause they's bigger or richer. Who else in yore bunch might be willin' tu speak for yu and do it in a reasonable manner?"

An older man, around forty, stepped forward with a smile and spoke up. "I reckon I should have tried to keep Mort, there, out of this, but he sort of pushed his way in. He was in a mix-up down in southern Wyoming just before we became a territory back in sixty-three. It was really ugly from what I understand and he lost a couple of cowpokes to the squatters. That doesn't excuse his bullying attitude, but I didn't feel much like bustin' in on him.

"Name's Con Reiger. I run cattle around thirty miles north of here. We heard about this railroad comin', then someone spread the word that farmers was organizing, so we decided to organize ourselves and come down here to find out what's goin' on and what their reason was."

"It don't much matter what their reasons are, Mister Reiger; this hyar's a free country an' they kin do as they please. I know firsthand what it's like tu hev men push people around what's been free all their lives. I kin tell yu right now, my people killed a lot of yore people an saw jist as many of our own killed over this thing of men pushin' men around 'cause of a lust fer power.

"I don't like tu kill a man, but I hev, and if this gets bad, I will again. Thing is, yu cattlemen seem tu think yu hev the right tu try an' dictate tu others what they kin do. Thet makes me killin' mad, so all o' yu best walk easy right now; an' if big-shot hyar wants tu get up and hev it out, I'm worked up into a right smart heat fer fightin', any way he wants."

"Hey, redskin, you say you're a rancher, so what you sidin' with these farmers for?" The question came from the back of the cattlemen's group.

"Cause the Comanche was in the same spot once, feller, an' iffn yu got the guts tu come up hyar an' ask me, I'll show yu what a Comanche does tu an idiot like yu."

Hiram Cogswell stepped in between Reddy and the cattlemen, holding his hand up for silence.

"Men, I think this whole thing has been ridiculous from the start; and if you men will just be quiet long enough to hear me out, I can settle this once and for all."

"We don't need to hear any farmer's lies and such!" It was the same voice from the back.

"Mister, I'm walkin' back thet way, gun drawn, an' if yu interrupt one more time I'm gonna bore yu. Thet goes fer any man what speaks out of turn. Yu got this Comanche mad, now jist SHUT THE BLAZES UP!"

A silence fell over the entire crowd until Reiger spoke. "Men, I've tried to get this same message to you, but you all got too worked up to listen. Now I join our Indian friend here in telling, not asking, you to be quiet. We ranchers have ALWAYS gotten along with the farmers in this region until Mort, there, started getting all worked up about this organizing thing. Some of these farmers have been our friends for years. Some have even had sons and daughters marry our youngsters. What changed all that?"

There was a general muttering going on for a bit until Hiram spoke again.

"We farmers are definitely organizing. The thing is, you ranchers need to do the same thing in the same way. I admit to being the instigator of this, and with no apologies.

"Back east, farmers are organizing into different groups. One is called the Grange, but there are others, in order to better market their crops. We have, thanks to the Twin Forks Ranch men, a spur going in here from the railroad. It will have loading docks, and loading ramps and pens for livestock.

"The railroad won't put cars here for one or even two farmers when we need them. But if we organize and build storage bins, warehouses, and holding pens for our goods, we can store up until the railroad sees fit to give us the cars we need. Then we can ship together and have a ready market for our goods. You cattlemen stand to benefit just as much as we farmers."

Reiger addressed the two groups. "See what I was trying to tell you hotheads last night at the meeting? We needed to listen first instead of coming in here mouth first."

It was then that Mort Sandford started struggling to his feet. He swayed a bit as he tried standing still, then looked around for his attacker. He found him standing in front, poised for action.

"Yu feel froggy, big man?"

Hiram Cogswell stepped between them and looked at Sandford. "Mister, we've turned this into a peace parley, and these men with you understand a lot better just what we farmers stand for and what we intend. I suggest you think about what went on here for the last few minutes before you get any more ideas of causing trouble. Should you not want to do that, I'll be more than glad to accommodate you myself. But you leave this Indian alone; I want no dead men on my farm, and that's what you'll be if you cross him."

The big man looked at the burly, shorter man and sized him up, apparently arriving at a common sense decision. He turned on his heel and strode to his horse. After missing the stirrup on his first attempt he finally made the saddle and spurred off at a gallop.

Hiram turned to Reddy. "Friend, we've just met, but you don't seem anything like Dan described you. He said all four of you were reasonable men with fair outlooks on life. You, my friend, are a hothead. And dangerous."

Red Elk looked him in the eye for a long minute, then nodded. "Yore right, Mister, yore right. I did git hotheaded thar. But, I saw men tryin' tu tell other men what tu do and how they could do it and whar they could do it. Thet spelled reservation tu me, and thet calls fer fight. I apologize fer flyin' offn the handle."

He turned to the ranchers. “Men, I apologize tu all o’ yu, too. I was outta line.”

Reiger held out his hand to Reddy and then to Cogswell, then turned to the still-mounted men and looked steadily at them as though questioning them. One by one, they all dismounted and started to mingle with the farmers, shaking each hand in turn.

Reddy glanced at the house just in time to see rifles disappear from a door, a window, and from around the one corner of the house. Hiram’s wife and two of his three boys had been ready for trouble! His liking for this settler and his family took a huge leap. These were people to tie to!

Hiram called on everyone to arrange themselves before his front porch and get comfortable. As soon as that was done, he spoke of the benefits of organizing, both for the farmers and for the ranchers. After a long discussion and several questions and answers the group started selecting officers for a joint organization. Cogswell was the only one nominated for a president, with Reiger becoming vice-president.

Their first order of business after that was to determine the location of the railroad spur the U.P. had promised. Reddy knew that George Searcy would go with the decision of these men and said so. Before the next hour was gone, there was a strong, cohesive organization under way and both farmers and ranchers knew they had leadership they could count on.

The next step was to look over the land and decide where to place the storage terminal.

Hiram spoke, “I really don’t want to give up any land for such a place, the space needed is big enough to seriously hamper my acreage at this stage of development. Is closer to town advisable?”

In answer to Hiram, a rancher stepped forward. “About five miles outside of town is a spot on my land that isn’t the greatest forage in the country. There’s enough space there for whatever we need. Figure out what you need, the rest of you furnish the building materials, and the land is the combine’s; that’ll be my share. Fair enough?”

A cheer went up and the deal was agreed to. After another

hour of mostly visiting, the men, all but Hiram, Reiger and Reddy, rode off for their respective homes. The other three mounted and rode toward the railroad crew to see if Searcy was there.

§ § § §

Crews were grading a half mile ahead of the track crew, the trace chains of the teams jingling with a musical harmony to the cacophony of the teamsters' shouts and the crack of the bull-whips. Dust rose from everywhere and tried to choke all who dared invaded the space. The teamsters wore their neckerchiefs over their faces to help with their breathing and the three visitors soon mimicked them.

A half-mile ride through the choking cloud brought them to the track crew with its gandydancers and the ring of steel on steel as the hammers of the spikers drove the huge spikes into now latent ties. Men hustled and bustled everywhere in what appeared to be total confusion, but the riders couldn't help but notice that the steel rails appeared magically at the proper time and place right after the ties and barely in advance of the swinging, ringing hammers.

Begrimed men were everywhere, some without shirts, others still shirted, but all soaked with sweat that caught and captured the floating dust particles to turn the men brown. It looked as though each one would weigh an extra few pounds from the dirt by evening, but they would have sweated off more than they gained in the process.

Reddy guided the other two through the activity to a group of tents over a quarter of a mile east of the track-layers. This would have been the morning starting place for the day's track crew. A white, or rather, what used to be white, tent larger than the rest was Reddy's destination. He dismounted and poked his head in the opening, then motioned for the other two men to follow.

The rancher simply dropped his reins to the ground, knowing his horse would stay as though it were tied, but Hiram had to find a place to tie the work horse he had ridden. Being a practical man, he owned only harness horses and used a wagon for travel most of the time.

George Searcy bounded from behind the table strewn with

maps, drawings and the like and circled it with his hand extended, a happy smile on his face.

"Reddy! Man, it's great to see you! I was just plotting out where the best place to pick your spur off the main track might be. What are you doing, just visiting?"

"Wal, thet's the main reason, but not visitin' yu. Came up tu see Mister Cogswell, hyar. We want tu make sure he's cared for an' such as far as our ranchin' goes with him."

"Hi, Hiram. He's told me about your deal with him, Reddy, and might I say it's a great move for both parties! I see a real prosperous partnership in the future there."

"I think so myself. George, this hyar's Con Reiger, cattle rancher hyar 'bouts. Him and Hiram been workin' up a company for sellin' goods."

"I've met Con. Hi, Con, welcome back to the U.P. Reddy, I've purchased cattle from Con to feed my men. And you probably don't know that Hiram and I have talked about his caring for selling my herd of harness stock when we finish this job in a few weeks."

"Naw…nobody ever tells me nothin'. I'm jist a worthless redskin, I guess."

"Hey, I haven't had a chance to tell you anything, fella. You busted in over there in the middle of a problem, took care of part of that problem like some Texas tornado, and then when we had the company formed, we came right over here.

"Don't you try to play the 'poor me' part right now, Mister Red Elk, you're just too much chained lightning for that."

This was a long speech for Hiram Cogswell when there wasn't need for a speech, and Reddy chuckled at him.

"I dunno 'bout the chained lightnin' part, but we ain't got properly acquainted yet."

"Well, we'll care for that this afternoon come dinner time. Reiger, you'll join the family and me in feeding this redskin?"

"He'll do nothing of the kind," said Searcy. " He, along with the two of you, is going to eat some of his own beef right here. I'll get the cook moving on it right now. Then, Reddy, I have a question for you. You don't have to answer it, of course, but I've been curious about the four-man partnership down on Twin

Forks Ranch. You know, how it came about."

"Yu get thet cook to work and I'll be glad tu tell yu all about it."

Searcy returned to the office tent in a few minutes and poured them all a drink from the lemonade pitcher he had carried back. They all found portable chairs and Reddy started his tale.

"Back some four years ago I was headin' fer a meetin' with my cousin, Joe Five Ponies, in the canyon area down around the Arizona border. It was gettin' nearly too late tu get down into the canyons before the first snow hit. I knew iffn I was still on top thet I would be stranded up thar and likely freeze or starve, so I was getting' right nervous.

"I rode real late because of thet, and I saw a fire thet had burned real low with a couple o' hosses nearby. I snuckered up on them, made friends with them so's they wouldn't wicker, and made myself at home. Whoever thet wrangler was, he needed tu be getting' down outta thar as much as I did.

"I hed found a couple of prairie hens' nests thet day and had the eggs with me so I figgered on a proper breakfast outta them. I eased thet feller's gun outta the holster beside him and unloaded it careful like, then put it back. Then I jist rolled up and slept fer a few hours.

"Woke up early, found some bacon he hed in his grub pack, kicked thet fire up and started makin' breakfast with them eggs n' bacon. I heard him stir a bit an' figgered he'd throw down on me so I jist spoke up real quiet like an' informed him thet his shootin iron was no longer loaded. Then I told him breakfast was ready an' he better stir his stumps 'cause we hed tu be gettin' down outta thar as fast as we could 'cause the snow was a comin'."

"Well, you obviously made it, since you're here. Who was the fellow?"

"Wal, George, thet feller was none other than Dan Kade. An' come first light I saw one of the, if not THE, most beautiful mares I'd ever seen in my life. It was the mare Sheba from down Arizona way, the same one what foaled thet red stallion Melodi Sweeny was ridin' when they was hyar!"

"Wow, that is some horse, so the mare had to be something."

"Yessir, the best. And fast? Like greased lightnin'. Thing

is, Dan and I made it, as yu said, and when we met my cousin Joe in Wild Hoss Canyon he hed two others with him, one of which was Bear Rollins. The four of us been together ever since. Fact is, the only way we'll split up is when we croak."

"Reddy, I appreciate your sharing that with us. It's not a good idea to ask personal questions like that, but my curiosity has been pushing at me since the first day I met you four. Thanks."

"Don't mention it, George. Now, about this company these fellers have formed, do yu think it's a good idea, and will it work?"

"Of course it's a good idea; and if run properly, will become one of the largest and strongest companies around here. I happen to know a bit about this sort of organizing and can help, providing they want help."

"Mister Searcy," spoke up Hiram, "We'll take all the help you want to give. I had some knowledge of this from back east but never saw the inner workings and how the thing operated for sure."

"I'll make a suggestion right now that you find someone who is knowledgeable to run the thing. Don't look at it as a company business, look at it as a co-op. You need a full-time man who can starve for a year to kick it off right. No wages, but, instead, shares of the co-op. Then when he gets it on solid ground, renegotiate a salary for him, issue shares to the members, and you'll be growing before you know it. The U.P. will be glad to work with you as far as train schedules go."

"George, whar yu goin' after yu get this road done?"

"I'm not sure, Reddy. I really haven't given it much thought, except I plan to get out of the building roads rut. I have a wife and two sons in Saint Louis and I want to be a family man from now on. I've been building railroads for twenty years now and it's time for someone else to take over."

"Iffn yu don't mind a suggestion from a renegade redskin, why in tarnation don't YU take the job iffn they want yu?"

Searcy leaned his chair back, linked his hands behind his head and looked from one person to the next for several minutes. No one spoke.

"I never thought about it, Reddy, but the thought really is an attractive one. That would, of course, depend on a few things. For one, my family would have to approve. They're used to the city life back there and this might be a bit lonely for them.

"Then there's the matter of the co-op offering me the job. They would need to present it to the membership to vote on it. I truly don't know how this might go, but if these two gentlemen will think on it together, I will, too. What say, gents?"

"I think this renegade redskin, as he calls himself, is pretty sharp. What say you, Con, do we think on it together?"

"Absolutely. WE need to have this thought through and ready to put before the membership as soon as George says 'Yes', which he's gonna do, for I can see it in his eyes."

The cook and two helpers entered the tent just then. They were laden down with many plates, each steaming with wonderful-smelling food. The three dug in like a wolf-pack on the hunt.

Two hours later, as the three riders emerged from the dust cloud of the graders, there was a spirit of promise for the future. Reddy knew that Dan had tied the Twin Forks crew to a good man in Hiram Cogswell and also that Cogswell and the co-op had found an equally good man in Con Reiger. The years would no doubt prove this as the newly formed co-op became a powerful influence on the lifestyle of the area producers of crops and cattle. It was a good feeling.

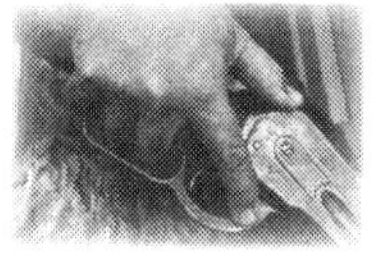

THIRTEEN

Early September was threatening to arrive when Dan Kade was summoned to Boomstick by George Searcy to examine the plans for grading the roadbed to a point just north of the Twin Forks Ranch. They needed to establish not only the specs for the grading but also the Y for a turn-around for trains. It was expected that only a couple of cars would make the trip to the T Bar F for loading. Twin Forks Ranch would also build the loading pens.

Ted and Melodi Sweeny were preparing to return to Sunny Springs but wanted to see the work thus far completed on the new railroad, so had ridden along with Dan. It would only take a couple of extra days to satisfy their curiosity and then they would depart in the wagon. Ted figured that "Flash and Dusty both air getting' too blamed fat with all this rest, so we need tu work 'em a bit anyhow."

Dan took them straight north from the ranch to a point just south of the Cogswell farm, where they stopped atop one of the higher hills. With field glasses they could see the steel ribbons approaching from the east. It appeared they would pass just on the north edge of Cogswell's place, an ideal routing for him and his family. After watching the grading crew through the glasses for a while, the trio rode on in to the farm yard. They were greeted by Missus Cogswell.

"Hello, Mister Kade. Get down and come on in, it's good to

see you. Hiram is out with the railroad crew trying to make sure they build that railroad just the way he wants it!" She chuckled loudly at her humor.

Dan laughed as he swung his leg over the saddle and replied, "Now, Missus Cogswell, please call me Dan."

"I will if you call me Eleanor."

"Okay, Eleanor, it's a deal. If we're to be partners in this farming and ranching thing, we need to be on a first name basis."

"I agree. Now, if you're going to bring friends here, I think I need to be on a first name basis with them, too!"

"Oh my, I am SO sorry. How impolite can I be? Eleanor Cogswell, these are my friends from down in Utah, Melodi and Ted Sweeny. They, my dear lady, are on their honeymoon!"

"Wonderful!" she replied, clapping her hands with joy.

They led the horses to the hitch-rail at the porch and tied up, then plopped down in the shade for a visit. Since it was after lunch and Hiram wouldn't be back for a while the visit was only long enough to fulfill the obligatory neighborliness and then they rode to the railhead. There they found the Cogswells watching the progress of the grading.

Dan was told that George Searcy had ridden the train back to Boomstick the previous day and didn't plan to return soon. After a brief visit with Hiram and his boys the trio rode east until darkness fell. They made camp in a swale with a lively little spring at one side. The next morning found them underway at daybreak, as was the custom of the times.

Two hours before noon the second day found them seated in the diner in Boomstick discussing the future plans for Twin Forks Ranch with Searcy. As soon as they had eaten, Ted and Melodi toured the town, stopping at each business and doing a little shopping as they did. Ted kept reminding Melodi that they had no pack horse and were relying on just their saddlebags. He found a little fist in his ribs each time he said something. They had learned the name of Joe's new fiancé before leaving the ranch so they looked her up for a visit. By the time they had made their rounds of all the town Dan and George were finished with their preliminary plans. The next step would wait until the tracks were laid clear into the town of Twin Forks. That was roughly a week away.

Dan suggested they spend the rest of the day in town before starting the journey back to Twin Forks Ranch, and the young couple quickly agreed.

"A hotel bed sounds really good for a night!" exclaimed Melodi. "We have several days of using the ground for a mattress ahead of us!"

After arranging for their two rooms, they trooped out for another tour of the town. As they walked along the boardwalk, they were seen from the saloon window by a rough, grizzled observer.

§ § § §

"Look thar!" grumbled Cannon. "Thet's the gurl we're after! She's up here whar she'll be even easier pickin's. Man! Luck is finally with us."

"It's about time something went right," replied John Smoots. "We can take her and get out of here. I don't like this marshal the least bit."

"I'll take care o' him afore we leave, don't you worry. Whar are the men you got from the other side o' the mountains?"

"Camped north of town. Listen, you leave that marshal alone. I've been seen talking to him too many times, and I don't want my name to come up if he's killed. You understand that, Cannon?"

"Yeh, yeh, I got it. Fer a fast gun, you seem tu be really skeered o' bein' known."

"Listen, you big, stupid jerk, when you hire a gun out like I do, a low profile is best. I'll try to find out what I can about those three and see if anyone knows their plans."

§ § § §

Sitting at the restaurant table that evening, the three from Twin Forks discussed their plans, not noticing the small man seated at the next table, eating slowly and quietly. Smoots listened carefully to them, drinking in every word. He not only learned their plans to depart at daybreak, but also picked up the information that Bear Rollins was a partner and was at the Twin Forks Ranch. As soon as he knew that information he quietly withdrew and began a quest to find where the T Bar F was located.

The old hostler at the livery stable provided detailed directions as to how to locate the ranch, and the little gunman then slunk out of town to the camp where four additional outlaws resided. He had hired them on his last trip to the eastern edge of the mountains where he and Cannon had sold their stolen stock. Cannon was there, and when Smoots gave him the information the burly outlaw was ecstatic.

"We'll wrap this up this week, get our money fer the gurl next week, and be out of hyar fer southern weather right after thet! An' the world will be rid of Rollins and the gurl both!"

"In other words, you don't plan to release the girl even when you get the money?"

"You ketch on quick. She's caused old Cannon way too much trouble tu let'er go. I'm gonna skin her jist like I do Rollins."

"No, Cannon, you're not. I hired my gun to you to kill one man and kidnap a girl for ransom money. I won't be a party to murdering any girl."

"Reckon I'll do as I please once she's mine. Iffn I gotta care fer you first, thet'll be my pleasure."

"You can't 'care for me' first, Cannon. I'll never turn my back on you, and you can't match me. We'll get the cash and I'll take the girl back."

"We'll see, mister high hat, we'll see."

§ § § §

The next day found the six outlaws ten miles east of town before first light. They had moved their camp the night before so they could be ready for the capture. They had orders to shoot the two men with Melodi on sight. As a result, they were armed with loaded rifles at the ready when the three riders came in sight.

One of the new men drew down on Dan Kade in preparation to fire when Cannon kicked his foot with the admonition to "Wait 'til they're closer," but all he succeeded in doing was to cause the fellow to jerk when startled and fire. The bullet sailed harmlessly over the heads of the trio and they pulled up for a second. Then Dan and Ted yelled together, “Get out of here!” and they turned north and put their horses to a dead run.

“Mount up! Get after them!” yelled Cannon. He was fit to be tied over the mistake, and had he not been in such a hurry, he probably would have shot the offender even though it had been his own fault. Within a minute there were six riders mounted and spurring their mounts in pursuit.

Dan looked over his shoulder as Blue stretched out in his run to see both Ted and Melodi still close behind. He was relieved to see he wouldn’t have to hold the big horse in too much because of the speed of the other two horses. They let them run all out for two miles and then hauled them in for a possible long haul.

Ted yelled to Dan, “Where should we head for?”

“I sorta know the mountains up ahead, hunted horses there a few times a couple of years ago when we still worked for Allie’s dad. We’ll lose them there!”

Ted looked over his shoulder, as did Dan, and they saw the six riders strung out behind them a quarter of a mile. They both knew their horses could run the others’ into the ground; but here was a rider on a pinto stretching out in front of the other five, and he was gaining. Apparently, his pony was as fast as theirs, for he was leaving his friends behind as he pursued.

“Ted, you and Melodi keep going and head for that notch you see just to the right. When you get there, wait for me and give the horses a breather. Don’t go any deeper than a few feet and I’ll find you. I have to stop that pinto.”

With that, he pulled his Winchester from the saddle sheath and levered a shell into the chamber. Dan had recently begun carrying the longer-barreled rifle in a 44-40 caliber and knew the range to the pinto was marginal at the least. He hauled Blue to a skidding stop, turned his right side to the pursuer, and leaped off all in one motion.

“Stand, Blue!” he cried out and then, leveling the rifle over the now stock-still saddle, pulled the sights onto the pinto. Dan Kade hated nothing more than hurting a horse, but knew that was the best target at that range.

When he fired, Blue stood perfectly still. He saw the bullet kick dirt a foot to the right of the running horse and low. Adjusting his aim, he fired again and saw the puff of dust pop from the chest of the fleet pony as it tumbled head over heels and catapulted the rider from the saddle. The man stopped tumbling and lay still for a moment. By the time he stirred Dan and Blue were once again at full speed after the other two fugitives.

As he checked over his shoulder once again he saw a rider pull up by the prostrate comrade and then saw the burly form of Cannon fly by and kick at the good Samaritan. The big one was apparently the leader, for the fellow leaped back to his saddle and came on.

The delaying tactic pushed the pursuers back a bit and by the time Dan reached the notch he had extended his lead by several yards. He cut into the entrance and found Ted waiting, rifle at the ready. "Great shot!"

"Follow me, and watch out for the brush and limbs; it's really thick in here!"

Dan pushed on by Ted and Melodi and pulled Blue to a trot. That was possible for less than another quarter mile and then they were down to a walk because of the thickness of the trees and underbrush. Not one of them was wearing chaps so they were experiencing cuts and painful scrapes from the growth through which they were riding.

Ted rode last so as to keep Melodi between him and Dan and much of the time he caught only glimpses of the tail of Flash. Dan led them in a twisting, seemingly meandering route deeper and deeper into the forest. It was an hour later when Dan stopped in a little glen overlooking the stream some twenty feet below.

"Okay, we start climbing from here. The notch narrows and becomes impossible to pass through. I want to get to the eagles' nest today before sundown, and maybe we can make a stand there. I don't know what those men are after, but it's probably the horses and anything else we might have on us."

Melodi blanched and spoke up, "I know what they're after, Dan, and it's me. When you stopped to slow them down back there before we hit the forest, I got a look at the man who made sure they all stayed after us, the one who didn't let the fellow stop for his friend? He looked like the man who kidnapped me, Cannon. I couldn't tell for sure at that distance, but I'm pretty sure it's him."

Ted and Dan looked at each other for a minute of silence, then Dan spoke up again. "That settles it. We make a stand when we get to eagles' nest. If that's really him, we need to stop this once and for all. Bear told us all what happened; and if a man like that is going to continue his efforts, Ted and I will see to it there's no more problem!"

The last was said with strong feeling and even Ted felt a chill at the tone of Dan Kade's voice. There was now a death sentence on Cannon, bad man of the mountains.

"What's so special aboot this hyar eagles' nest, Dan?"

"It's a promontory point a few hundred feet above the valley floor that juts out over it several feet. There's a large rock on the top, right out at the edge, that's sort of balanced there and looks like a nest. I'm told there's even a hollowed-out center on the top that makes it even more like a nest. Thing is, it overlooks all the routes to the top in a manner that provides total protection to anyone there. I've seen it from a distance and, believe me, I wouldn't want to have to approach it if someone there didn't want me to!"

"Wal, I hope thar's a good overhang, as yu put it, 'cause we're gonna get real wet iffn they ain't; look at them clouds comin' thar. I think we're in fer it."

Dan looked to the west and agreed. "Rest's over, let's ride. It gets pretty rugged from here and we're several hours away yet."

That stretch of mountains wasn't nearly as high as those of the Sawtooth range, or the range to the west, for that matter; but they were much more rugged and jagged, so progress was quite slow. The rain Ted had predicted started an hour later in a slow, steady fall. The three stopped to don their slickers and then moved on.

As they ascended they came to many spots where the trail became narrow and on the very edge of the chasm. The cliff to their left alternated between straight down and a gradual slope, but it was in no way passable as far as descending into the bottom of the chasm. Even if they could have, the stream at the bottom traded places with waterfalls and pools so often as to present a barrier to passage of even the heartiest of mountain goats, had they desired to travel there.

Pines and spruces decorated the sides of the mountain where possible, and mighty oaks and maples lived in harmony in many places, tolerating not only each other, but the aspen as well. As the altitude increased, the larger growth of trees gave way to all aspens and pines that held their own among the mighty boulders spotting the slopes. It was at a place where the trail swerved out to the edge of the curvature of the mountain that they could look back and see the followers, even in the now-heavy rain. They stuck to the trail like bloodhounds! There looked to be about the same quarter mile distance between the two parties as before. Dan grunted his displeasure at the sight and urged Blue to a faster pace. The fifty caliber Sharps Melodi told him Cannon relied on could reach them easily at this distance, should he decide to unlimber it.

As the rain fell heavier and the darkness approached, they came out once again to the edge of the forest and could see the promontory ahead. It jutted out some hundred feet over the bottom a thousand feet below and, like its namesake, seemed to command authority over its surroundings. The huge stone balanced on the very point looked, indeed, very much like the nest of the mighty eagle. All it needed to finalize the impression was the piercing cry to echo among the lofty peaks.

"There's supposed to be a protected shelf directly under the point. Bear told me that's the place to hole up in a storm. I'd say it sounds good; I'm soaked!"

The wet trail was treacherous by now, but the three rode some of the finest horses the land had ever seen, so the riders trusted them and put them to the task. They rounded a point and, as though they had entered an auditorium, they found themselves under the protective shelving of rock that protruded over them for some fifty yards, making a cave of massive proportions that would shelter both riders and horses from the storm. It was situated such that they could see the back-trail and that leading forward for well over the quarter-mile distance Dan had been told about. Riders were visible through the darkening shadows mixed with the rain, and Dan let no time lapse before his 44-40 spoke a nasty message to those following. The slug spanged off a rock and set the horses of the outlaws to jumping nervously on the dangerous trail.

In a matter of seconds the heavy boom of a Sharps fifty bellowed out and the lead missile beat around in the cave, ricocheting off the underside of the roof and burying itself in the dirt of the floor. They moved the horses back to the back of the shelf and somewhat around a corner that afforded total protection from that sort of problem.

"We're lucky there's no lightning," Dan offered. "This is the last place I'd want to be in an electric storm! Melodi, be sure you stay around the corner, but see if you can find some wood for a fire. We need to try and dry out. It's going to be really miserable for a while if we stay wet."

Melodi complied with his request while he and Ted set up a watch over the trail. "It looks tu me like we're not gonna need tu watch very long. If they try tu come this way in the dark, they'll save us a lot of ammunition!"

"I agree. We can't see all that good, anyway, so the only watch we need for now is one of us right here. Tomorrow we'll get a better idea of the possible ways they can try for us. At least they'll be more miserable than we will! Come on rain, come hard and cold!"

"Yore a nasty man, Dan Kade. A real nasty man!" chuckled Ted. "Whatever happened to 'vengeance is Mine, sayeth the Lord?'"

"Vengeance is one thing, wearing down the enemy is another, my fine-feathered friend. And just maybe their hired hands don't share the same fervor for capturing us as the leader does."

"Good point, pard, good point."

Melodi showed up with her arms full of dry, nearly rotten limbs that she said had been laid in store by some previous visitor to the shelf. They started a fire, with Ted standing the first watch on the trail; and after Dan warmed up, he came to Ted with steam still rising from his clothes to relieve him. Dan's clothes were still slightly damp, but he was much warmer. Ted spent several minutes rolling out a bedroll for Melodi before standing close to the fire and slowly turning around to dry himself as much as possible. Mel had gone after more of the rapidly burning dry wood. They settled in for a long, miserable night with the only true comfort being the knowledge that their pursuers would be even worse off.

§ § § §

Dawn failed to break the next morning; it simply sneaked into the area amidst the copious dropping of water from the night's rain. The rain had stopped, but great amounts of water ran over the edge of the cave roof in miniature Niagaras that misted into the interior of the open cave and saturated anything they touched. Leather saddles and saddle-bags glistened with a covering of the mist while the three humans struggled to warm themselves before a fire that was nearly non-existent. The meager wood supply had gone the route of ashes and smoke, and only a small, not-quite-red bed of glowing embers remained to warm bare hands.

Ted was on watch at the corner of the rock ledge and saw movement below.

"They're stirrin' down thar, people. Get ready fer action."

He and Dan had carefully wiped the moisture from their weapons and Dan quickly joined Ted at his post. "I figure that guy with the Sharps will start the ball by sending ricochets at us. We better move around the corner where the horses and Melodi are. If they get brave and slither up the trail, we'll just have to meet them when they round this corner here."

"Listen, what's on the other side of this cave? Thet trail oot of hyar, whar would it take us?"

"Just deeper into the rough mountains. The farther in we go, the rougher it gets. I think this is the best place to make our stand, Ted. We can do this; they can only pass two men at a time around this corner. Remember, the horses had a dickens of a time making it and they're great mountain horses."

"And how far air we from the top?"

"Maybe fifty or sixty feet."

"Stay hyar a bit. I want tu take a look at thet cliff on the other side of hyar."

Dan nodded and the Texan slipped around the corner of the cave's interior and down the trail on the other side for a few yards. As he stood looking up he heard the first singing of a leaden missile off the roof of the cave on the other side.

"I reckon it's Katy-bar-the-door now, Mister Sweeny. Get yoreself to it!"

The side of the cliff where he stood sloped up for the first twenty feet or so, then sheered straight up from there for at least the fifty feet Dan had estimated. There were, however, many cracks and crevasses all the way to the top. Ted returned to the cave and started removing his spurs. He then searched out a leather thong long enough to tie a makeshift sling to his rifle.

"I'm goin' up to the top, Dan. Maybe I kin give them a little discouragement from thar."

"You sure you can make it?"

"Naw, but if I cain't, I kin always slip back down. Mel darlin', kiss yore old cowboy fer luck, then keep Dan's guns loaded for him."

As soon as Melodi had complied he slung the rifle over his shoulder and disappeared around the corner. He smiled at the gumption his bride had shown by not begging him to be careful, or to not go at all. She was a true prize!

The cliff was slippery from the rain, but fear of heights and a desire to live kept the cowboy from being careless. He picked his way up the first twenty feet quite easily, then began to pick and choose the handholds and footholds very carefully. An hour later he was like a human fly on the face of the cliff a mere ten feet from the top, but was having a hard time finding another place to grab. It was then he heard a sound from up there! Someone or something was causing a scraping sound that indicated much activity. He slowly eased his pistol in its holster after removing the safety thong from the hammer. Then he resumed his search for the next handhold.

It took another half hour before Ted could get near the top, and by then he had lost his hat and scraped his hand several times. The noise had subsided a bit, but he was still cautious of making any more noise than necessary. His eyes were glued to the rim in search of any presence whatsoever.

The sounds of rifle fire had been evident for a long time during his climb, and he thought he heard a cry of pain from down the trail. "Hope old Dan cared for one o' them," he thought to himself.

§ § § §

Below, Dan had been engaged in a battle of patience with those trying to ascend the trail. The Sharps had ceased to speak, probably due to a shortage of ammunition, but the smaller saddle guns had continued their occasional barrage. Dan was bold in peering out from time to time in search of targets. He had never believed in shooting at air, and that was his opinion of those who shot when no target was in view.

He had been focusing on a spot about a hundred yards down the trail where a flash of red had caught his eye fifteen minutes before. Someone had slipped in where a depression in the cliff existed and was waiting a chance to move closer. He drew aim on the general area and waited.

The noise on top was loud enough he could hear it, and he hoped Ted either heard it or was causing it. As he passed that thought through his mind an arm protruded from the spot he was watching and was quickly followed by a shoulder and torso. Wasting no time, Dan drew down on the torso and fired, drawing fire from further down the trail but hearing the cry of pain from his target. The man was now down in full view of Dan and was attempting to crawl back down the narrow ledge. Dan let him go, having no desire to kill needlessly. Besides, now the rest had someone they would have to take care of, and that should tie another man up for a while. He could hear cursing from someone down there and figured it to be the burly leader.

Ted moved several feet to his left before resuming his journey upward. He could now hear an axe thumping against wood. He slipped over the edge when he reached the top and hunkered down behind one of several large boulders. When he peeked out he saw two men lugging a long pole to the eagles' nest rock. They placed it over a rock, wedged it under the edge of the eagles' nest boulder and tried to pry the huge stone free to tumble it over the edge. It refused to move.

"Listen, get back down there and bring everyone but Cannon back to pry this thing loose. If we can roll it over the edge it'll bash in the roof of that overhang they're under and either force them out or kill them. I'm tired of this game and I really don't give a hang which happens!"

Ted's grip on the sixgun he found in his hand tightened and he forced himself to wait while the fellow trotted off in the direction of the others. The speaker looked familiar, but Ted couldn't place him. He wore two guns tied down in the manner of many professional gunmen and thousands of would-be gunmen. As soon as the other man was out of hearing, Ted stepped out from his cover.

"Just set tight thar, mister. Yu don't wanna make me nervous. Ease those guns outta yore holsters and drop them. One at a time, mind yu, and real careful-like."

Smoots turned slowly, not reaching for the guns, and laughed at Ted.

"So you can shoot me down and brag that you're the one who dropped John Smoots? I don't think so, dead man."

"So yu think yore a famous gunslinger or something like thet? I'll tell yu, Mister John Smoots, thet yore as good as daid right now. Yore tryin' tu kill… or worse… my wife and good friend down thar, and yu just decided for me thet I'm gonna do somethin' I had promised myself I'd never do again. I'm gonna put this away, and yore gonna see thet yu ain't who yu think yu air. Raise yore hands over yore haid so I can slip this iron away, then we'll see who the gunman is hyar."

Smoots laughed derisively and did as told. "Your little woman down there is going to be a widow soon. Tell me, which gun would you like me to carve YOUR notch in, the right or left? I'll give you your choice."

"Thet's a real tinhorn trick, feller, and proof tu me thet yu ain't really a gunman tu be feared. I'll give yu yore own choice; yu want those guns tu be sent tu yore next of kin, or buried with yu?" Ted then slid his weapon into the holster and stood waiting.

Smoots' body jerked as he grabbed both guns. The right pistol was nearly level and was fully cocked when the first lead slug struck his ribs on the right side. It turned him a bit sideways and numbed the hand holding the gun, which he dropped. The left gun continued its upward travel with his thumb pulling back the hammer until the second slug took him in the stomach, bending him over like a fist had punched him there.

The little gunman plopped down on his rear and tried valiantly to raise the gun again, but to no avail. He finally dropped his hand to the ground and laid back, legs pulling up and then scooting back straight. He looked up at Sweeny with a confused look on his face.

"Who…are…you?"

"Don't matter much. Yu wasn't as fast as yu thought yu were, and now yore goin' south. Yu have any kin I should tell?"

"No…no one who would give a…..I'm gut shot, that's bad. Help me so I don't suffer through that like they say. You have to do it, mister, you…you have to."

"Stand up hyar, mister gunman, and look around yu." With that, Ted pulled the little man to his feet and supported him. They moved to the edge of the cliff in plain sight of the men below and Ted pointed to the stream a thousand feet below. It was all he could do to hold the man on his feet, but he was determined to do so.

"Look thar, mister. Ain't thet beautiful country? A man could really like spendin' eternity thar, don'tcha think?"

"It is…beautiful. But what…what does that have to do with me? You gotta stop this bleeding, mister. I might make it if you do." His voice was getting weaker with each expenditure of breath and he was getting heavier in Ted's grasp.

"The bleedin's gonna stop soon, feller. Look down thar, see those jagged rocks? Thet's yore restin' place. Coyotes cain't get to yu thar, and if yu land just right, yu can look up at the sky all the rest of forever. So long, friend."

Ted gave the dying man a huge push from the edge and dropped flat so as to not be a target to Cannon's fifty Sharps. Smoots catapulted several feet out, arms and legs splaying out as he tumbled over and over on his flight to the rocks below. He was silent all the way down, because life had left him even as

Ted pushed.

The plunge of John Smoots, former gunman, was seen quite plainly by the three remaining hired toughs and they looked at each other, two of them holding the wounded man between them, then they eased their way back through the trees to their horses.

The wounded man was helped into the saddle and they rode quickly to the faint trail disappearing into the forest. Cannon heard the horses and wheeled to see the wounded man just entering the trees. He bellowed a curse and fired his rifle at the rider who was propelled from the saddle when the huge slug took him in the back. The act was seen plainly from above by Dan and Ted.

Dan opened fire at Cannon, but the man was moving quickly toward his horse to pursue the deserting hirelings. He forgot all about those above him in his rage at the fleeing toughs.

"Melodi, start saddling the horses, we're leaving!" yelled Dan. "Ted get down here as quickly as you can; it looks like they're bailing out!"

"I'm way ahead of yu, Danny boy! I'll meet yu down the trail a ways! I can get thar a lot faster then climbing down hyar! Safer, too!"

In a matter of less then fifteen minutes Dan and Melodi were descending the trail with Dusty following. Ted emerged from the trees just a bit higher than where the outlaws had been and leaped to saddle as they arrived. Dan spurred Blue ahead to clear the way just in case any of the attackers doubled back.

It was several hours later when they rode clear of the trail on the south edge of the forest just a few yards from where they had entered the day before. They pulled up for consultation.

"I don't see any sign of them, but there are tracks heading off that way in the general direction of Boomstick. Looks like two horses that way and two the other direction, maybe southwest a bit."

"You're right, Ted. One of these heading west isn't carrying a rider and the other has a big man on him. See how deep the tracks are in comparison to those over there?"

"Thet must be Cannon! He's leading the other horse so he can switch off and cover ground much faster. Why the different direction?"

"He's headed to our ranch! Remember, that gunman was asking about Bear way back when he was in town. He'd been asking around for a couple of days as to how to find Bear."

"He hates Bear and me both! He threatened Bear when we were in Salt Lake City just before they ran him out of town last year! Dan, we've got to warn him!" Melodi was nearly panicked with her plea.

"Bear can take care of things, but I'm going to head that way anyhow. Listen, you two, Blue hasn't had anything to eat, just like us, for nearly two days now, but I'll try and make good time anyway. You head to Boomstick and care for yourselves and your mounts, and Blue and I will head for Twin Forks. As soon as you can, you follow. Your horses can make it in a day with hard riding, but you be really careful on the way. No telling where those outlaws went or what they have in mind."

"Tell yu, Dan, I think when they saw their gunman go over the cliff they lost heart and gave it up."

"You may be right, Ted, but be on the lookout anyway. I'll see you when you get to the ranch."

He wheeled Blue and spurred the horse into a run. He would run him an hour and then walk him fifteen minutes, then canter an hour and walk him again, then back to the run. If Blue had been fed recently he would simply have run him several hours before the walking rest, because the horse had endurance to spare. As Ted and Melodi watched him go, they looked at one another and then turned in the same direction.

"If he can do it, so can we. Right, Ted?"

Ted just nodded and kept Dusty beside Flash. The race was on between the three of them and Cannon. As they rode, Ted looked to his guns to insure they were battle-ready. Little did he think that up ahead of them, Dan was in that very act himself. By the time the newlyweds had made their decision, Dan and Blue were out of sight. Because Dan had learned the art of the fastest travel while still preserving his horses, he made better time than his followers, so by evening he was a few miles ahead of them when they stopped for the night. They failed to realize that Dan would ride through the night.

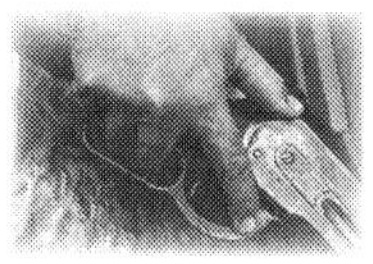

FOURTEEN

Allison turned as Lucinda came through the back door into the kitchen carrying little Ira.

"He's a mess, Allie! You don't want to know what he's been into out there. Honestly, I just turned my back for a moment to finish hanging up the clothes when he tied into something in the yard. I'll clean him up before I go berry-picking."

"Thanks, Lucinda. I can get him, though; you go ahead. I put a clean apron over there by the door for you to carry the berries in."

"Thanks, Allie. But are you sure you don't mind? His condition is my fault."

"That's what you think, girl. I've had this youngster for nearly a year now, and believe you me, nothing is the fault of the one watching him. Come here, you miscreant little boy. I'm gonna scrub you into tomorrow!"

Bear stepped through the front door, rifle in hand. "Did I hyar someone say somethin' about berry-pickin'?"

"You sure did, Bear. Lucinda is going back up the creek to that blackberry patch and plans to make some pies. You probably won't want any."

"Ha! No more than three or four just for me! Listen, girl, I'm goin' with yu. I saw bear tracks up thet way a coupla days ago, an' it's best yu don't wander up thar alone."

"Well, if you're going, you better get a hustle on, 'cause I'm leaving right now."

The two went out the back door as Allison picked up the grubby Ira and hauled him to the tub on the dry sink. She poured some hot water from the tank on the wood stove and then cooled it to suit her for the impromptu bath. Stripping the smelly clothes off the wiggly youngster, she proceeded to scrub away his indiscretions. As she pulled clean clothes from the drawer in the bedroom she heard hoof-beats down by the river. Not thinking much about it she returned to the kitchen, where Ira remained on the dry sink and began the task of dressing the whirling dervish she called son. She had just completed the wrestling match when she hear footsteps crossing the porch. They were heavy, almost like Bear's, but not quite. In the three years Allison had lived there she had come to recognize the sounds of each rider's walk, and this one was strange to her.

A shadow darkened the open doorway and then she was confronted by a big, unkempt man in buckskins. "Whar's Rollins?" he growled.

"Mister, please step back out on the porch and I'll call him for you. I don't appreciate someone barging in like you just did without knocking. You need to learn some manners."

"I'll teach you manners, woman. You belong tu Rollins?"

"I don't BELONG to anyone. Dan Kade is my husband. Now step out of here."

"Not likely. I come tu do damage tu people like you who think they can order Cannon around. I guess I can start with the likes of you."

Allison gasped as he drew a huge knife from his belt and started forward.

"Yu know, I think I know how tu get Rollins here. A few screams from thet kid o' yorn and then you, and I bet he shows up. I'll start by lettin' you watch me whack the arms offa thet kid. Then I'll start skinnin' you!"

As he started around the table that separated them, Allison grabbed a butcher knife from a drawer and backed against the dry sink, pushing Ira behind her.

"Mister, you try to touch my baby and I'll kill you."

"This is gonna be fun, lady. I'm gonna really enjoy this!"

As he started forward there were footsteps hurrying across the porch and a cry from the doorway.

"Hey! Stop!"

Cannon whirled to his right, slinging the knife as he did and reaching for his sidearm. The knife clattered harmlessly against the doorjamb and the room was filled with the crash of a gunshot. The first ball brought a grunt from Cannon as it smashed into his chest. His gun came free of the holster and another ball struck an inch from the first drawing another grunt with the shock.

He sank to his knees, still trying to raise the weapon now in his hand, but a third shot barked and a little round hole appeared in his forehead. The room was filled with blue smoke and Allison could not even see her rescuer for the cloud drifting by the door. She grabbed Ira and lifted him as she slipped by the table opposite where the prostrate figure of Cannon lay to approach the figure by the door. As the smoke cleared a bit she saw Skinny seated in the doorway. He had his knees doubled up, his arms around them with his pistol still hanging from his right hand. His head was buried in his arms and he trembled violently.

Allison quickly sat down beside him facing the opposite direction, still holding a confused but quiet Ira in her left arm, and drew Skinny to her with the right one. She held him there as he trembled and she cried softly.

"It's okay, Skinny. You had to do that. You did right. Just sit here a while. Here, let me put that gun down for you."

She reached for the pistol and placed it on the floor beside him as he buried his face in her shoulder and continued his shaking.

§ § § §

Bear perked his head up when he heard the shots. They were faint from where he and Lucinda picked berries, but he said, "Small-bore pistol. Must be Skinny practicing again. Thet boy's getting' tu be a good shot."

"If you don't quit eating more than you put in my apron, we're never going to get any pies done, you big lug."

"Aww, I know it gurl, but thet's the way of it with us hardworkin' fellers. We need tu be always replenishing our energy."

"Well, I guess we have enough for some pies now, so let's get back. I want to have some done in time for supper."

The two started down the creek toward the house and when they were in sight of the main house Bear could see the big dog crouched by the back door, tail lowered and quivering with his scruff raised.

"Wait hyar, gurl, thar's somethin' wrong down thar." As he approached carefully he heard horse's hooves thundering up from the river. "Thet kin only be Blue," he muttered.

As Bear entered the back door Dan hit the porch with a leap from the saddle.

He knelt by Skinny and Allison as Bear saw the body of Cannon and cautiously approached it.

"Allie, where's he hit? Let me look."

She looked up at Dan through watery eyes and smiled through the haze, "He's okay, dear. He just needs some time to wrestle with what he had to do. Dan, this young man is a hero. Look in there where Bear is."

Dan rose with a pat on the shoulder of Skinny and then that of Allie and strode into the dining area. Bear was examining the body, which he had rolled over.

"Two hard shots in the chest, an' one dead center up top, Danny boy. Thet little thirty-six did the job for him. This gent's hurt his last person, for sure. I hate tu even bury him on Twin Forks land. Never saw a man this rotten anywhere, so this is good riddance."

"Looks like it's hard on Skinny, though. I understand the feeling, I'll never get used to the idea of taking another man's life. I was weak for days after the first time!"

"I know, Danny, but thar's some jist needs tu be shot on general principles."

"I'm not sure I hold with that, my friend, but we're all different. At any rate, let's get this body out of here and see if we can get this blood cleaned up."

They each grabbed an arm and dragged Cannon out the back door. They then scouted around for a place of burial that would be unobtrusive when done. They finally settled on a spot way back in the woods and disposed of him once and for all. It took the better part of an hour before they returned to find Skinny on the couch with a coffee in hand and a tray of food beside him. Allison was doing her best to settle the youngster down and felt the stimulant might do the job.

Dan left the house to care for the horses but found that someone had already unsaddled and rubbed down all the mounts. He checked over each one and when he got to Blue, the monster horse nuzzled him and whickered gently as if to say all was well. Dan twisted and scratched his big ears and then went on to the others.

The two horses Cannon had ridden into the ground would never run again. They were both wind-broke, and Dan wasn't even sure he shouldn't put them out of their misery. His gentle nature took over and he applied some liniment and gave them extra oats. Neither one seemed excited about anything but breathing hard so he left them to their stall and went back to the house.

"Thanks for caring for Blue and the others, hon. Those two others look really bad."

"I didn't do it, dear, Skinny did."

"I'm sorry, Skinny, thanks to you for that. What do you think about those other two horses? Should we keep them around or do them in?"

"They'll be fine, Dan. But they won't be worth the hay they eat. I think we should just turn them loose on the other side of the river and forget about them."

"I tend to agree. Let's check with the rest and then take a vote on them."

It was nearly dusk when Red Elk and Joe rode in from upriver, where they had been checking the herd for possible health or bear problems. They were allowed to care for their animals and enter the main house before they were told of the day's tragedies.

"I wondered where those two poor nags out there came from. Reddy said they must have been turned out by some farmer and ended up here looking for charity. Man, that guy must have ridden them into the ground!"

"How long was he hyar before yu got hyar, Dan? Blue looks okay, gave me the evil eyes when I rubbed my hands down his laigs. He looks sound."

"We were several minutes late, even though we traveled all night with few stops. He's amazing. I don't think I have any idea what he's capable of, even after these many years of riding him." The last was said through shining, wet eyes. Dan's love for the horse was exceeded only by his love for his family and partners.

Lucinda called them to the table as she piled mounds of steaming food in place. They crowded noisily to their customary places and stood while Dan returned thanks for the day's safety and provisions. The meal began with the passing of many bowls, plates, and much chatter. The talk would soon die out when the individual plates were full and under attack.

It was only after those plates were empty, Ira was safely encased in a layer of poorly-aimed food remnants, and Lucinda and Allison were serving blackberry pie that conversation resumed.

"Skinny, air yu up tu tellin' us what happened hyar?" asked Reddy.

"I can. I saw the horses outside, nearly falling down, and knew there must be trouble, so I ran up from the barn and came in the door. The guy was there with a knife as big as Blue and Allie was on the other side of the table with a knife.

"I hollered and he threw that knife at me and grabbed his gun. I shot quick and he still tried to draw, so I shot again. When he still tried to raise his gun I was more careful and…well, I…"

"Never mind, Skinny, we get yore drift. Yu did fine, youngster, jist fine."

"Skinny, do you carry your gun with the hammer on an empty chamber even though it's not a cartridge gun, or did you have three shots left?" asked Dan.

"I didn't have any shots left. I've been out of powder for a week now."

"Oh, wow. That took guts, mister. Listen, that heathen won't be needing his pistol any more; you take it. I imagine it's a caliber same as some of ours. I think we all use forty-fives. If not, we'll get you some forty-four ammo."

"Thanks, but I'd rather not. It would only remind me of this thing. I'll buy a different gun come payday."

"Look here, Ted sent these with me," Dan said as he rose from the table and walked to the fireplace. He reached up on the mantle and took down two short barreled pistols that had been those of John Smoots. "This guy used these so he could draw faster with the short barrels, so the guns are a tad lighter, which is good for you right now."

The lad took the guns and carefully looked them over. Then he swallowed hard and spoke, "I don't know, these notches are the same thing. I don't want anyone seeing them and thinking I'm some sort of killer."

"Look, Skinny, he notched each of them on the outside of the grips so people could see them when they were holstered. We can take the plain grip from one and put it on the other so one pistol has plain grips and the other has all the notches."

"Hey, that should work!"

Reddy spoke up then, "I kin take the one with the notches and cut them down enough tu make a usable spare with no notches. Yore right, Skinny, we don't need no two-bit show around hyar."

"Elroy."

They all just looked at him and then he spoke again, "My name isn't Skinny, it's Elroy. My folks named me Elroy, so that's it."

Reddy was seated directly across from the lad and stood up, pushed his chair back and walked around the table. The teenager stood to face the Indian.

"Give me a shake on thet, Elroy. I want tu apologize in advance fer the times I'll probably forget or slip an' call yu Skinny, 'cause it shore kin happen, but I'll try an' not let thet be. From now on, yore Elroy, or maybe jist Roy."

"Elroy, please."

Reddy smiled his explosive smile that lighted the whole room and nodded. "Elroy it is."

Elroy nodded and shook the Comanche's hand again only to be hugged by the impetuous Reddy. He then returned to his seat at the table. Allison and Lucinda both had glistening eyes at this acceptance of Missus Robins' boy as a man. The title came not from the taking of another life, but from the willingness to meet life no matter what it threw at him. The entire table was silent for a minute and then the rest of the "family" lined up to solemnly shake the hand of Elroy Robins.

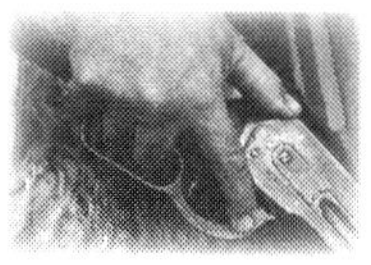

FIFTEEN

As George Searcy crossed the river that October he could hear the ring of axes in the forest behind the Twin Forks Ranch buildings. He tied up at the hitchrail in front of the main house and dismounted. Mounting the steps he paused at the open door and knocked on the side jam.

"Who's there?" came the cry from deep in the house. "Come on in; I'll be right there."

He recognized Allison's voice and waited patiently until she emerged from the bedroom in the back carrying Ira.

"Oh, hi, Mister Searcy. I was just getting our little man up from his nap. It's good to see you; what brings you out today?"

He reached for the youngster and cradled him as he probed the little ribs playfully, getting the desired squeal from him.

"Allison, what do I have to do to get you to drop the 'Mister' thing? After all these months I feel like family here. I came to let everyone know the situation up on the line. I assume all the others are in the back where all the noise is?"

"That's right, all but Lucinda, and she's cooking up a storm for those hungry guys."

"Lucinda?"

"Yes. You haven't been here since she came to work for us. I had too much on my plate to keep Ira from trouble and cook, too, so we found help. If you wouldn't stay away so long you'd know that,' she said as she gave him an admonishing look.

He laughed easily and nodded his agreement. These Twin Forks ranch folks were his kind of people. Allison led him out the back door and through a small grove of pinions to the location of all the frenetic activity. It was nearly a hundred yards to the level spot chosen for Joe's house. A huge pile of recently felled and peeled logs blocked their path, so they rounded the stack and found Bear and Reddy on the other side. They were flattening the sides of logs with the axes while Dan was notching the ends of some for interlocking at the corners of the new structure.

Joe was carefully gauging just where to dig for the foundation and marking off the perimeter of that part of the structure. The house was to be rather large, though not as large as that of Dan and Allison. Their house had been built with lumber from a sawmill, while Joe elected to use the raw materials at hand. Molly had been there to look over the site and she and Joe had designed it together, right down to the porch overlooking the stream that ran by on its merry way to the river out in front of the main ranch buildings.

Joe saw the two onlookers first and quickly left his task to greet them. The rest soon joined them, and George motioned for them to sit on the log pile.

"I wanted to let you know the U.P. is done with the line to Twin Forks town, the siding near Cogswells, and has started the spur this way. We'll be at the end in less than two weeks, thanks to the excellent grading job the people you hired have done. We'll have a celebration in November in Twin Forks and I need for you to take a major part.

"Also, we'll be having an auction of the horses during that week. I got a telegram from Jim Branson down in Utah, and he and Ted agreed they don't want any of the teams back if we can sell them here. Ted seems to be making a little headway in persuading Jim to go back into cattle-ranching.

"I guess they had a real go-round over that when Ted told Jim he was just too ignorant about cows to make a go of it alone! I talked to Melodi when I was in Salt Lake City a week or so ago and she seemed to get a real kick out of it. It seems Ted's folks are firmly entrenched and wanting to work with her dad on the cattle proposition."

"Shore, and thet's good tu hyar. Ted's real smart on cows, and thet'll keep the critters away from us!" Reddy was always quick to mention his dislike of "those cantankerous critters," whenever possible.

"They won't have problems with rustlers with Ted around, at least not fer long," exclaimed Bear. The Texas cowboy had established his reputation on their range and it would likely drift down to the Sunny Springs territory soon.

"So, when is the wedding, Joe?"

"Not 'til we get this house done and ready to move in. I would hope by Christmas, because I can't think of a better Christmas present than a new bride!"

"That's the spirit. Well, listen to this: as soon as we're done with the road I'll have around twenty men out of a job. Suppose we see to it they stay employed for another couple of weeks or so and have them come here to help? I don't think the railroad would begrudge you that in thanks for all the help you men have given in the building of this spur during the summer."

"Wow, that would be great, George, but are you sure about that?"

"I am positive. After all, Reddy there says he can't wait for you to move out so it will be quieter in their bunkhouse."

"Oh, he did, did he?"

"Wal, now thet yu mention it, Bear, Skin…err, Elroy and I were just talkin' aboot thet same subject a while back an' we agreed we were kinda tired aboot you droopin' round thar like a lovesick calf and makin' the mood o' the whole place like an undertaker's parlor."

"Is that so, cousin? Well, I'll tell you what, I can camp back here for the remainder of the time so I can actually sleep instead of laying awake nights trying to figure out whether I'm hearing one of George's trains or your snoring!"

Allison intervened by handing Ira to Dan and grabbing Reddy by the ear and dragging him over to Joe, whose ear also got the grip of her strong fingers. She gently shook each and scolded them for "acting so juvenile in front of company."

"Allison Kade, what is it about Comanche ears that all

you white women want to grab, shake, and try to stretch them? You're just like Molly and her mother!"

"Sometimes, my dear Indian brother, you and this…this… whatever he is, need more than just your ears pulled, but I'm not that bloody yet. If I live around you two much longer, that may change! Now behave yourselves, at least while George is here."

George spoke up, laughing as he did so. "Actually, Allison, this is why I come here. These four characters are so bonded together that I would worry if they failed to carry on so."

Bear's head snapped up at just that moment. "Hush everyone! I hyar somethin'."

Bear's hearing was uncanny, and he cocked his head as he concentrated. "Thar's a wagon comin' 'cross the river. I hyar the hosses splashin' 'n the axles squeakin'."

They all tried to hear, but it was a while before Reddy nodded and Joe started walking toward the house. It was then they heard a shout from in front of the house. Joe arrived ahead of the rest and let out a whoop of joy as he saw Molly Clements jumping down from a large wagon pulled by two teams and loaded to the gills with lumber, furniture, and the like.

Molly ran to Joe and leaped to throw her arms around him, wrapping her legs around him at the same time. She knocked him over with the rush and had to extract herself quickly to get up. Her full-skirted dress had flown embarrassingly high when she forgot herself and she stood blushing for a moment until Joe made it to vertical again, then they embraced in a bit more gentle manner.

"Looks like those two know each other," said Searcy with a smile.

Ann Clements spoke quickly at that comment, "You don't know the half of it, George. I came out to make sure that renegade redskin was not just erecting a tee-pee for my dear daughter. Come here Joe, I need a hug."

Joe smiled at his future mother-in-law and complied meekly. Molly, Allison and Lucinda shared greeting hugs and then all the others gathered to greet Molly and her parents with hugs and handshakes. They all talked small talk for a bit and then Joe grabbed Molly by the hand to lead her back to the building site.

Reddy started to follow, but Allie reached out and grabbed his arm and silently shook her head "No." He caught on and stayed where he was.

"I swear, you men have no grace whatsoever when it comes to love. Those engaged people want some time alone, Reddy."

"Hey Allie, I stopped. Yore getting' awful protective of my poor cousin, there, ain't yu?"

She laughed aloud at that and nodded. "Someone has to be, or you other three would never stop riding him. Yes, you too, husband of mine!" She glared at Dan as he stood mouth open and ready to speak in defense of himself. He never got out a sound.

The group looked the wagon load over as they made their way to the house, commenting on the usefulness of each item and the thoughtfulness of the gift.

Back in the glade, as Joe and Molly stood arm in arm, Joe's heart suddenly swelled with the knowledge that here was his soon-to-be-established future. The woman snuggled close to his right side with her arm around his waist felt soft and warm as her long hair was blown into his face by the breeze now coming up the stream. He could almost feel her heart beating with his as a lump formed in his throat and his eyes glazed over with moisture.

All the past; the mission school, his years with Reddy at his side, the love of Bear Rollins and Dan Kade as brothers, the numberless horse hunts with them, and lastly, the necessary violence that weighed so heavily on his heart, seemed to flood over him in a rush, and then slipped away as though nothing but the positives remained as he contemplated just what the great love of this dear girl beside him was doing in his life.

As these thoughts consumed the couple, Dan Kade had his arm around Allison in just the same manner as Joe did Molly, and the same type of thoughts were rushing through his mind. Blue nuzzled his shoulder as they stood there in the place where he had drawn Allie away from the others as they stood watching the lovers from afar.

As he thought back to the violent escape from Arizona years before, the lonely months on the trail through rugged canyons as a fugitive, the fear of reprisal from the law, the great trust of old Ira Stevens, the great mare, Sheba, and finally, the all-consuming love of this wonderful life's companion and mother of his child beside him, the memories got the better of him and he cried out from his total inner being a prayer to his Creator, God, and Protector above, the absolute reliance and gratitude he felt at that moment. The shadow of vengeance had dissipated and was replaced by the flitting shadow of an eagle soaring high above on his hunt. Dan Kade had been, and now was, blessed as never before and life was good.

Will Riley Hinton was born and raised in the foothills of the Appalachians in southeast Ohio. He grew up on a farm with a grandfather who had made his living with horses and as a result, Will literally grew up on them. Having a mother who encouraged his active imagination along the lines of role playing and storytelling at a young age contributed greatly to his creative writing.

He was consumed by a love of horses, books, and airplanes. He served a hitch in the Navy and afterwards spent time as a part time flight instructor and crop duster. Will is married and has two grown children with five grandsons and two great grandchildren. Not surprisingly, his reading preferences are westerns and folklore.

Glossary.

The Grange - A fraternal organization for American farmers that encourages farm families to band together for their common economic and political well-being. Founded in 1867 after the Civil War, it is the oldest surviving agricultural organization in America.

Sarsaparilla - The sarsaparilla plant is mostly a vine, found primarily in Mexico, Central America and South America. The most valued portion of the sarsaparilla is the root which was often mixed with sugar water. Thus a popular beverage called sarsaparilla was born, years before other chemists would invent other medicinal drinks like the original Pepsi and 7-Up. The taste was similar to our modern root beer.

Gandydancer - is a slang term used for early railroad workers, especially those in the Southern United States, who maintained railroad tracks in the years before the work was done by machines. No one knows the origin of the term for certain, but it is generally thought that it was a combination of gandy, from the Chicago-based Gandy Manufacturing Company, maker of railroad tools, and the "dancing" movements of the workers using a 5 foot rod ("gandy") as a lever to keep the tracks in alignment. Another typical explanation was the practice of those laying the steel rails in place that had them straddling the rail and carrying it with a swaying motion much like the waddle of a goose, or gander. It looked much like a dance. (I chose this explanation in the text because it's the most colorful.)

Grulla dun - Most misconceptions of this term is that it refers to the color of a horse, but it's more of a breed. The color of the grulla is typically a mousy color, but can also be more of a silver blue. The grulla often has four black legs, black mane and tail, and all duns have a stripe down the spine of the same color as the mane and tail.

Steeldust - Another term that causes the misconception of color reference. Steeldust is actually a breed that was the forerunner of our wonderful quarter horse. Steeldust was a stallion from whom came a strain of horses that were revered for their quickness, speed, and ability for working cattle. He was a beautiful blood bay, nearly a sorrel, but his decendents sometimes varied in color.

Sharps fifty - One of the rifles that truly won the West. While this terminology was typically reserved for the Winchester 73, the Sharps played just as big a role in its day. The rifle had a phenominal range and accuracy for the time. The range was upward of 1000 yards while throwing a lead slug weighing 475 grains at 1200 feet per second. This one-half inch of lead would drop anything it hit.

U.P. - The initials of the Union Pacific Railroad, used by most when referring to the railroad that was the first to reach the ocean to our west.

6574671R0

Made in the USA
Charleston, SC
09 November 2010